MISS SILVER INTERVENES

MISS SILVER INTERVENES

PATRICIA WENTWORTH

LARGE PRINT

Oxford

Copyright © Patricia Wentworth, 1944

First published in Great Britain 1944
by
Hodder & Stoughton

Published in Large Print 2007 by ISIS Publishing Ltd.,
7 Centremead, Osney Mead, Oxford OX2 0ES
by arrangement with
Hodder & Stoughton, a division of Hodder Headline

British Library Cataloguing in Publication Data
Wentworth, Patricia
    Miss Silver intervenes. – Large print ed.
    1. Silver, Maud (Fictitious character) – Fiction
    2. Detective and mystery stories
    3. Large type books
    I. Title
    823.9'12 [F]

ISBN 978–0–7531–7828–7 (hb)
ISBN 978–0–7531–7829–4 (pb)

Printed and bound in Great Britain by
T. J. International Ltd., Padstow, Cornwall

CHAPTER
ONE

Meade Underwood woke with a start. Something had waked her — some sound — but she did not know what it was. It had startled her back from a dream in which she walked with Giles Armitage — Giles who was dead. But in her dream he wasn't dead, but warm and alive, and they walked together and were glad.

She listened for the sound that had waked her with bitter resentment in her heart. Only once before had he been so near to her in a dream. Sometimes he called her in a voice which wrung her heart, sometimes he whispered and she could not catch the words, but in this one dream there had been no words at all, only a deep and satisfied content.

And she had waked. They had found each other, and she had waked and lost him all over again. She sat up and listened. It was the third time she had waked like this in the night with that sense of a sound heard in sleep. There was no sound now. Her waking memory had no knowledge of what the sound had been. Wind? The night was still. A passing car — the hoot of an owl — a bat brushing against the window — someone moving here, or in the flat overhead . . . She rejected these things one by one. A car would not have startled

1

her. It wasn't an owl — not that sort of sound, not a cry at all — somehow she did know that. And not a bat. Who had ever heard of a bat blundering up against a window? The floors in this old house were much too solid and thick to let any sound come through from above, and in the flat around her no one stirred.

She had turned instinctively to the window. There was a moon, but its light was thickly veiled. A luminous mist hung there like a curtain, hiding the night sky and the trees which should have been massed against it — two old elms, relics perhaps of a time when the garden boundary was a hedgerow and the place where the house now stood an open field. She went over and looked out. The old-fashioned sash window, too heavy to move without a pulley, was open as far as it would go. That is to say, the top half had been pulled right down behind the lower pane. Meade had therefore two thicknesses of glass to look through, and the mist beyond that again.

She put her hand to the pulley and raised both panes. Now the bottom half of the window was clear. But the mist was still there, white with the light of the unseen moon but quite impenetrable. She could see nothing at all. Leaning out over the sill, she could hear nothing either. The still misty night, the moon veiled, the house asleep, only Meade Underwood awake, brought her back from her happy dream to a world where Giles Armitage lay drowned beneath the sea.

She kneeled down by the window and stayed there, her elbows on the sill, her thoughts bitter and sad. There hadn't been any sound at all. She had waked and lost her dream of Giles because she was a coward, because her nerves still played her false, startling her out of sleep with an echo of the crash which had roused them all three months ago in mid Atlantic. She ought to be over it by now, she ought to be well. She wanted to be at work, too busy to hear what she had heard that night or see what she had seen. Her ribs had mended and the broken arm was sound again. Hearts take longer to mend than bones. She would not have minded dying with Giles, but he had died alone, and she had waked in a hospital ward to hear that his life was gone and hers was left to her.

She kneeled there, bringing up her courage to meet an agony of depression, fighting it back inch by inch — "I shall be able to work soon, and then it will be better. They'll let me join something. I'm doing half a day at those parcels now — that's better than nothing. Everyone's so kind, even Aunt Mabel — I wish I liked her better. But she's been so kind. Only it'll be much easier when I can get right away and not have people being sorry for me."

The mist came chill against her face, her breast, her bare arms. It pressed against her eyes like a bandage. Mary Hamilton's lament came wailing through her mind: "They'll tie a bandage roon ma een and no let me see to dee." Horrible! That was what it had been like on the night when the ship went down — when Giles went down. A shudder went over her from head to foot. She wrenched away from the thought and sprang up. How many thousands of times had she said, "I won't look back — I won't remember." If you keep the door shut upon the past, it can't get at you. It's gone, it's dead, it's over. No one can make you live it again except yourself — that traitor self which creeps out to unbar the bolts and let the enemy past creep in upon you again. She would have no traitors in her citadel. She must look to her bars and wait until the enemy tired and fell away.

She got into bed and lay down. The stillness of the night came nearer. Strange to think of this big house and all the people in it, and no sound, not so much as a breath, to show that it was inhabited.

Perhaps it wasn't. When we are asleep, where are we? Not in the place where our bodies lie without sight or sense. Where had she been herself before she waked? She had walked with Giles —

The barred door was opening again. She thrust it to. "Don't think about yourself. You mustn't! Do you hear — you mustn't! Think about all the other people in the house — not about yourself or Giles — *Giles* —"

The house — the people —

Vandeleur House — four stories and a basement set in what had once been a field bordered by a lane when Putney was a village in the days before London swallowed it up. A big square house, shorn now of most of its grounds and turned into flats. Vandeleur had lived and painted there — old Joseph Vandeleur who had been called the English Winterhalter. He had certainly rivalled that celebrated court painter in the number of times he had painted Prince Albert, Queen Victoria, and all the little princes and princesses. He had painted Mr Gladstone and Lord John Russell, he had painted

4

Dizzy and Pam, he had painted the Duke of Wellington and the Archbishop of Canterbury. He had painted all the lovely ladies of the day and made them even lovelier, and all the plain ones and made them interesting. A tactful man, a charming host, a liberal friend, he had painted his way to fame, fortune, and a well-dowered wife.

Vandeleur House had been graced by the presence of Royalty. A thousand candles had lighted its chandeliers. Five thousand roses had decorated it for a ball. Now, where the large, well-garnished rooms had been, there were flats, two to each floor — eight flats, and a basement given over to central heating, luggage-rooms, and a caretaker. The large kitchen no longer sent out generous steaming meals, course upon unnecessary course. Instead each flat had its kitchenette, an exiguous slip of a room into which had been crowded a sink, an electric cooking-stove, and some cleverly planned cupboards. The fine staircase had given place to a lift and a narrow concrete stair, cold and uncarpeted, winding its way from floor to floor about the lift-shaft.

All this was familiar and present to Meade Underwood's mind. She began to go over the flats and the people in them. It was better than counting sheep, because there was more to fix your attention. There was so little about sheep to hold the thought or to keep it from slipping back to that closed and bolted door. But you could be interested in people. She began to go over the people in her mind, counting them up.

Begin at the bottom. Old Bell in the basement — James Bell — old Jimmy Bell, porter and caretaker.

With a warm, fuggy layer tucked in between the furnace and one of the luggage-rooms. A cheerful old man, Jimmy Bell. Face like a withered apple, and a bright blue eye. "Morning, miss — morning, Mrs Underwood. Oh, yes, it'll clear. Why, it stands to reason rain can't keep on falling." Perhaps it couldn't — perhaps the sun would shine again some day.

Flat No. 1 — old Mrs Meredith, who went out all bundled up with shawls in a bath-chair. How dreadful to be nothing more than a bundle of shawls. Better to be unhappy, better to be anything that was alive than to have forgotten what it was like to live. Better to break your heart for a dead lover than to have lost the memory of love. She pulled away from that. Mrs Meredith's companion, Miss Crane, an easy, tattling person — large round glasses and a plump pale face. Mrs Meredith's sour-faced maid who never spoke to anyone. There they were, the three of them, asleep now. She wondered if Packer's trap of a mouth loosened at all or fell open in sleep.

In the other ground-floor flat, Mrs and Miss Lemming. She felt sorry for Agnes Lemming, the drudge of a selfish mother. She wouldn't be so plain if she took any trouble over herself. But it was Mrs Lemming who had the new clothes, the permanent waves, the facial treatments, and who still carried herself with the air of a beauty and got away with it — lovely white hair, and those fine eyes, and a really marvellous complexion. Poor Agnes, she had a nice smile, but so little use for it — all the work of the flat to do, and endless errands to run besides. "I wish they'd call her up. It would give her a chance to be a human being instead of a slave. I suppose she must be thirty-five."

Number 3 — the Underwood flat. Just now it contained herself, Aunt Mabel, and, in the slip of a maid's bedroom, Ivy Lord. Uncle Godfrey was away in the north. She loved Uncle Godfrey — quiet, gentle, shy — Wing-Commander Underwood, with a D.F.C. Now how in this world did he come to marry Aunt Mabel? They simply didn't belong. Perhaps it was because he was shy and she saved him the trouble of talking. Anyhow there they were, nearly sixteen years married and very fond of each other. An odd sort of world.

Over the way, in No. 4, Miss Garside — elderly, dignified, aloof. "Thinks herself somebody," to quote Aunt Mabel. "And who is she anyway?" Well, Miss Garside was Miss Garside. She came of an intellectual family. She had what Mrs Underwood stigmatised as "highbrow" tastes. Her figure and her ideas were equally unbending. The eyes which looked past her neighbours quite possibly saw the stars. Meade thought she might be anywhere, in any time. Not here. I wonder where she is now.

Easier to speculate about Mr and Mrs Willard in No. 5. She could picture him sleeping neatly, without a wrinkle in sheet or pillow. He would, of course, have taken his glasses off, but otherwise he would be just the same as when he was awake — dapper even in pyjamas, his hair unruffled, his gas mask handy. Of all the people in the house, she could feel least sure that he would have escaped into a dream. Does a Civil Servant ever escape? Does he ever want to?

Mrs Willard in the other twin bed with the bedside table between her and Mr Willard. In the daytime both beds had spreads of rose-coloured art silk embroidered in a rather frightful pattern of blue and purple flowers which had never bloomed outside the designer's imagination. Now at night they would be tidily folded up and put away. Mr Willard would see to that.

It was not in Mrs Willard to be neat. She had hair which had stopped being brown without getting on with the business of going grey. It had more ends than you would have thought possible, and they all stuck out in different directions. She had rather a London accent, and she wore the most distressing clothes, but she was nice. She called you "Dearie", and somehow you didn't mind. Where did she go to in her dreams? Meade thought it would be a nursery with lots of jolly children — something very small in a cot, twins in rompers, grubby little schoolboys bouncing in, a girl with a long fair plait . . . But Mrs Willard hadn't any children — she had never had any. Poor Mrs Willard.

Opposite in Flat 6, Mr Drake. Or perhaps not. He was often out quite late — later than this. You could hear his step on the gravel before the house. She wondered if he was out now, or only away in a dream. And what would Mr Drake's dream be like? An odd-looking person — black eyebrows like Mephistopheles, and very thick iron-grey hair. What he did and where he went when he wasn't in his flat, nobody seemed to know. Always very polite if you met him in the lift, but no one got farther than that. Mrs Willard opined that he had a secret sorrow.

Up to the top of the house now. No. 7 was shut up. The Spooners were away. Mr Spooner, torn from his warehouse (wool), his stout form most unbecomingly clothed in khaki, but still cheerful, still facetious, still talking about the "little woman". Mrs Spooner, in the A.T.S., youngish, prettyish, anxious, trying to be bright. Trying very hard. She came up sometimes. Perhaps her dreams were giving her back the world which had been snatched away — a little pleasant world with little gossiping bridge parties; a new frock, a new hat; going with Charlie to the pictures and coming home to a cosy little supper — a trivial world, but all she had, not to be found anywhere now except in a dream.

The eighth flat, and the last. Miss Carola Roland — stage girl with a stage name. Meade wondered what she had started with. Not Carola, and not Roland — there wasn't any doubt about that. Whatever the pretty, pert child had been called, and whatever colour her hair had been then, at somewhere in her twenties she was still pert, still pretty, and the perfect peroxide blonde.

Meade was getting sleepy. Carola Roland — she's frightfully pretty — wonder why she lives here — dull for her — she won't stay — wonder why she came — wonder what she dreams about — diamonds and champagne — bubbles rising in a full golden glass — bubbles rising in the sea — the rocking of a ship . . . She was back in her own dream again.

In the room next door Mrs Underwood slept heavily, her hair in wavers, her face well creamed, her shoulders propped upon three large pillows, her window open, as Meade's had been, at the top. The moonlit mist was close against the double panes. It hung like a curtain across the gap above them. Something moved in the mist, moved across the panes, across the gap. There was a faint creaking sound, as if a hand had leaned upon the frame of those double panes. There was another sound, much fainter, audible only to the finest waking sense. But no one waked, no one heard anything at all. Something as light as a leaf slipped to the floor inside the window and lay there. The shadow passed on, passed Meade's window, open at the bottom now. No handhold there. Nothing but smooth, cold glass above and empty space below.

Moving without haste and without delay, the shadow went by. It passed across the window and was gone. There had been no sound at all.

Meade was in her dream, but Giles wasn't there any longer. It was dark. She wandered in the dark, seeking him desperately and in vain.

CHAPTER
TWO

In a moment of relaxation Miss Silver rested her hands upon the Air Force sock which she was in process of knitting and contemplated her surroundings. A feeling of true thankfulness possessed her. So many poor people had been bombed out of their homes and had lost everything, but her modest flat in Montague Mansions remained unscathed — not even a window broken.

"Quite providential," was her comment as she looked about her and noted the blue plush curtains, their colour a little dimmed after three years of wear but they had cleaned remarkably well; the brightly patterned Brussels carpet; the wallpaper with its floral design, a trifle faded but not noticeably so unless one of the pictures was removed. She saw all these things and admired them. Her eye wandered from the engraving of Landseer's *Monarch of the Glen* in a contemporary frame of yellow maple to similarly framed reproductions of *Bubbles, The Soul's Awakening,* and *The Black Brunswicker.* Her heart was really quite full of thankfulness. A comfortable and tasteful room in a comfortable and tasteful flat. During the years when she had worked as a governess for the meagre salary which was all that a governess could then command she had never had any grounds for hoping that such comfort would be hers. If she had remained a governess, there would have been no plush curtains, no Brussels carpet, no steel engravings, no easy chairs upholstered in blue and green tapestry with curving walnut legs, Victorian waists, and wide well-padded laps. By a strange turn of events she had ceased to be a governess, and had become a private investigator, and so successful had the investigations proved that they had made possible the plush, the tapestry, the walnut, and the Brussels pile. Deeply and sincerely religious, Miss Silver thanked what she was accustomed to call Providence for her preservation throughout two years of war.

She was about to resume the sock, which she was knitting for her youngest nephew Alfred who had just entered the Air Force, when the door opened and her valuable middle-aged Emma announced, "Mrs Underwood." There came in one of those plump women whose clothes fit them with unbecoming exactness. Mrs Underwood's black cloth suit moulded her too frankly. She wore a little too much face powder, a little too much lipstick, and it would have been better if she had dispensed altogether with eye shadow. The waves of her hair, under one of the odd hats just then affected by the ultra smart, were too set, too formal, too fresh from the hairdresser's hands. Her skirt was too short and her stockings too thin for a pair of buxom legs, and if her shoes were not so tight as to be excruciatingly painful they very much belied their appearance. She advanced with a bright smile and an extended hand.

"Oh, Miss Silver, I am sure you have not the least idea who I am, but we met a few weeks ago at Mrs Moray's — Mrs Charles Moray — dear Margaret — such a charming person — and as I happened to be passing I thought I must come in and see you! Now don't say you have forgotten our meeting, for I should never have forgotten you!"

Miss Silver smiled and shook hands. She remembered Mrs Underwood very well, and Charles Moray saying, "Poor old Godfrey Underwood's fiasco and the most crashing silly bore in the Home Counties. She hangs round Margaret's neck like the Ancient Mariner and the albatross. No resolution — that's what's the matter with Margaret. Does she take the woman out and push her under a tram? No, she asks her to tea, and I shall probably throw the milk-jug at her if it goes on."

Miss Silver said briskly,

"How do you do, Mrs Underwood? I remember you very well."

The lady sat down. There were two rows of pearls upon her bosom. They rose and fell a little more rapidly than was natural. Their owner had presumably come up in the lift, yet from the evidence of the pearls she might very well have taken the three flights of stairs at a run.

Rejecting such an absurd supposition, Miss Silver wondered why Mrs Underwood should be nervous, and whether her visit was to be regarded as a professional one. She said, breaking in upon some negligible remark about the weather, "I beg your pardon, Mrs Underwood, but it is always best to come straight to the point. Had you any special reason for wishing to see me, or is this merely a friendly call?"

Mrs Underwood changed colour. It was not a becoming change. Beneath the powder her skin was suffused with an ugly pinkish mauve. She laughed on rather a high note.

"Oh, but of course — any friend of dear Margaret's — and I just happened to be passing. Quite a coincidence in its way. There I was, walking down the street, and when I looked up and saw Montague Mansions just across the way I felt I really couldn't pass you by."

Miss Silver's needless clicked. The Air Force sock revolved. She reflected on the sad prevalence of untruthfulness — a distressing fault which should be wisely and firmly corrected in the young. She said a little primly, "And how did you know that I lived here, Mrs Underwood?"

That unbecoming flush came up again.

"Oh, Margaret Moray mentioned it, you know — she just happened to mention it — and I felt I could *not* pass your very doorstep without coming in. What a nice flat you have here. A flat is so much more convenient than a house — don't you think so? No stairs. I don't wonder maids won't go to those basement houses. And then if you want to go away you have only to put your front door key in your pocket, and there you are."

Miss Silver said nothing. Her needles clicked. She supposed that her visitor would presently come to the

14

point. Not a very agreeable speaking voice — high-pitched, and with something of the sound given out by china with a crack in it.

Mrs Underwood continued to talk.

"Of course there are drawbacks. When I lived in the country I adored my garden. I delight in a garden, but my husband was obliged to be nearer his work — the Air Ministry, you know. And then when he was ordered up north, well, there I was with the flat on my hands, and if it hadn't been for the war, I could have let it a dozen times over, but of course nobody wants to take flats in London now. Not that it's really in London — Putney, you know — one of those delightful old houses which used to be right in the country. It belonged to Vandeleur, the artist, who made such a lot of money painting the royal family when Queen Victoria had all those children, so of course he became the rage and made a fortune, which artists hardly ever do, but I think he had private means as well. It must have been a dreadfully expensive house to keep up. I believe it stood empty for a long time after he died, and then they turned it into flats. But the garden isn't what it was — of course gardeners are almost impossible to get — and I would like to be nearer my husband, but as for getting anything reasonable, well, I did go and see a bungalow just the other day — three rooms and a kitchen, and they were asking five and a half guineas a week for it —"

"These exorbitant prices should be controlled," said Miss Silver briskly.

"So I decided to stay where I was."

"Very sensibly, I am sure."

"Though, as I said, there are drawbacks, living at such close quarters with other people. There are eight flats, and — well, I expect you know how it is, you come up in the lift with people, so you can't help knowing them by sight, can you?"

Miss Silver supposed not.

The pearls rose and fell. Mrs Underwood went on.

"So in a way you know them, and in a way you don't. And the ones you wouldn't mind being friendly with aren't always the ones that want to be friendly with you. Miss Garside now — I don't know who she is to give herself such airs, but she's got a way of looking across the lift at you as if you were on the other side of the street and she'd never seen you before and wouldn't know you from Adam if she met you again. Downright rude I call it. Then on the other hand there are people you don't know anything about — and I'm sure I haven't got anything against anybody, and you can't be too careful what you say, but Meade is a very attractive girl, and though she's my husband's niece and not mine, I don't make any difference on that account, and I'm very pleased to give her a home while she wants one — but having a girl in the flat, well, you have to be more careful than you would be on your own account."

Miss Silver began to see a glimmer of light.

"Has anyone been annoying your niece?"

"Well, she's my husband's niece — I told you that, didn't I — but as I said, I don't let it make any difference. Oh, no, nobody's been annoying her, and I'm

16

sure the flats are all let to a very good class of people —
I wouldn't like to give a wrong impression about that."

Miss Silver wondered just what impression she did
wish to convey. Whilst she had been talking about the
late Mr Vandeleur and his house her breathing had
been normal. Now it was becoming hurried again. That
there was something on her mind was certain. Whatever
it was, it had been sufficiently urgent to take her
through the successive stages of applying to Margaret
Moray for Miss Silver's address and then bringing her
from Putney to Montague Mansions. But there the
impulse appeared to have failed. It was not the first
time that a visitor who might have been a client had
come as Mrs Underwood had come, and in the end
gone nervously away with a fear unspoken or a call for
help withheld.

The idea that this plump, fashionable lady might be
the prey of some secret terror brought no smile to Miss
Silver's lips. She knew fear when she saw it. Mrs
Underwood was certainly afraid. She said, "It is very
important to get the right impression about everyone.
Things are not always what they seem — are they?"

Mrs Underwood's eyelids came down. It was as if
she had pulled down a blind, but not quite quickly
enough. In the instant before it fell terror had stared
out of the window — the sheer naked terror of the
creature in a trap.

Miss Silver looked across her knitting and said,

"What are you afraid of, Mrs Underwood?"

Plump gloved hands fumbled in a shiny bag. A
handkerchief came out. The powdered face was

dabbed. The voice which had been so high and sharp fell to a murmur about the heat.

"So warm — so very close —"

There were little glistening beads of sweat on the upper lip. The handkerchief dabbed, and came away stained with lipstick. Tragedy in caricature — rather horrid. The lady was so plump, so smart, so underbred, so *frightened*. Miss Silver preferred a client who engaged her sympathies, but her sense of duty was inexorable. She said in a kind, firm tone, "Something has frightened you. You came here to tell me about it, did you not? Will you not do so?"

CHAPTER
THREE

Mrs Underwood gave a little gasp.

"I don't know, I'm sure. Well, really it's nothing. It's such a very warm day, don't you think?"

"I think that something has frightened you," said Miss Silver, "and I think that you had better tell me about it. If we share our troubles we halve them."

Mabel Underwood drew a long breath. With a sudden drop into simplicity she said, "You wouldn't believe me."

Miss Silver smiled. She said, "I can believe anything, Mrs Underwood."

But the moment of simplicity had passed. The pearls rose and fell rapidly.

"I'm sure I can't think why I said that. Girls do walk in their sleep once in a way, and it's nothing to make a to-do about."

"Has your niece been walking in her sleep?"

"Oh, no — not Meade. But I'm sure if it were, it wouldn't be at all surprising, poor girl, after all she's been through."

Miss Silver had picked up her knitting again. The needles clicked encouragement.

"Indeed?"

"Oh, yes. She was torpedoed, you know — at least the ship was. She took her brother's children out to America last year, after he was killed in France. Their mother is American, and she was out there visiting her people and quite distracted, poor thing, so Meade took the children out to her. And then, of course, she couldn't get home again, not till June. And the ship was torpedoed and she was all smashed up, poor girl, and lost her fiance as well — at least they hadn't given it out, but she met him in the States. He was on one of those hush-hush missions — something about tanks, I believe, but perhaps I oughtn't to say so, though I don't suppose it matters now, because he was drowned. Of course it was a most dreadful shock for Meade."

Mrs Underwood had certainly found her tongue. Miss Silver recalled Charles Moray's "A gushing gasbag", and Margaret's "Charles, *darling* — gas doesn't gush!" She gave a slight cough and said, "Naturally. But you say it is not your niece who walks in her sleep."

Mrs Underwood dabbed at her lips.

"Well, I don't know — I didn't think about it being Meade — I thought it might be Ivy."

"Ivy?"

"The maid, you know — Ivy Lord. I wouldn't keep her, but they're so scarce and difficult to get, you have to put up with anything."

The needles clicked. Miss Silver said, "What makes you think this girl is walking in her sleep?"

Mrs Underwood gulped.

"There was a letter on my floor."

Miss Silver said, "Yes?" and saw the mauvish colour run up into the plump, pale cheeks.

"How could it have got there? I keep on trying to think of ways, but there aren't any. I mean it wasn't there when I went to bed and that's flat. And if it wasn't there then, who put it there — that's what I want to know. The flat was all locked up for the night, and there was just me and Meade and Ivy inside, and the very first thing I saw when I woke up in the morning was that bit of paper lying right under the window."

"A bit of paper, or a letter?"

Mrs Underwood dabbed her forehead.

"It was a bit torn off my own letter, and it was lying there right under the window. And someone must have come into my room in the night and dropped it, for it wasn't there when I went to bed — I can swear to that." The dabbing hand was shaking. She dropped it into her lap and it lay there, clutching the handkerchief.

Miss Silver leaned forward.

"Why does this frighten you so much? Is it because of something in the letter?"

The hand had stopped twitching and was clenched. Mrs Underwood said in a quick, breathless voice, "Oh, no — of course not — it was just a bit of business letter — it wasn't important at all. I just didn't know how it got there, and that frightened me. Very stupid, I'm sure — but this close weather and the war — well, it plays tricks with your nerves, don't you think?"

Miss Silver coughed.

21

"I am not troubled with nerves, I am thankful to say. They must be very disagreeable. Was it a letter you had received, or a letter you had written?"

Mrs Underwood had taken out her powder compact and was attending to her face.

"Oh, one that I had written — nothing of any importance — just a torn piece, you know."

"And you had not posted it?"

The compact sagged in a shaking hand.

"I — well, I —"

"It had been posted then? It is really better to tell me the truth, Mrs Underwood. The letter had been posted, and that is why you were alarmed at finding a piece of it on your bedroom floor."

Mrs Underwood opened her mouth and shut it again. Miss Silver was reminded of a fish gasping. Not an attractive resemblance. She said in her kind, firm voice, "If anyone is blackmailing you —"

Mrs Underwood put out both hands as if to push something away and said, "How did you know?"

Miss Silver smiled. It was a perfectly kind smile.

"It is my business to know that sort of thing. You are frightened about a letter. That naturally suggests blackmail."

Put like that, it seemed quite simple. Mrs Underwood experienced a sort of relief. The worst, or almost the worst, was over. She had not thought that she could tell anyone — not even when she got the address from Margaret, not even when she came up in the lift and rang the bell — but since this dowdy, governessy person had guessed, there was no doubt that it would be a relief to talk about it. She needn't tell her everything. Something in her shuddered and said, "Oh, no — *never!*" But they could talk it over from the outside, as it were — they needn't go farther than that. Like an echo of her thought, she heard Miss Silver say, "You need not tell me anything you do not want to."

She sat back in her chair and said in her natural voice,

"Well then, if you must know, I *had* posted it. That's what gave me such a turn."

"You had posted a letter of which a fragment was found on your bedroom floor?"

"Well, yes, I had. And that is what upset me."

"Dear me!" said Miss Silver. "You wrote a letter and you posted it, and afterwards a piece of that letter was found lying under your window."

"That's right."

"Did you post the letter yourself, or did you give it to your maid?"

"Oh, no — I posted it myself, with my own hand."

"Did you make more than one copy of the letter?"

Mrs Underwood shook her head.

"It was as much as I could do to write it once."

Miss Silver knitted. After a moment she said, "Your letter was in reply to one from a person who is, or has been, blackmailing you. Do you know who this person is?"

The head with its tinted chestnut curls was shaken again. The mauvish colour rose.

"I haven't an idea. There isn't anyone I can think of. There was an address, so I went to have a look — right the other side of London, but I went. And when I got there, it was nothing but a tobacconist's shop, and they said a lot of their customers called for their letters there, and made out it was all on account of people being bombed out — and I didn't believe a word of it, but they wouldn't tell me anything. So I posted my letter at the end of the street and came away."

"You posted that letter on the other side of London?"

Mrs Underwood nodded.

"Yes, I did. And that's what gave me the turn, because how did it get back into Vandeleur House, and how did that Ivy Lord come by a piece of it to drop in my room? Because that's what she must have done. Don't you see, if she got a bit of my letter walking in her sleep, it means the person I wrote it to is right there in one of those Vandeleur flats — and if that isn't awful, I don't know what is. I feel like having a heart attack every time I think about it, but I just can't stop thinking. And if she wasn't walking in her sleep, well, that's worse, isn't it? Because that means she's in with this wretch, whoever he is. And there's something crazy about it too, because what's the sense of dropping a piece of my letter like that? It would be just going out of her way to get herself into a mess, and no gain to anyone. So when I hadn't had a wink of sleep for two nights, I remembered what Margaret said about you and I got the address and came. And that's the truth."

Yes, that was the truth, and a different woman speaking it — a woman who had been country born and country bred, and who still retained a vein of country shrewdness. Charles Moray's crashing silly bore was in abeyance.

Miss Silver nodded approvingly.

"Very well put, Mrs Underwood. You know, you should go to the police."

The head was shaken again.

"I can't."

Miss Silver sighed.

"They all say that, and so blackmail goes on. Have you paid anything yet?"

Mrs Underwood gulped.

"Fifty pounds — and what I shall say to Godfrey, I'm sure I don't know!"

"The money was in the letter you posted?"

"Oh, no, that was in the first one, getting on for six months ago, just after Godfrey went up north. And this time I said I couldn't pay anything. And I can't — I haven't got it to give, Miss Silver. And that was what was on the torn bit of paper — 'I haven't got it to give'."

Miss Silver's needles clicked.

"This person is threatening to tell your husband something. Why don't you tell him yourself?"

Mrs Underwood gave another of those distressing gasps. She said, "I can't!" and left it at that.

Miss Silver shook her head reprovingly.

"It would be very much better if you did. But I will not press you. What makes you think that this girl Ivy Lord may have been walking in her sleep? Do you know of her having done so on any previous occasion?"

Mrs Underwood stared.

"Why — didn't I tell you? That's what comes of being upset — I thought I had. Why, the first thing Ivy told me was all about how she walked in her sleep, and after she found her shoes which she'd cleaned the night before all muddy in the morning, her aunt said she'd better take a job in a flat, and not on the ground floor either, because it wasn't respectable for a girl to be going out lord knows where and lord knows when, with nothing on but her nightgown and a pair of lace-up shoes. I thought I'd told you."

Miss Silver shook her head.

"No, you didn't tell me. What do you want me to do, Mrs Underwood? Would you like me to come down to Putney and see your maid?"

But Mabel Underwood was getting to her feet. Handkerchief and powder compact had gone back into the shiny black bag. The country voice and country manner had retired behind the façade of sham gentility. She said with the old affected accent, "Oh, no — I couldn't dream of troubling you. I'm sure you've been most kind, but I wasn't thinking of anything professional, you know — just a friendly call — but of course quite in confidence — I can rely upon that, can't I?"

Miss Silver shook hands gravely. There was a hint of reproof in her voice as she said, "You can certainly rely upon that. Good-bye, Mrs Underwood."

CHAPTER
FOUR

Meade had been packing parcels for three hours. It tired her dreadfully. She came out into the street and walked to the corner. She hoped she wouldn't have to wait very long for a bus — not her usual one, because she had to go to Harrods for Aunt Mabel. It was this sort of extra that was the last straw, but she couldn't say so, because that would invite the immediate retort, "If you can't pack a few parcels, and do five minutes' shopping to save me going right across London, how on earth do you think you're going to get on in the A.T.S.?"

She had to wait nearly ten minutes for her bus.

It was just on half-past five when she came out of Harrods by one of the side doors and met Giles Armitage face to face. Giles, looking down, saw a girl in a grey flannel suit and a small black hat — a little creature with cloudy hair and lovely eyes. The hair was dark, and the eyes of a deep pure grey. They looked at him out of a small, peaked face, and all of a sudden they lit up and shone like stars. Colour rushed into the pale cheeks. Her hands clutched at his arm, and a very soft voice said,

"*Giles —*"

And then everything went out. The colour, the light, the breath which had carried his name — they all failed together. She gave at the knees, and if he hadn't been pretty quick with his arm she'd have been down on the pavement. A light little thing and easy enough to hold. It was rather like holding a kitten.

She knew him — that much was certain. He waved to a taxi which had just set down a fare, and put Meade in it.

"Get into the Park and drive slow. Go on till I tell you to stop."

He got in and shut the door. The girl was lying back. Her eyes were open. Her hands came out to him, and before he knew what he was going to do he had his arm about her. She seemed to expect it, and so in some odd kind of a way did he. She held on to his arm as if she would never let him go. It all seemed the most natural thing in the world. He had the most extraordinary desire to look after her, to put the colour back into her cheeks and the light into her eyes, yet as far as he could remember he had never seen her before. She was saying his name again: "Giles — Giles — Giles —" A girl doesn't say a man's name like that unless she is awfully fond of him. The inconveniences of losing one's memory obtruded themselves. What did you say to a girl who remembered what you had forgotten?

She drew suddenly away and said in a different voice, "Giles — what's the matter? Why don't you say anything? What is it? I'm frightened."

Major Armitage was a man of action. This had got to be tackled. He tackled it. Those very bright blue eyes of

28

his smiled at her out of the square, tanned face. He said, "I say — please don't! I mean you won't faint again or anything like that will you? I'm the one to be frightened really. Won't you have a heart and help me out? You see, I've been torpedoed and I've lost my memory. I didn't know anything could make one feel such a fool."

Meade slipped away from him into the corner of the seat. *Giles didn't remember her.* A frozen feeling gathered about her heart. She said, "I won't faint."

It hurt too much for that. He was Giles come back from the dead, and he was a stranger. He was looking at her just as he had looked the first time they met, at Kitty Van Loo's. And all of a sudden the frozen feeling went and her heart was warm again, because he had fallen in love with her then, at first sight, and if he had done it once, why shouldn't he do it again? What did it matter that he had forgotten? He was Giles, and she was Meade, and he was alive. "Oh, God, thank you, thank you, for letting Giles be alive!"

He saw the light and colour come back. It gave him the strangest feeling, as if he had created something. He said in a different voice, "Who are you?"

"Meade Underwood."

He repeated it, "Meade — Underwood — It's a pretty name. Did I call you Meade?"

Something flickered and went again, like the flash of light off a bird's wing. He couldn't catch it. She said, "Yes."

"Have I known you long?"

"Not very long. We met in New York, on the first of May, at Kitty Van Loo's. Do you remember her?"

He shook his head.

She looked at the bright blue eyes, at the crisp fair hair above the ruddy brown skin, and thought, "He's well — he's alive. What does anything else matter?" But she was glad that he didn't remember Kitty Van Loo.

"I don't remember a thing, except about the job I went over there to do. I don't remember going out there, or anything after Christmas '39. Everything since then has just run into a fog as far as my personal recollection goes. Why" — his voice changed — "I didn't even remember about my brother Jack being killed. He was with me at Dunkirk, and somehow I knew he was dead, but I couldn't remember a thing about it — not a thing. I can't now. I've had to get it all from a chap who was there with me. I can remember being in France, and getting away from Dunkirk, and the job I had at the War Office, but none of the personal things. I could tell them all about my job in the States — all the technical part. Funny, isn't it, but I can remember a fellow in my first regiment, an extraordinarily fine bridge player. He used to get canned every night, but it never affected his game. I've seen him so that he couldn't take in a word you said outside the play, but he knew every card that was out — never made a mistake. I suppose it's something like that. Well, we met at Kitty Van Loo's — and where did we go from there?"

He saw Meade sparkle. It went to his head a little. The whole thing was going to his head — this blend of

30

the strange and the familiar. She said, "Oh, we went places."

"Nice places?"

"Yes, nice places."

"Lots of them?"

"Lots of them."

"And when did you come back?"

She was watching him. She said, "In June."

She saw the blood run up under his skin.

"But so did I — at least that's what they tell me. That is to say, I started to come, and we were torpedoed." He laughed. "I was picked up by a tramp a couple of days later. I'd got hold of a grating, and I believe they couldn't get me to let go — had to more or less prise me off it. I don't remember anything about it myself. I'd been hit on the head, and the next thing I knew I was in a hospital ward in New York, and nobody knew who I was. Well, that's me. But you said June. I suppose the Atlantic wasn't by any chance one of the places we went together . . . Oh, it was? Well, I hope I saved your life."

Meade nodded. For a moment she couldn't speak. It was all too horribly, too vividly present again — the darkness, the noise, and those rending crashes — the rush of the water, coming in, sucking them down — Giles lifting her, heaving her into the boat. She said, "You put me into one of the boats."

"You were all right — not hurt?"

"My arm was broken, and some ribs. They're all right now."

"Sure?"

"Quite sure."

They looked at one another. There was a silence. Just as it became unendurable, he said, "How well did we know each other, Meade?"

She closed her eyes. The lashes lay dark against her cheek. In three months she had not heard him say her name. When she had dreamt of him he had not said it. Now he was saying it like a stranger. It hurt too much. He said in a quick, anxious voice, "You look all in. Can't I take you somewhere? Where would you like to go? I say, you're not going to faint, are you?"

The lashes lifted. She looked at him. It was very disturbing. She said in a whispering voice, "I won't if I can help it. I think I had better go home."

CHAPTER
FIVE

They said good-bye on the steps of Vandeleur House, with the taxi ticking away in the road on the other side of a massive Victorian shrubbery. There was daylight still, daylight falling into dusk — grey daylight — no colour, no sparkle, no sun. There would be a mist again tonight. Meade was in the very mood of the mist, so tired that she could hardly stand. Reaction from the shock of finding Giles, only to find that she was forgotten, had left her as dull and lifeless as the day. They had met, they were saying good-bye, and perhaps they would never meet again. The pain of that came through the dullness and pierced her. He might just go away back to his job and think no more of their meeting than that it was a queer sort of business and best let alone. She must face it. It might very easily happen. He had been landed with a stupid fainting girl — for all he could remember, a total stranger. Men hated girls who cried and girls who fainted. He had been kind. Giles was kind. She had seen him being kind to stray dogs and tiresome old women — but once you got rid of the wretched lost creature you didn't go out of your way to look for any more trouble. So here she was saying good-bye to Giles. She mustn't cry, and she mustn't faint. She must go through with it decently.

She put out a hand and he took it. Then he took the other one and held them both. Giles always had such strong, warm hands. He said in a serious tone, halting a little over the words as if there was some strong feeling behind them, "This is — all wrong — we oughtn't to be saying good-bye. It's hurting you, and I'd give anything not to hurt you. Will you *please* not be hurt, and let me go away and get hold of myself a bit? It's knocked us both endways. What's your telephone number?"

This was so exactly Giles that she caught her breath on a laugh that hurt.

"You asked me that in New York, the first time we met."

"I expect I did. Did you give it to me?"

"Oh, yes."

"Well, you'll have to do it again. What is it?"

She repeated the number, and watched him write it down just as he had done that first time. But he'd got a new notebook. The other must be somewhere bobbing about in the Atlantic with her New York telephone number washed out of it as completely as she had been washed out of Giles' memory.

He put the notebook back in his pocket and took her hands again.

"I'll go now — but I'll ring you up. You won't mind?"

No, she wouldn't mind. She said so.

He held her hands for a moment longer, and then went away to where the taxi was waiting, his footsteps crunching cheerfully over the gravel.

34

Meade watched him go. If he was going to ring up, it wasn't really good-bye. Her heart warmed a little. She went up in the lift and got out at the first landing. The Underwoods' flat was No. 3. She would have to tell Aunt Mabel, and the sooner she did it the better. She wished with all her heart that she had never told anyone about Giles. When you are all smashed up in hospital and a very kind uncle comes and holds your hand, things come out. Besides, she had to know about Giles. Uncle Godfrey had been most awfully kind, but of course he had told Aunt Mabel and Aunt Mabel had told everyone in the world, so now she had to tell Aunt Mabel that Giles was alive and that he had forgotten her, so of course they were not engaged any more. She must get it over.

She got it over. It wasn't easy. Mabel Underwood did nothing to make it easier. She meant to be kind, but actually she was the last straw.

"He doesn't remember you?"

"He doesn't remember anything."

"But how perfectly extraordinary! Do you mean to say that he doesn't remember his name?"

"He remembers his name."

"Or who he is — or about his job in the States?"

"He remembers that."

Mrs Underwood's voice became strident.

"And he doesn't remember you? My dear, it's too thin! He's trying to back out. Your Uncle Godfrey must see him at once. Don't you worry — young men have these sort of turns, but your uncle will put it right. It's not as if you hadn't anyone to stand up for you. Don't you worry — it'll all come right."

It was quite unbearable, but she had to bear it. Unkindness would have been easier. Aunt Mabel meant to be kind, but behind the kindness it was perfectly plain that she thought Giles Armitage a very good match for a penniless girl, and that she had no intention of letting him go.

Nothing lasts for ever. Meade was told that she didn't look fit for anything but bed, to which haven she thankfully repaired. "And Ivy will bring you your supper. I'm going up to the Willards for some bridge."

Blessed relief, even though she knew that the Willards would be told about Giles and treated to Mabel Underwood's views upon the management of recalcitrant young men. It wasn't any good thinking about it. Aunt Mabel was like that, and you just had to let it go.

She lay there and let everything go. No use thinking, no use planning, no use hoping, no use grieving.

Ivy came in with a tray — fish cakes and a cup of Ovaltine. Meade, sitting up in bed, thought, "She doesn't look any too good herself. I wonder if she is unhappy." She said on the impulse, "You look tired, Ivy. Are you all right?"

"Got a bit of a head — nothing to write home about."

A London girl, small and thin, with a pale, sharp face and lank brown hair.

"Where is your home?"

Ivy jerked a shoulder.

"Haven't got one — not to speak of. Gran's being 'vacuated. Ever such a nice lady she's got billeted with. Bottled four dozen of tomatoes out of their own garden, and fresh veg. coming in every day — we could do with a bit of that here, couldn't we?"

"Is that all the family you've got?"

Ivy nodded.

"Gran and my Auntie Flo — that's the lot. And Aunt Flo, she's in the A.T.S. — got one of those new caps they wear too — red and green on them — ever so smart they are. She wanted me to join up too, but I didn't pass my medical. That's on account of the accident I had when I was a kid on the halls."

"What halls?"

Ivy giggled.

"Music halls, miss — V'riety — me and me sister Glad. Boneless Wonders we was — acrobats, you know. But there was a naccident on the high wire and Glad was killed, and they said I wouldn't never be any good for it again, so I went out to service, and seems like I'll have to stay in it. Doctor said he couldn't pass me nohow."

Meade said, "I'm sorry," in her pretty, soft voice. And then, "Get off early to bed, Ivy, and have a good rest. Mrs Underwood won't be wanting anything."

Ivy jerked again.

"I'm not all that set on bed — seems like it don't do me any good. I get dreaming, you know — about Glad and me, and having to walk that wire. That's how I come to walk in my sleep when I was down in Sussex,

37

and Gran said it wasn't respectable and I'd better take and go in a flat where I couldn't get out."

Meade shivered, and then wondered why. It certainly wouldn't be easy to get out of Vandeleur House after Bell had locked up. Horrid to think of wandering up and down that circular stair in the dead of night. She said quickly, "You don't walk in your sleep now?"

Ivy's glance slipped away.

"Oh, I dunno," she said in a vague voice. "Aren't you going to have another fish cake? I made them the way Gran told me, and they come out lovely — tomato sauce and the least little bit of shrimp paste. Makes all the difference, don't it?"

When the tray was gone and the room was quiet again, Meade took a book and tried to read, but what the book was, or what the lines of print had to say, she never had any idea. There was a shaded lamp beside the bed. The light fell mellow across her shoulder, and across Mabel Underwood's pink sheets and the corner of a pink frilled pillow-case. This had been Godfrey Underwood's room, that was why there was a telephone by the bed. Uncle Godfrey and a pink frilled pillow-case — nothing could be more incongruous. But he wouldn't notice anything like that. The eiderdown bloomed with pink and purple paeonies, and so did the curtains. There was rose-coloured china on the washstand, and a rose-coloured carpet on the floor. There had been times when she felt that she couldn't bear it for another moment, but it was like everything else, you got used to it.

The telephone bell cut across her drifting thoughts. Under them she had been listening for it, straining for it, expecting it. Now that it had come, her heart knocked wildly at her side and her hand shook. Giles' voice said from a long way off, "Hullo! Is that you?"

She said, "Yes."

"It doesn't sound like you."

She caught her breath.

"How do you know what I sound like?"

At the other end of the line Giles frowned. How did he know? The answer to that was that he did. He said so.

There was no answer.

"Meade — are you there? Please don't ring off — I've got a lot to talk about. I think it's easier on the telephone — I mean we want to get the ground cleared a bit, don't we? You won't go away?"

"No, I won't go away."

"Where are you? Are you alone — can you talk?"

"Yes. My aunt has gone out. I'm in bed."

"Why? What's the matter?"

"Oh, nothing. I'm just tired."

"You're not too tired to talk?"

"No."

"All right, then, here goes. I've been thinking, and I want to know where we left off. It seems to me I've got to know that. Don't you see you've got to help me out? If I'd come back blind, you'd lend me your eyes to see with — read my letters for me, all that sort of thing — wouldn't you? Well, this is just the same, isn't it? I've gone blind, not in my eyes but in my memory. The

39

things I can't remember are like a letter that I can't read. If I ask you to read it for me, you're not going to say no, are you?"

"What do you want me to tell you?"

"I want to know how we stood to each other. We were friends, weren't we?"

"Oh, yes."

"Anything more? That's what I really want to know. Was I in love with you?"

"You said so."

"Then I meant it. I wouldn't have said it if I hadn't. What did you say?"

There was no answer. Her heart beat and her breath came quick, but there weren't any words.

"Meade — don't you see you've got to help me? I've got to know. Were we engaged?"

There was still no answer.

He said in an insistent voice, "Why, I've *got* to know — you must see that. Were we engaged? Was it given out?"

She wanted to laugh and she wanted to cry. It was so very much Giles — so dearly familiar — the urgency of his voice, the way he said her name, the way he never could wait if there was anything he wanted. Echoes out of the past: "Meade, I must know" — the same insistent ring. Then it had been, "Can you care for me?" Now it was, "Did I care for you?" She said as quickly as she could, "No, it wasn't given out."

There was a silence so utter and so prolonged that her heart contracted with fear. Suppose he had gone —

40

hung up and gone away. Quite easy to do. Perhaps that was what he had done — hung up and gone away out of her life. She found herself quick and hot to deny it. That wouldn't be Giles. He always said what he thought. He would tell her straight out — "I'm sorry. I can't remember. It's a wash-out." He wouldn't slink away like a thief in the night.

His voice came over the wire, strong and full.

"Well, that's that. We've got it over. I didn't want to spoil our lunch tomorrow. You will lunch with me, won't you?"

Meade said faintly, "I pack parcels from two to five —"

"*Parcels?*"

"For the bombed — clothes and things."

"But you could get an afternoon off, couldn't you, if you tried very hard?"

"It wouldn't be smiled on."

"I shouldn't worry about that. After all, I don't come back from the dead every day."

He heard her catch her breath.

"That's hitting below the belt."

"I always do. You'll come?"

"Oh, yes, I'll come. Where?"

"I'll be round to fetch you at a quarter to one. Go to sleep and dream about nice things. Good-night."

She went to sleep, and did not dream about anything. For the first time since that June night she slept and did not dream at all. Everything in her relaxed and fell into rest. The effort of the will, the strain of endurance, the hurrying memories, thought which would not be controlled, all went from her. She slept without consciousness or movement until Ivy came in to draw the curtains.

CHAPTER
SIX

After this, breakfast was not as bad as it might have been. Mrs Underwood, in pyjamas and a pink satin dressing-gown, discoursed volubly upon last night's bridge.

"They had that Miss Roland from the top floor for a fourth — Carola Roland. Plays quite a good game, but if she wasn't born Carrie Snooks or something like that, I'm very much mistaken. And she isn't as young as she looks either — not when you see her close to. Of course Mrs Willard's got no young people to consider, and I'll say that for Mr Willard, faddy and tiresome he may be, but there are worse things in a husband than that, and he isn't the sort that runs after blondes, though really you can't be sure about anyone. There was that Willie Tidmarsh that was some sort of cousin of Godfrey's, and I must say I did think his wife bullied him but they were a very devoted couple — one of those finicky little men, always getting up to open the door for you, and taking the temperature of the bath water, and putting new washers in the taps — got on my nerves. And, as I say, Bella did nag him, but you'd have thought after twenty-five years he'd have been used to it. And he went off with the barmaid from the

Bull, and I believe they were running a snack bar somewhere down in the west." Mrs Underwood paused to pour herself out another cup of coffee.

Meade asked, "What is Carola Roland like to talk to? She's awfully pretty."

All at once the hand with the coffee-pot shook. Some of the coffee went into the saucer. Mrs Underwood made a vexed sound.

"Pretty! She's made up till you don't know what she's like underneath! And what do you think she was wearing last night? Black satin trousers, a green and gold top, and emerald earrings about half a yard long. If it was done for Alfred Willard's benefit, she had her trouble for nothing — and as for Mrs Willard and me, she won't do either of us any harm." She put down her cup rather abruptly.

Meade said, "What's the matter?"

The flow of words had broken so suddenly. Mabel Underwood had such a curious faltering look. She repeated her last words in a fumbling sort of way.

"She won't — do either of us — any harm. Was that what I said just now?" Her eyes stared and blinked. And then before Meade could answer she caught herself up. "Of course it was — I can't think what came over me — everything seemed to go. But what I was going to say was, it's all very well for Mrs Willard and me, and you can't just sit at home doing nothing all through the black-out, so a fourth for bridge is a fourth for bridge, and it's a pity you don't play, but there it is. But it's quite different for a girl, and your uncle wouldn't like you to go mixing yourself up with this

44

Carola Roland — not at all. You can say good-morning and pass the time of day in the lift, but that'll be quite enough. I don't want Godfrey telling me I oughtn't to have let you get mixed up with her."

There was some more on these lines, and then Meade managed to intimate that she was going out to lunch with Giles. Her heightened colour provoked an embarrassing flood of kindness.

"There — what did I tell you! It'll all come right — see if it doesn't. And as for the parcels, I'll go and do them myself, and then that stuck-up Miss Middleton won't have a word to say. One pair of hands is as good as another, and she won't have anything to look down her long nose about. Goes on as if she'd a vinegar bottle under it and was trying not to sneeze. I couldn't do with her for long, but I can put in an afternoon or two to let you off. And mind you put on something pretty, for I'm sick to death of seeing you in grey, and no need of it now he's come back."

Meade's lips trembled into a smile. No need to wear mourning for Giles, because Giles was alive. She went down into the luggage-room to get out coloured things that she had packed away. There was a suit she had had in the spring — skirt and jumper of green and grey wool, and a green coat. It might be too warm for the jumper, but there was a little checked shirt which would do instead. She could wear her grey hat with the green quill which she had taken off it.

She was coming through the hall with the clothes over her arm, when she ran into Miss Crane, who was always in a hurry but never in too much of a hurry to talk. Of course it must be very dull being old Mrs Meredith's companion, but she was dreadfully difficult to get away from. The lift was at one of the upper floors, so she could not take refuge there. There was nothing for it but to let Miss Crane have her say.

The near-sighted eyes peered through very round, large glasses.

"I'm in such a hurry. How busy you look. Are you packing, or unpacking? Green is such a sweet shade, I always think. But I don't believe I have ever seen you in it before. I do hope it means that you are going out of mourning. So sad — so very sad. But perhaps I shouldn't touch upon a painful subject. Pray forgive me. It was most thoughtless, but I had no intention. Oh, no, none at all. It is always a pleasure to see young people enjoying themselves when one has not many enjoyments of one's own. Mrs Meredith is a sad sufferer and needs a great deal of attention. A very great deal. I find it hard sometimes to keep my spirits up. And it is so necessary for her. She is affected at once. That is what I am always telling Packer. Her spirits are not always as even as one could wish. She is inclined to moods. And Mrs Meredith is affected immediately. So I do my best to be cheerful."

Miss Crane had a way of talking with her head pushed forward and her large, pale face uncomfortably near one's own. Her soft, husky voice never seemed to have quite enough breath behind it, yet her short gasping sentences followed one another without any perceptible pause. She had a shopping basket on her arm, and wore the elderly black felt hat and

46

weather-beaten raincoat which were her invariable garb. She touched the basket now and said with the effect of a whispered confidence,

"Fish, Miss Underwood. Mrs Meredith does fancy a nice fresh bit of fish, you know. Fried with breadcrumbs. And if I don't hurry, as likely as not he'll be sold out. And the meat ration is a thing she can't be expected to understand, poor dear. So if you won't think me rude —"

Meade said, "Oh, no, of course not," and turned thankfully towards the lift. It was coming down. The cables swayed and creaked. The lift stopped at the ground level. The door opened and Carola Roland stepped out, looking as if she had just come off a mannequin parade — very highheeled shoes, very shiny and new; very sheer silk stockings; the shortest of smart black suits; the smallest of ridiculous tilted hats; and the largest and most opulent of silver foxes. A gardenia in the buttonhole — the white flower of a blameless life, no doubt, — and above it lips of sealing-wax red, a perfectly tinted skin, enormous blue eyes, and hair of the beauty-parlour's gold. She gave Meade a ravishing smile and said in a voice which very successfully imitated the Mayfair model, "Oh, Miss Underwood, isn't this marvellous news about Giles? Mrs Underwood was full of it last night. But she said he's lost his memory — that isn't true, is it?"

The clothes on Meade's arm weighed suddenly heavy. She couldn't keep the surprise out of her eyes or out of her voice as she said, "Do you know him?"

Miss Roland smiled. The smile displayed a glimpse of pearly teeth. She said mellifluously, "Oh, yes. But do tell me if it's true about his memory. How too dreadful! Has he really lost it?"

"Yes."

"Altogether? Do you mean he can't remember anything?"

"He remembers about his work. He can't remember people."

The scarlet lips smiled again.

"That sounds very — odd. Well, if you're seeing him just ask him if he remembers me. Will you?"

Still with that amused smile, Carola Roland passed on, was silhouetted for a moment against the open doorway, and then disappeared down the steps.

Meade got into the lift.

CHAPTER
SEVEN

At half-past eleven Mrs Underwood went down in the lift. She walked to the corner of the road and took a penny bus, after which she went into a call-box and shut the door.

The bell interrupted Miss Silver in the midst of an earnest calculation as to whether her coupons would provide sufficient wool to make her niece Ethel a new blue jumper, and at the same time enable her to knit a couple of pairs of socks for Lisle Jerningham's baby. She turned with reluctance to the telephone and heard her own name in a high, affected voice.

"Miss Silver?"

"It is Miss Silver speaking. Good-morning, Mrs Underwood."

A breath was sharply drawn.

"Oh! How did you know who it was?"

Miss Silver coughed.

"It is my business to remember voices. Is anything the matter?"

The voice wavered.

"Why, no — not exactly. I'm speaking from a call box. Perhaps I shouldn't have troubled you."

A woman does not leave her own flat with its convenient telephone and ring up from a call-box unless she has some reason for wishing to make quite sure of not being overheard. Miss Silver said crisply, "It is no trouble. Perhaps you will tell me why you called me up."

There was a gulp, and then, "I'm frightened."

"Please tell me why. Has anything fresh occurred?"

"Yes, it has — in a way —"

"Yes?"

"Well, I went upstairs for some bridge last night — the people on the next floor — I often go there. Sometimes her sister comes in to make a fourth — she lives quite near and Mr Willard sees her home. And the Spooners from the top floor used to come down, but they've gone away — he's been called up and she's joined the A.T.S. — so once or twice it's been Mr Drake from the flat opposite, but he's very stand-offish and it wasn't a great success, so last night they had the girl from the other top-floor flat. Her name is Carola Roland — at least I don't suppose it is for a moment, but that's what she calls herself. And oh, Miss Silver, I had such a dreadful shock!"

Miss Silver said, "Yes?" in her most encouraging manner.

Mrs Underwood took up the word and echoed it.

"Yes, I did. I felt better after talking to you, you know. And then Meade came in — that's my niece. And the young man I told you about — the one she was going to be engaged to — well, it seems he wasn't drowned after all, but there's some talk about his having lost his memory, which is a thing that's very easy to say and no doubt very convenient, but he'll find he's got her uncle to reckon with. So you can imagine I'd plenty to think about, and what with packing Meade off to bed, for she looked like fainting on her feet, and getting ready to go up to the Willards, it's the real truth I never gave a thought to what I told you about. I went up, and we had a nice little supper — just the three of us — Miss Roland didn't come in till afterwards. It was Mrs Willard's birthday and she'd had a present of eggs from her sister in the country — her married sister, not the one who comes in for bridge — and she'd made an omelette with a tomato purée and we had some very good soup and a grapefruit jelly. Quite a dinner-party, as I said to her, and I told Mr Willard he was a lucky man to have a wife who can cook like she does. And then Miss Roland came down, and we had coffee and began our bridge. Well, I'm telling you all this for you to understand that I wasn't giving a thought to you know what. I was enjoying myself. I'd better cards than I've held for a long time, and they were all most interested about Giles Armitage turning up like that, and his memory going — if it really has. Mr Willard told us about a man he used to know who drew out five hundred pounds and went to Australia, and when they traced him he couldn't remember who he was, or being married, or anything, and he'd just had his banns put up with a good-looking widow. Miss Roland laughed and said that sort of memory was very convenient — and then she opened her bag for a cigarette, and it was

51

then when she was getting out the case that I had my shock."

"What happened?"

The voice dragged and came slowly, as if it needed those extra breaths to force the words.

"There was a letter — at the bottom — of the bag. I think — it was — my letter. There was — that corner torn off —"

Miss Silver said, "This is a grave accusation, Mrs Underwood."

"It was the same paper — greyish blue. It had the corner torn off."

"Did you see the writing?"

"No, I didn't. It was all folded up — I only saw it for a moment — then she pushed her case down on to it and shut the bag."

Miss Silver took time to think. Then she said in her firmest voice.

"You will have to make up your mind whether you wish me to take up this case professionally."

Mabel Underwood said in a blundering sort of way, "Oh, I don't know — what could you do?"

"I could make some enquiries. I could probably find out who is blackmailing you. And that would almost certainly have the effect of putting a stop to it."

Mrs Underwood gulped and said abruptly, "Would it be expensive?"

Miss Silver named a modest sum.

"We could agree on that to cover a preliminary enquiry. Then if you wished me to go on, I would tell you what I considered would be a fair fee. You had better think the matter over and let me know. If you desire me to take the case, I should like to see you as soon as possible."

Mrs Underwood hesitated. She couldn't really afford the fee — she couldn't afford to be blackmailed. She didn't feel as certain of her ground as she had when she came out. When you spoke about things they slipped away from you. A letter might very easily get torn lying around in a bag. She might be making a fool of herself. It mightn't be her letter at all.

She said, "Oh, well —" And then, "Yes, I'll think it over and let you know."

CHAPTER
EIGHT

Giles had said that he would call for Meade at a quarter to one. He arrived at half-past twelve and found her ready. He might have lost his memory, but she hadn't lost hers, and he had always been at least a quarter of an hour too early for every appointment they had had. It heartened her a good deal to find that he hadn't changed.

She opened the door before the bell stopped ringing, and there he was, very cheerful indeed and coming straight to the point.

"You're ready? Splendid! Come along! I thought we'd go into the country. I've got a car *and* some petrol. This is where you find out who's your friend."

It was at this point that Mrs Underwood emerged. Impossible not to present Giles. Impossible not to wish that it might have been avoided, or at least postponed. Mabel Underwood had spared no pains to make an impression, and an impression she certainly made. Hair waved, face made up, figure tightly restrained, black suit, extravagant hat, tight shoes — how you did wish she wouldn't. The best manner too — the drawled, "Major Armitage"; the "I have heard all sorts of charming things about you from my little niece." The references to Uncle Godfrey — "I'm sure he's as devoted to her as if she was really his daughter."

Meade felt her colour rise and her heart sink down like lead.

They got away at last. Giles said, "Don't let's wait for the lift — it's only one flight."

As soon as they were on the stairs he slipped a hand inside her arm, looked down at her with laughing eyes, and said, "I haven't met her before, have I? I don't suppose one could live through it twice. Is she always as grand as that? It's going to be a most awful strain if she is. I say, darling, she won't want to live with us, will she?"

Everything in Meade broke into answering laughter. Did he know that he had called her darling? Did he know what he had just said? Or had his tongue run away over a familiar course? It didn't matter. Nothing mattered whilst he looked at her like that. Her own tongue run away too. She whispered, "Hush! I'll tell you a secret. She was a farmer's daughter, and when she lets herself be she's one still, and oh, so kind. She doesn't know I know, but Uncle Godfrey let it out."

Giles said, "I'd love to see her milking a cow."

"But that's what she'd like really. When they retire they'll go into the country, and they'll be much, much happier. I oughtn't to have laughed — it was horrid of me. She tries to be grand because she thinks it's good for Uncle Godfrey's career. She's been frightfully kind to me — you don't know —"

He put an arm round her waist and jumped her down the last three steps into the hall.

"Give the conscience a rest," he said in a teasing voice. "You've got some laughing to make up, haven't you? Come along!"

On the entrance steps they met Agnes Lemming coming up. She carried a heavy shopping bag and she looked very tired — Agnes always did look tired. Her abundant brown hair was bundled into a black beret and hardly showed at all. Her face was colourless, with dark smudges under the eyes. She wore an unbecoming purple coat and skirt. Her steps dragged. It was not in Meade to pass her without a word. She said, "Good-morning," and, "This is Major Armitage."

Agnes Lemming smiled. It was a very nice smile. Her brown eyes were soft and pleased.

"Yes, I know. I am so glad." Then the smile went out. She went on in a nervous hurry. "I'm afraid I mustn't stay — I am late. My mother will wonder where I've been, but I've had to wait so long for everything today — the shops were so crowded."

As the car turned out into the road, Giles said, "Who was that? Ought I to know her?"

Meade shook her head.

"Oh, no. She's Agnes Lemming. They have one of the ground-floor flats."

"Who beats her? Somebody does."

"Her mother. I do honestly think Mrs Lemming is the most selfish person in the world. She makes a slave of Agnes and nags at her all the time. I don't know how she stands it."

56

"She's due to crack up any moment, I should say. Don't let's talk about her — let's talk about us. You look a lot better today. Did you sleep?"

Meade nodded.

"You didn't dream we were eloping, or anything like that?"

"I didn't dream at all."

He gave her a sharp sideways glance and said, "Been dreaming a bit too much."

She nodded again.

He took his left hand off the wheel and put it down over one of hers.

"That's all finished with. Now we're going to enjoy ourselves. You shall tell me everything we did and said in New York, and then I'll give my mind to improving on it."

She didn't tell him everything, but she told him a good deal — all the pleasant outside things they had done — where they had dined, and where they had danced, and what plays they had seen.

It was when they were having lunch at a country road-house that she asked him suddenly, "Do you know a girl called Carola Roland?"

Something happened when she said the name. She had an odd feeling that she had broken something, like throwing a stone into a pond and seeing the whole reflected picture of sky and trees break up. But that was just a feeling. What she actually saw was a tightening of the muscles about his throat and jaw. A small intent spark came and went in the bright blue eyes. He said slowly, "You know, that kind of rang a bell. But I'm not there. Who is she?"

"She took one of the top-floor flats about a month ago. She's an actress."

"Young?"

"About five or six and twenty — perhaps a little more — I don't know. She's very pretty."

"What like?"

"Golden hair, blue eyes, lovely figure."

He burst out laughing.

"The perfect blonde — gentlemen prefer her! Is that it? Not my style, darling."

"She's *frightfully* pretty," said Meade in a burst of generosity. "And — and — you mustn't call me darling."

"I didn't know I had. Why mustn't I? It's extra-ordinarily easy."

"You don't mean it," said Meade — "that's why."

He laughed.

"Break for refreshments! Here comes the waiter. The sweets look appalling. I should have cheese if I were you — we'll both have cheese. It's a serious food much better suited to a nice ethical problem than hair-oil jelly or paving-stone puffs. This seems to be honest unadulterated Cheddar — one of the things I haven't forgotten. As the poet laureate would no doubt have said if he had happened to think of it:

'English beef and English cheese
Are things at which I never sneeze.'

"And now that we are alone, why mustn't I call you darling?"

Meade lifted her lashes, and dropped them again upon a sparkle.

"I told you why."

"Did you?"

"You don't mean it."

He was buttering a biscuit.

"Look here, is this thought-reading? Because if it is, you're right off your game. Try something easier. For instance, is this butter or margarine? It looks like butter, but it tastes like marge."

"Perhaps it's half and half."

"Perhaps it is." He leaned across the table. His eyes laughed into hers. "There you are, you've said it — half and half. *Perhaps it is, darling.*"

Meade said, "Oh!" It was just a soft breath. Her heart beat. She must play his game, and play it as lightly and easily as he did. If only she didn't care so much. It would be pleasant and easy enough if she could go back, as he had gone back, to the first enchanted days when they were playing at love. That was what he had done. And all at once she found that she could do it too. She could meet the laugh in his eyes and give it back.

He said, "Half a loaf's better than no bread, isn't it? Presently we'll have cake. Meanwhile, you know, it's really a most interesting point — are we engaged or not? Because if we are, of course I call you darling, and I think you ought to call me something a little warmer than Giles. And if we're not, why aren't we? I mean, who broke it off? Did you? No, you didn't, or you wouldn't have come gallivanting out with me like this, and you wouldn't have been in mourning because you thought I was dead, would you? Well then, are you going to tell me that I broke it off?"

She couldn't look at him any longer She wanted to laugh and cry. She wanted to cry with his arms round her. She said in a soft, quivering voice, "Didn't it just break of itself — when you forgot?"

"Of course it didn't! You don't break things by forgetting about them. Suppose we had been married, my having a bang on the head wouldn't unmarry us, would it? . . . All right, I'm glad you see reason about that. Then it can't disengage us. If you want to stop me calling you darling, you can just break it off."

"Or you can."

"Darling, why should I? I'm liking it most awfully. No, if you want it done you'll have to do it yourself. I didn't give you a ring, did I?"

She shook her head.

"No."

"Meanness — or lack of time? When did we actually get engaged?"

"The day we sailed."

"How inartistic — no time for anything! But it lets me out on the score of being mean. It's a pity you haven't got a ring though, because it would be so easy for you to push it across the table and say, 'All is over between us', wouldn't it?"

Laughter won the day.

"I can still say, 'All is over between us'."

"But you won't, will you — not before we've had coffee? It would cast such a blight. Look here, I've got a splendid idea. We'll go back to town and get you a ring, and then you can break it off with the proper trimmings. How's that?"

"Perfectly mad," said Meade.

"'*Dulce est desipere in loco*.' Which means, broadly speaking, 'You've got to have some fun sometimes.' Come along, we'll skip the coffee — it's certain to be foul. What sort of ring shall we have — emerald, sapphire, diamond, ruby? What's your fancy?"

Meade was shaken with that queer laughter.

"Oh, Giles, you *are* a fool!" she said.

CHAPTER
NINE

A number of things happened that afternoon. None of them appeared at the time to have any special significance, yet each was to take its place in a certain dreadful pattern. It was like the weaving of threads in a tapestry picture — light for gay and dark for grave, red for blood and black for the shadow which was to fall across Vandeleur House and everyone in it. No thread had any value taken singly, but all together they wove the picture.

Mrs Underwood, packing parcels under Miss Middleton's gimlet eye, was having it brought home to her that she couldn't let her thoughts stray to Carola Roland without being pulled up.

"Oh no, Mrs Underwood, I'm afraid that won't do. That knot will slip."

Insufferable woman. She hoped Meade would be properly grateful, and that she was making good use of her time with Giles Armitage — such a good-looking man — and an excellent match. If only nothing went wrong. That wretched letter — "I don't see how I can find the money without Godfrey knowing. I haven't got any jewellery worth two-pence . . . Miss Silver — I can't afford her either. Besides, what could she do? I must do something. Suppose they don't wait — suppose they tell Godfrey. They mustn't — I must do something. If that was my letter in Carola Roland's bag . . . Perhaps it wasn't — there's a lot of that sort of paper about —"

"Really, Mrs Underwood, this won't do at all . . ."

Giles and Meade, with the car run off the road on to a common where the late gorse bloomed.

"Meade — darling!"

"Giles, you mustn't!"

"Why mustn't I? I love you. Have you forgotten that?"

"It's you who have forgotten."

Arms very close about her, lips very near her own.

"Not really — not with anything that matters. It's only my stupid head that's had a crack. Everything else remembers you. Oh, Meade, don't you know I've got you under my skin . . .?"

Miss Garside, grey and restrained, picking up the ring which a stout Jewish gentleman in spectacles had just pushed across the counter in her direction. It was the sort of push which is almost a flick. It carried contempt. She said, "But it was insured for a hundred pounds."

The Jewish gentleman shrugged.

"That is not my business. The stone is paste."

"You are sure?" For a moment horrified incredulity pierced the restraint.

The Jewish gentleman shrugged again.

"Take it anywhere you like, and they will tell you the same."

Mrs Willard, on the couch in No. 6, weeping slow, agonised tears, her face buried in a frilled cushion. The couch was part of the suite which Alfred and she had bought when they were saving up to get married. The suite was here — new covers just before the war — but Alfred . . . Crunched up in a tear-soaked hand was the note she had found in the pocket of the coat she had been going to take down to the cleaners. Not such a very damning note, but more than enough for poor Mrs Willard who had had no practice in looking the other way. Alfred might be fidgetty and Alfred might be cross; he might reprove her unpunctuality, her untidiness, her easy-going lack of method; he might omit to praise her cooking; but that he should be unfaithful, that he should go straying after blonde persons from the floor above was unbelievable.

But she was believing it. She lifted a disfigured face, straightened the moist note out, and read it again:

"All right, Willie darling, lunch at one as usual. Carola."

It was the "as usual" which ran the sharpest needle into Mrs Willard's lacerated heart. And how dared she call him Willie? A chit of a girl half his age . . .

Carola Roland, smiling sweetly at a little man with thin greying hair, very neat, very dapper, the eyes behind an old-fashioned pince-nez gazing at her rather after the fashion of a fish seen through the glass of an aquarium. Mr Willard would have been much horrified if anyone had been so rude as to tell him that he was goggling. Miss Roland was not unaccustomed to being goggled at. It did not offend her in the least. She regarded it as a tribute. She allowed Mr Willard to pay for her lunch and to buy her an expensive box of chocolates. Wartime London can still provide them if you know where to go. Miss Roland knew . . .

The afternoon being fine, old Mrs Meredith went out in her invalid chair, Parker pushing it, and Miss Crane walking sedately on the right-hand side. A performance, getting the chair down the steps — Bell summoned from the basement, and the chair lowered cautiously, with the three of them easing it down and old Mrs Meredith nodding solemnly among her shawls and never saying a word.

They went down to the shops. Miss Crane assured Agnes Lemming that Mrs Meredith enjoyed it all very much — "She does like a bit of life . . ."

Agnes had come down for the second time, to change her mother's library book. Mrs Lemming had not cared for the one which had helped to make the shopping-basket so heavy in the morning.

"Perhaps, Mother, you could change it yourself on your way out to bridge —"

Only when desperate with fatigue did Agnes venture on a suggestion like this. It wasn't any good — it never was — but sometimes when you were desperate you had to try. Mrs Lemming's delicate eyebrows rose in an indignant arch.

"On my way? My dear Agnes, since when is the library on the way to the Clarkes? Are you really as stupid as you make out? You had better be careful, or people will think you are not all there."

Coming back from the town, Agnes did not feel that she was really there at all. Her feet moved because she made them move, but her head felt light and odd, and rather as if it might float away and leave her body behind. Everything seemed to have that inclination to float away. Only her tired, aching feet went plodding on along the hard uphill road. All at once there was a hand under her elbow and a voice in her ear.

"Miss Lemming — you're ill."

She came back with a start to find that it was Mr Drake from the flat opposite the Willards who was addressing her in a tone of concern.

"You're ill."

"Oh, no — only tired."

"The same thing. I've got my car. Let me give you a lift."

She managed her shy, nice smile, and then she couldn't manage anything more. The next she really knew, she was lying on the couch in the sitting-room of her own flat and Mr Drake was boiling a kettle on the gas-ring. It was so extraordinary that she blinked once or twice. Mr Drake and the kettle declined to be blinked away. He looked round, saw that her eyes were open, nodded approvingly, and said, "Good girl! Now what you want is a nice cup of tea."

She wanted it more than anything else in the world. It was a good cup of tea. When she had finished it Mr Drake filled it up again. He also produced a bag of buns and a cup for himself and sat down.

"Do you like buns? I am very fond of them. These are almost pre-war — they have currants and citron peel in them. I was taking them home to have a solitary orgy, but this is much nicer."

Miss Lemming ate two buns and drank two more cups of tea. There had not been quite enough lunch to go round, and she had said that she wasn't hungry. During the last cup she discovered that she was being reproved by Mr Drake.

"Bell said that you were out all this morning. What made you go off down into the town again? You should have taken a rest."

She was so used to being in the wrong that she found herself apologising.

"I had a book to change."

"And why didn't you change it this morning?"

"Oh, I did. My mother didn't like the one I brought."

Mr Drake's peaked eyebrows went up until they threatened to touch his thick iron-grey hair. He looked quite terrifyingly like Mephistopheles. He said with the abruptness of a shy man breaking bounds,

"Your mother is a damned selfish old woman."

Miss Lemming stared at him. Her heart beat painfully. The tea-cup chattered in her hand. In all her life no one had ever said such a monstrous thing to her before. And he had sworn — actually sworn. She must find words to reprove him. She found none. Something inside her said, "It's *true*."

He took the cup out of her hand and set it down.

"It's true, isn't it? Who should know that better than you? She's killing you. And when I see someone being killed I can't just stand by and hold my tongue. Why do you put up with it? Why don't you go and get yourself a job? There are plenty going."

Miss Lemming stopped shaking, and said with directness and simplicity, "I did try about two months ago. You won't tell anyone, will you, because they said I wasn't strong enough, and if my mother knew she would be most terribly hurt. She — she doesn't understand that I'm not as strong as I used to be. It's no good, Mr Drake — I can't get away."

The eyebrows relaxed. Mr Drake's whole expression relaxed.

"It isn't always easy," he agreed. "But there is generally a way. Take my own case. I was — well, very much out of the world for some years, and when I came back I found myself without any money, or a job, or friends. It really didn't look as if there was any way out of that. I had — well, I had rather a bad time of it. And then I was left a business — rather an odd sort of business, and I don't suppose you would approve of it, but it did offer me a way out. I may say that I have never regretted taking it, though there are times when I might have wished for something more congenial. At those times I remind myself that it provides me with the means to live comfortably, to keep a small car, and to do more or less what I like with my spare time. The fact is, if you cannot get what you want, common sense suggests that you should put your mind to wanting what you can get."

A little colour rose to Agnes Lemming's cheeks. The ugly black beret had either come off of itself or been removed by Mr Drake. The mass of brown hair which it had hidden fell to her shoulders. It had once been very curly, and still retained enough wave to make the fall becoming. Mr Drake observed this. He noticed also that it matched the brown of her eyes in an unusual and, to his mind, very attractive manner. The eyes brightened as she said, "What did you want?"

"Oh, I wanted the moon," said Mr Drake — "the moon, and the stars, and the seventh heaven. We all do when we are young, and when we can't get them we say they don't exist, and we fill our bellies with the husks which the swine do eat, and then we get a pretty bad go of indigestion."

Agnes Lemming had a nice soft voice. She said very softly indeed, "What was your moon?"

He was looking past her to the window, with its uninspiring view of gravel sweep and massed Victorian shrubbery, but what he saw was something very different. He said, "Oh, a woman — just a woman. It generally is, you know."

"What happened?"

"I married her. A fatal thing to do. Moons should be left in the sky. Seen close, they lose their glamour and turn into dead worlds. To leave the metaphor behind, she changed her mind and went off with somebody else. I spent what was very nearly my last penny on the divorce. Rather ironic. There you have my story. What about yours?"

"I haven't any." The soft voice held a tragic note.

"No — she's sucked you dry, hasn't she? Are you going to stay and let her finish you?"

"What can I do?" said Agnes Lemming sadly.

Mr Drake removed his eyes from the window and looked at her with a peculiar and intent expression.

"Well, you could marry me."

CHAPTER
TEN

Four people wrote letters that evening. They too were to form part of the pattern.

Carola Roland wrote to someone whom she addressed as "Toots darling". It was a gushing, girlish letter.

"Missing my Toots so dreadfully. Am just longing for us to be together, but of course I do see we've got to be ever so careful until your divorce is through. I'm living exactly like a nun here — you needn't be afraid about that — but I don't mind a bit *really*, because I'm always thinking about you, and when we can get married, and what a lovely time we'll have . . ."

There was a lot more in the same vein.

This letter was not posted, because Miss Roland suddenly lost interest in it. She was, in fact, visited by a very bright idea. When you are bored beyond tears, bright ideas are exceedingly welcome. Miss Ronald was bored to such an extent that any distraction was welcome. She had even snatched at Alfred Willard. Anyway writing to Toots was the last word in boredom. It wouldn't do him any harm to be kept waiting for her letter. She believed in keeping men waiting — it made them keen. Toots had got to be kept keen enough to come down with a wedding ring and a handsome settlement as soon as his divorce was made absolute. He might be a bore — he was a bore — but oh, boy, had he got the dough!

She pushed the letter inside a very fancy blotter, took a bunch of keys out of her handbag, and went down to the luggage-room. The bright idea was a positive Catherine-wheel of malicious dancing sparks.

She came upstairs again presently with a packet of letters and a large signed photograph. Setting the photograph conspicuously on the left-hand side of the mantelpiece, she sat down to read the letters . . .

Mr Drake wrote to Agnes Lemming:

"My dear,

I must write, because I want you to have something which you can read when I am not there to say these things. You have lived long enough in prison. Come out and see what the world is like. I can only show you a very small corner of it, but it would be your corner and mine, and it would be a home, not a prison. I know what life looks like to a prisoner. Come out before it destroys you. When she has killed you, how will your mother be any the better for it? You say you could not leave her alone, but it is not your companionship she wants, it's your service. Give her a paid servant who can leave if the chain is pulled too tight. You are not a daughter, you are a slave. Slavery is immoral and abhorrent. These are hard words, but you know perfectly well that they are true ones. I have wanted to say them for a long time now. Do you remember the day. I carried your basket up from the town? It started then. The thing weighed a ton — your arm was shaking with the strain. I could have sworn at you for the patience in your eyes, and for the smile you gave me. People oughtn't to be patient and smile under an intolerable tyranny. I found myself unable to get you out of my mind. I discovered that you are that most infuriating of human beings, the saint who invites martyrdom. It is a reckless act on my part to ask you to marry me. You will try to destroy my moral character and turn me into a monster of selfishness, but I am forewarned and, I hope, forearmed. My best weapon is the fact that I desire nothing so much in the world as to make you happy. I believe that I can do it. As this is not an argument that would appeal to you, I will add that I have not had much happiness myself, and that you can give me all that I have missed and more. Won't you do it?"

Agnes Lemming wrote to Mr Drake:

"We mustn't think of it — indeed we mustn't. If we could be friends — but that would not be fair to you. Don't think of it any more. I ought to have told you at once and most definitely that it would never, never do. If only you are not unhappy . . ."

This letter, like Miss Roland's, was never sent. It became too much blotted with tears. Painfully, and with the expenditure of a good many matches, Agnes contrived to burn the sheet.

Mrs Spooner wrote to Meade Underwood:

"It may be in the bottom drawer, or if it isn't there, will you be so kind as to look through all the others? One of those woven spencers with a crochet edge. I should be glad of it to wear under my uniform now the evenings are getting so cold. Bell has the key of the flat."

CHAPTER
ELEVEN

Mrs Spooner's letter arrived at breakfast time next day. Meade read it, and enquired in a laughing voice, "What on earth is a spencer?"

It was a bright sunny morning. Her heart laughed and sang. Her cheeks had colour and her voice faltered. Everything in the garden was quite extraordinarily lovely.

Mrs Underwood, looking across the table, said, "Good gracious — he's not writing to you about underwear, is he?"

"It's not Giles — it's Mrs Spooner. She wants a spencer out of her chest of drawers, and I shouldn't know one if I saw it. What do I look for?"

"It's an underbodice — long sleeves and high neck — at least they're generally that way. What does she want it for?"

Meade's eyes danced.

"To wear under her uniform now that the evenings are getting chilly."

Mrs Underwood dropped a saccharine tablet into her tea and stirred it.

"Funny what a difference men make," she observed with apparent irrelevance. "If you had got an invitation to Buckingham Palace the day before yesterday it wouldn't have raised a smile out of you. Now Mrs Spooner writes and asks you to find her a spencer — and if there's anything duller than that, I don't know what it is — and anyone would think you'd just had a love letter. Why, I thought so myself. And all because you've got your young man back. I suppose it's all right and you're quite sure of him now?"

Meade nodded.

"Has he said anything about getting you a ring? I wouldn't make too sure unless he has."

Meade laughed and nodded again. Giles wanting to give her a ring so that she could break off their engagement with the proper trimmings — what would Aunt Mabel make of that? She resisted the temptation to find out and said, "Yes, he wants to give me a ring. But I won't let him buy one — not in war time. He's going to see about one of his mother's. Her things are all in a bank somewhere. He wants me to go down with him and get them out."

Mrs Underwood nodded approvingly. That certainly looked like business. A man doesn't give a girl his mother's jewellery unless he means to marry her. Then she said sharply, "Oh, he remembers about his mother's rings, does he?"

"He remembers everything before the war. Then it gets fainter and fainter — all the personal part of it —"

She stopped because Mrs Underwood was tossing her head.

"Well, that's what he tells you — and perhaps better not look into it, so long as he means to do the right thing now."

Meade went down to the basement and got the key of Mrs Spooner's flat. Bell was busy, so he called out to her to take it.

"Hanging on hooks right along the front of the old dresser, all the keys in a row — that's where you'll find it, miss, if it isn't a trouble. Can't make a mistake — one to eight they run, all along the front of the dresser — put my hand on them in the dark I can. Number seven's the one you want."

He was down on his knees scrubbing the old stone floor. As she passed him with the key in her hand, he looked up, nodding and smiling.

"Rare old job these floors, and the water goes cold on you that spiteful or I wouldn't have troubled you. Just put it back when you've finished, will you, miss?"

Meade said she would and it wasn't any trouble. Then she went up in the lift and let herself into Mrs Spooner's flat, which was No. 7 at the top of the house.

She found the spencer at once. It was a horrible affair of natural wool with mother-of-pearl buttons down the front and a crochet edging round the high neck. It smelled of napththalene. It would certainly be warm, but oh dear, how it would tickle! She hung it on her arm and came out upon the landing, to find the door of the opposite flat wide open and Miss Roland standing there.

"Oh, Miss Underwood — good morning. I saw you come up. That's the Spooners' flat, isn't it? They had gone before I came here. Rather nice to have the floor to oneself, I think. Come in and see my place."

Meade hesitated.

"Well, I ought to send this off —" She indicated the spencer.

Carola Roland looked at it. It might have been a black beetle. She wrinkled her nose and sniffed.

"How foul!" she said frankly. "Here, hang it on the door knob and just take a look at my flat. Not bad, is it? You've no idea what it was like when I came."

Meade didn't want to be rude. She felt friendly towards the world. She was also a little curious. She ignored the suggestion about the spencer, but she crossed the little lobby and followed Carola into a highly modernised version of the current Vandeleur sittingroom. Ceiling, walls, and floors had been painted with a matt grey paint. The colour scheme was blue and grey — pale blue carpet, blue and grey brocaded curtains and upholstery, pale blue cushions. On the mantelshelf a silver statuette — a naked dancer poised on one foot, faceless, curveless, arms outstretched. Meade's first thought was, "How strange —"; her next, "How beautiful!" because it had the beauty of flight. Yes, that was it — the beauty of flight. And then she stopped seeing it, because at the end of the shelf, leaning back against the wall, there stood a large unframed photograph of Giles.

Carola Roland came past her and picked it up.

"Good — isn't it?" she said. "I suppose you've got one too." She set it down again.

Yes, it was good. It was Giles. It had his signature across the corner — "*Giles*".

Carola turned a smiling face.

"Well? Did you ask him if he remembered me?"

78

Meade said, "Yes."

"And did he?"

"I'm afraid he didn't. He doesn't remember anything since the war."

"How very, very convenient!" said Carola Roland. Her bright idea was fairly blazing. She had meant to have some fun out of it, but it looked — yes, it really looked as if there might be money in it too. "Nothing at all? Do you really mean it? Why, I'd love to be able to do that! Wouldn't you?"

"No — I should hate it."

Carola Roland laughed.

"Want to keep your memories? I don't. Fun while they last, but what's the good of remembering them? Anyhow Giles and I are all washed-up."

Meade put out a hand and took hold of the back of one of the brocaded chairs. The smell of naphthalene from Mrs Spooner's spencer was suddenly more than she could bear. She let it slip down on the floor. Then she said in a steady enquiring voice, "Giles and you?"

Miss Roland smiled a brilliant scarlet smile.

"Didn't he tell you about me? Oh, no — of course he's forgotten all about everything. But he might just have happened to mention me before he lost his memory. Sure he didn't?"

Meade shook her head.

"Was there any reason why he should?"

Carola was helping herself to a cigarette from a shagreen box. She struck a match and set the tip glowing before she said, "Reason? Well, that's just as you happen to look at it. Some people might think he would mention that there was one Mrs Armitage already before he asked you to marry him? I suppose he did ask you to marry him? Your aunt seems to think so."

Meade's hand closed tightly on the back of the chair. She said, "We are engaged."

The scarlet lips emitted a puff of smoke.

"Did you hear what I said? I don't believe you did — or you didn't take it in. I expect it was a shock, but that's not my fault, is it? You can't expect me just to hold my tongue and let Giles go on forgetting me. I've got my allowance to think about. What about that? He was giving me four hundred a year. And can I do with it — oh, boy!"

Meade felt nothing. It was just as if it was happening to somebody else. It couldn't be happening to her — and Giles. She looked at the photograph on the mantelpiece and she looked at Carola. There are things you can't believe.

She said, "Miss Roland —" and was met by a bright glance and a wave of the cigarette.

"But I'm not. I *said* you hadn't been listening. Roland is just my stage name. Rather good, don't you think? But my real legal name is Armitage. That's what I've been telling you — I'm Mrs Armitage." She turned back to the mantelpiece, picked up the photograph, and slightly altered its position. "He's not handsome, but there's something attractive about him, don't you think? At least I used to think so till I found out what a cold, grasping devil he could be."

Meade stared at her, her eyes wide and blank. It didn't seem to mean anything. It didn't seem to make sense. She said in a horrified whisper, "It *doesn't* make sense —"

Carola dropped the photograph and came back. She was angry, but there was amusement behind the anger. She had always wanted to get a bit of her own back on Giles, but she couldn't have hoped for a chance like this. There was a packet of letters lying on a little gimcrack table with twisted silver legs and a glass top. She picked up the one that lay uppermost and said, with the Mayfair accent gone, "Oh, I'm a liar, am I? All right, Miss Meade Underwood, you take a look at this, and then perhaps you'll be sorry you spoke! I suppose you know Giles' writing when you see it."

A sheet of paper was being held up in front of her. The writing on it was Giles' writing, very black and distinct. Everything had become quite extraordinarily clear and distinct — the edge of the paper; the way it was creased; Carola's hand, long fingers, and scarlet nails; and a ring with a single diamond, very bright — Giles' letter.

The writing said, "You are making a mistake if you think that sort of argument will have any effect on me. You are just appealing to sentiment, and I haven't any use for it. To be completely candid, it makes me see red, so I advise you to drop it. I will allow you four hundred a year provided you undertake to stop using the name of Armitage. If I find that you are breaking this condition I shall have no hesitation in cutting off supplies. You have, as you say, a perfect legal right to the name, but if I find that you are using it the allowance will stop. It's a good name, but I hardly think

81

it is worth four hundred a year to you. And that, my dear Carola, is my last word."

Meade lifted her eyes to Carola Roland's face and saw the malice there. She said on a quick-caught breath, "He doesn't love you."

The blonde head was shaken.

"Not now. But isn't that just like Giles? Blows hot and cold — falls for you one day and forgets all about it the next. He did that to you too, didn't he? Well now — am I a liar, or am I Mrs Armitage and do you apologise? It's there in Giles' own writing — you can't get away from that."

Meade stood up straight and stiff.

"Are you divorced?"

Carola laughed.

"Oh, no, nothing like that — just all washed-up — like I said. Some day perhaps he'll remember and tell you all about me. That'll be something for you to look forward to, ducky!"

Meade stooped and picked up the woollen spencer. She turned with it in her hand. There seemed to be nothing to say. The door to the lobby was open, and the outer door beyond that again. Perhaps she really would have said nothing if the sound of Carola's laughter had not followed her. Everything in her fused in a white hot flame. She stood on the threshold and said in a ringing voice of anger, "No wonder he hates you!"

After that it was the most frightful anticlimax to find Mrs Smollett only a yard or two away on her knees, doing the landing. She had a seething pail of soapsuds and she was swishing away at the cement floor with her scrubbing-brush. Just how much had she heard of that frightful conversation with Carola Roland? The scrubbing-brush was making a lot of noise, but Meade had a dreadful conviction that the noise had only just begun. With those two doors wide open, she would have heard it. And if it had only just begun, she was quite certain that Mrs Smollett must have heard every word. Nothing to do but to walk past her with a "Good morning, Mrs Smollett", and so down the stairs.

CHAPTER
TWELVE

Mrs Smollett told Bell all about it over an elevens in the basement. She was a large woman with hard apple red cheeks and little dark eyes which saw everything. As she sipped from her cup of tea she observed that the skirting under the dresser had not been dusted, and that one of the eight keys was missing from its hook. When she remarked upon the key, Bell told her about Miss Underwood coming down to fetch it.

"She's got something to get out for Mrs Spooner seemingly."

Mrs Smollett took a lump of sugar out of a screw of paper and dropped it in her tea. War or no war, tea without sugar was a thing she couldn't abide. She stirred vigorously and said, "Well, that wasn't where she was coming out of, Mr Bell. Miss Roland's flat she was in, and both doors open right through to the lounge so I could no more help hearing what they was saying than if I was in the room with them. And 'Giles and I are all washed-up', she says — that was that Miss Roland. And, 'Didn't he tell you about me?' she says."

Bell shook his head.

"You shouldn't have listened, Mrs Smollett — you really shouldn't."

Mrs Smollett set down her cup with a bang.

"Oh, I shouldn't, shouldn't I? Then perhaps you'll tell me what I ought to ha' done! Put cotton wool in my ears which I hadn't any handy, or gone away and got all behind with my scrubbing?"

"You could 'ave coughed."

"And give myself a sore throat? Not likely! If people don't want you to hear what they're saying they should shut their doors! Here, this Giles, he'll be Major Armitage — he'll be Miss Underwood's fiongsay, won't he? Fancy it's turning out he's been carrying on with Miss Roland!"

"It's none of our business, Mrs Smollett. She's a very nice young lady that Miss Underwood, and I'm sure I wish them happy."

Mrs Smollett gave a loud snorting laugh.

"Likely, isn't it, with them two girls both wanting 'im and ready to scratch each other's eyes out! 'We're engaged,' says Miss Underwood, and, 'I'm Mrs Armitage,' says Miss Roland, and she gives her a letter to read."

"Oh dear me, you shouldn't say things like that — you really shouldn't."

Mrs Smollett tossed her head.

"It wasn't I that said them! It was them two. 'I'm Mrs Armitage,' Miss Roland says, and Miss Underwood says, 'He don't love you.' And when I heard her coming out I got down to my scrubbing so as not to upset her by letting her know I could hear what was going on. And she turns right round in the doorway and calls out to Miss Roland something about hating her, and then off down the stairs all in a flash. Funny ain't it — I mean that Miss Roland calling herself Mrs Armitage. I mean that would be bigamy, wouldn't it? Or do you suppose it'd make a difference him having lost his memory? What do you think, Mr Bell?"

Bell pushed back his chair and got up.

"I think I got my work same as you got yours."

There was distress in his wrinkled, ruddy face. A talker, that's what Mrs Smollett was. And he'd no objection to talk provided there wasn't any tittle-tattle or nastiness about it, which he didn't hold with and never would — taking away people's characters and such.

"I got a nice lot of hot water on the stove for you. I'll just fill your pail," he said.

But when he had filled it, Mrs Smollett was in no hurry to go.

"Funny how Miss Garside stopped having me in to clean up her place, wasn't it? She don't have anyone else, I suppose — evenings when I'm out of the way?"

Bell shook his head. He wasn't any too happy about Miss Garside, and he didn't want to talk about her affairs.

Mrs Smollett flounced — if the word can be applied to so large a woman.

"Well, I've got the right to know whether I give satisfaction, haven't I? Used to have me in regular three times a week, and stopped dead as you may say. 'I shan't be wanting you any more, Mrs Smollett,' she says, and, 'Here's your money for today,' and goes into her room and shuts the door." She bent to the handle of the pail but straightened up without lifting it. "Here, Mr Bell — did she ever get those bits of furniture of hers back again? Told me they'd gone to be mended but I couldn't see anything wrong with them myself. Very nice pieces they was, like what you see in the antique shops — walnut cabinet and writing-desk, and a set of chairs with backs like a lot of ribbon plaited. Funny if they all wanted mending together, isn't it? Here now, you might as well tell us, have she had any of them back again?"

Bell looked distressed. This was tittle-tattle. He didn't like it. He said as sharply as he could bring himself to speak, "I got something else to do than take notice of what people has mended. And water don't stay boiling, Mrs Smollett — yours will be cold."

He got a toss of the head.

"I've no call to scald my fingers, have I?" She lifted the pail. "Nasty marks those things left where they'd been standing — that wallpaper isn't half faded, only you didn't rightly notice it till they'd gone. And if you ask me, Mr Bell, I'd say she'd sold them."

CHAPTER
THIRTEEN

The events of this day were to be collected, catalogued, sorted, and re-sorted. Everything that everyone did or said, however trifling, however unimportant in itself, came to be scrutinised and put under a microscope. There are days like that, but you don't know until afterwards that the small, foolish things you do or the hasty words you say are going to be raked up, and picked over, and brought into judgement. If you had known, you would of course have behaved quite differently. But you don't know — you never know — until it is too late. Only one of the people in Vandeleur House had any idea that what was said and done that day might make all the difference between safety and disaster.

Meade came back to No. 3, and made a neat parcel of the spencer, which she addressed to Mrs Spooner in Sussex. Mrs Underwood asked her why she was looking like skim milk, and lectured her for climbing the stairs when she might have taken the lift.

"But I did take the lift, Aunt Mabel."

"Then what are you looking like that for? When are you seeing that young man of yours?"

The skim-milk colour gave way to a momentary scarlet. Mrs Underwood received a startling impression of fragility. Then the dark head was bent over the parcel.

"He'll be at the War Office all day. He's going to ring me up as soon as he knows when he can get off."

Mrs Underwood was dressed for the street. She pulled on a pair of gloves and said, "Here, I'll take your parcel, and I'll go and pack for you this afternoon. Get Ivy to make you some Ovaltine and have a lazy day. He'll be wanting you to go out with him tonight as likely as not. I shan't be back till half past seven."

It was a fearfully long day. Meade went into her room and lay down upon the bed. She couldn't think, and she couldn't feel. Everything was suspended, waiting for Giles. But this inability to think or feel was not rest, it was the extremity of strain. Thought did not function because it was stretched rigid between two opposite poles, the impossible and the actual. It wasn't possible that Giles should be married to Carola Roland — Giles was married to Carola Roland. Only one of these things could be true. Yet there they were, the two of them, each making an impossibility of the other, and between them her own thought, in suspense.

Across the landing, Elise Garside sat staring at the bare wall which faced her. Six months ago the wall had not been bare. A tall, slender walnut cabinet had stood against it with, on either side of it, one of her ribbon-back chairs. The whole effect had been delicately formal. Now the wall was bare. The cabinet with the Worcester china tea-service which had been one of her great-grand-mother's wedding presents had gone. The chairs had gone, not only the two but the whole set, and gone, as she most bitterly knew, at a tenth of what had been their value before all values had been lost in a dissolving world.

The paper which covered the wall was, as Mrs Smollett had said, a good deal faded. The imprint of the cabinet remained, blue upon a ground of silver-grey. The chair backs had left faint shadows. On Miss Garside's right another patch of blue showed where the bureau had stood, whilst above the high mantelshelf several small blue ovals and a large rectangle proclaimed the departure of six miniatures and a mirror. The furnishings which remained were sparse and of no value — a threadbare carpet whose colours had gone down into a grey old age, a few chairs with chintz covers pale from much washing, a bookcase, a table, and Miss Garside.

She sat quite still and faced the empty wall. She also faced an empty future. She was sixty years of age. She had no training and she had no money. She would not be able to pay the rent of her flat on quarter day, and she had nowhere to go. Her only living relations were an incredibly aged aunt, bedridden in a nursing home, two young serving soldiers in the Middle East, and a niece in Hong Kong. Until six months ago she had been quite comfortably off. Then the industrial concern from which she derived her income failed, and she had nothing left. All her eggs had been in the same basket. Now there was no basket and no eggs. There was no money at all. The diamond ring which she had failed to sell was in her hand. She turned it to and fro without looking at it, until her eyes were caught by a flash from the stone. She stared now at the ring, a fine solitaire diamond set in platinum. That was what it looked like, and that was what she had always believed it to be. But it wasn't — it was a sham. Uncle James' wedding present, and a sham. There hadn't been any wedding, because Henry Arden had been killed at Mons. But Uncle James had been most lordly and open-handed about the ring. "Oh, keep it, my dear, keep it! Bless my soul, I don't want it back!" Uncle James, rolling in money, playing at being generous, and cheating her all the time. He had had the name for being mean — but to be as mean as that! Life was very surprising.

She turned the stone. It flashed and made a rainbow as bravely as if it had been real. That Miss Roland who had taken the top flat had one just like it. It had winked at her only yesterday from a long hand with scarlet nails when they went down in the lift together. She wondered whether that stone too was a sham. Girls like Carola Roland often had very valuable jewellery given to them. It might easily be real. Looking back, she remembered how bright the stone had looked — brighter than her own, because she had slipped her glove down to make sure that the ring was there. And then she had pulled on her glove in a hurry because the rings were so much alike and that offended her pride.

She went on thinking about the rings and how much alike they were.

CHAPTER
FOURTEEN

Mrs Underwood packed parcels for the bombed until a quarter to five. Then she had a few straight words with Miss Middleton and went out to play bridge. In the course of the words she informed Miss Middleton that she wouldn't be coming again, and that, "My niece isn't really strong enough, and I think it would be very much better if you made arrangements to fill her place. She comes home quite worn out, and I'm sure I don't wonder."

At 5.30 Agnes Lemming met Mr Drake by appointment in the town. She had intended to tell him with all the firmness to which she could constrain herself that he must stop thinking about her, and that they must never meet again, but as it turned out she did nothing of the kind. The reason for this change of purpose was really no reason at all. It was trivial, it was inadequate. It was also, one would have said, quite out of Agnes Lemming's character. But it sufficed. There is, after all, such a thing as the last straw. Julia Mason's parcel was the last straw.

Julia was a cousin, good-natured and extremely well-to-do. She was the kind of woman who buys clothes and doesn't wear them, or wears them three times and then gets bored to tears. Periodically she sent parcels to the Lemmings. One had arrived by the midday post, and it had arrived addressed, not to Mrs Lemming, but to Agnes. Opened, it was found to contain a delightful tweed suit in one of the soft shades between brown and sand with the least coral fleck in it. There was a long coat to match with a warm fur collar, shoes, three pairs of stockings, a felt hat, a handbag and gloves, and a jumper and cardigan in a dull coral shade. Tucked inside the cardigan was a letter from Julia.

Dear Agnes,
I do hope you'll be able to make use of these things. I must have been off my head when I bought them. They are too tight, and I look a fiend in the colour. Marion has given me all her coupons, so I can get something else. She's just gone back to America, so she doesn't want them . . .

Agnes picked up the coat and slipped it on, tucked a fold of the jumper inside it to try the effect of the colour, and pulled on the hat. The effect was quite magical. These were *her* clothes — designed for her, made for her — exactly right. As a rule Julia's things were too big. These fitted. And generally they were the last things on earth which Agnes Lemming could or should have worn. These were *hers*.

And then Mrs Lemming came in, picked up the cardigan, and walked over to the glass. When she turned round she had a pleased, excited look.

"What a charming colour! I don't always care for Julia's taste, but this is really very charming indeed. Just take off the coat and let me slip it on. Why, it couldn't be better! The shoes won't fit me — you can have those, and the stockings. Tiresome that Julia's feet should be larger than mine — women's feet seem to get bigger and bigger — but the other things will do beautifully. The skirt may want a little alteration. You can do it this afternoon, and then I can wear it to go down to lunch with Irene on Saturday — it's just right for the country."

A little colour had come into Agnes' face.

"Julia sent those things to me, Mother. I — I should like to keep them."

Mrs Lemming had slipped out of the long coat and was trying on the cardigan. It was a very good fit, and it suited her. But then most things did suit her. She was nearly sixty, but she still had elegance and beauty. Her grey hair was most becomingly waved. Her dark eyebrows arched perfectly above dark, brilliant eyes. She had remained slender without becoming thin, and her complexion was still remarkable. She contemplated herself with pleasure and turned a smiling face.

"Really, my dear, Julia won't mind who has the clothes. She just wants to get rid of them — they wouldn't suit her at all."

Agnes said, "No." And then, "She sent them to *me*, Mother. I should like to keep them."

Mrs Lemming's smile became tinged with malice.

"Well, my dear, I'm afraid you can't. Really, you know, you are being a little absurd. At your age you

94

should have enough sense not to make yourself ridiculous by wearing completely unsuitable clothes."

Agnes lost her colour, but she stood her ground.

"Julia sent them to me. Here is her letter — you will see what she says."

Mrs Lemming let the letter fall upon the dressing table.

"That is quite enough of this nonsense. I need the clothes, and I am going to keep them. You can tell Julia they did not suit you, and you can have my old grey instead. By the way, the grey skirt is exactly right — you can alter this one by it. Get it done this afternoon. I am going on to the Remingtons, so I shan't be back till after seven. And for goodness sake clear up all this mess! I must fly!"

Agnes cleared up the mess, but she did not alter the skirt. She lay down on her bed and rested.

At a quarter past four she made herself a cup of tea, and then slowly and carefully she dressed to go and meet Mr Drake. She had beautiful hair. She took pains with it. Then she went into Mrs Lemming's room and used her powder. She even added a touch of colour, and was surprised to find what a difference it made. Then she put on the new clothes. First the shoes and stockings — beautiful soft shoes and fine stockings. Next the skirt which she hadn't altered, and the soft coral jumper. She would be too warm if she wore the short coat of the suit as well as the top coat. She had a fancy for the latter with its becoming fur collar. She put it on and packed the short coat and the coral cardigan back in Julia's box. Next hat, gloves, handbag. Julia had done the thing thoroughly — gloves, shoes and handbag were a perfect match. She looked at herself in Mrs Lemming's long glass and thought, "This is me — this is what I'm really like. I needn't be a slave." Then she went to meet Mr Drake.

He did not know how much afraid he had been until he saw her coming towards him. It is not easy to break old tyrannies. He looked, and wondered at the change in her.

"My dear — you've come! Do you know, I've been afraid all day that you wouldn't."

She shook her head.

"I would have come — whatever happened. But I meant to tell you I couldn't come again."

"And now?"

"I want to talk to you."

They found a corner in an almost empty tea shop. When he had given his order he said with a smile which transformed his face, "Well, now we can begin. It will take them ten minutes to produce that tea. I want to talk to you, and you want to talk to me. Which of us talks first?"

Agnes said, "I do." If she didn't talk first her resolution might fail, and if it failed she would go back of her own slave will and never be free again.

He went on smiling at her with his eyes and said, "Very well. What is it, Agnes?"

Her hands were clasping one another tightly. Her feet in Julia's new soft shoes were cold, but her cheeks burned. In Mr Drake's eyes she was as beautiful as a dream, and he thought that the dream was going to come true. She said in her soft voice, hurrying a little,

"Did you mean — what you said — yesterday?"

"Yes, I meant it. Didn't you get my letter?"

"Yes — I got it. I — loved it — very much. I thought you meant it. You do, don't you? You want to marry me?"

"More than anything in the world, my dear."

The waitress brought the tea on a gimcrack tray — war buns, war cakes. Agnes drew a long breath and waited. When the girl had gone away she said in a whispering voice, "Could it be soon?"

Mr Drake nodded. He was under an extreme pressure of emotion. A tea-shop with a languid waitress and a few dallying customers is a definite handicap upon the emotions. He wanted to take the woman he loved in his arms and make ridiculous and romantic speeches, and all he could do was to nod at her across a flimsy table and say, "Just as soon as you like."

Agnes took another of those long breaths.

"How soon could it be?"

Mr Drake's heart was now beating so hard that he found it very difficult to remember the little he knew about the rules for getting married. He said rather stumblingly, "I think it takes about three days."

"I want to be married in church —" And there she caught herself up. "You must think this very strange. You won't understand, but I will try and tell you. You said that about my being a slave, and I knew it was true, but I didn't think I could get away. I was going to tell you so, and see you once and say good-bye. And then something happened. I can't tell you about it. It was something you wouldn't think — no, I can't tell about it — you wouldn't understand — I don't understand myself, but it made me feel as if I couldn't go on. Only you see I don't know how long I shall go on feeling like that, and if we were married I couldn't go back, but if we weren't — I might." Her voice broke. She said with a gasp, "I'm so dreadfully afraid — about that."

"About going back — do you mean now?"

She shook her head.

"Oh, no, of course I must go back — now. I didn't mean that — I didn't mean going back with my body at all, I meant going back with my mind — slipping back again after I'd climbed a little way out."

Mr Drake took both her hands and held them.

"Agnes, look at me! And listen to me! You're never going back like that — not even if you say you want to, not even if you tell me you've changed your mind! You are not going back! And now we'll set about finding out just how soon we can be married."

CHAPTER
FIFTEEN

Giles didn't ring up. He walked in after six o'clock and found Meade in the drawing-room, huddled in one of the big chairs. Ivy shut the door behind him and went away. She thought him ever so nice, and Miss Meade ever so lucky only nobody would have thought it the way she'd been looking all day. She went back into her slip of a kitchen and sang in a shrill, childish voice:

> "I like your lips, I like your eyes,
> You like my lips? You like my eyes
> To hypnotize you?"

Meade got up, a white little ghost of the girl he had kissed last night. He kissed her now, and found her shaking and cold.

"My sweet, what is it?"

But she only shook and shook.

He sat down in the chair and rocked her in his arms.

"Silly little thing! What's the matter?"

He could feel her little body shaken with sobs, but no voice, no words.

"Meade darling, what is it — what's the matter? Can't you stop crying and tell me? Look here, you must!"

Yes, she must. And when she had told him, they would never sit like this again. It would be all over, and finished, and done with. Just for a moment more she let herself feel the warmth, the strength, the love that held her. Then she lifted her head from his shoulder.

"Giles — you said you didn't know her —"

"Lots of people I don't know. Which particular one? And why have you been crying yourself into a jelly?"

"Carola Roland — you said you didn't know her."

"It sounds a pretty phoney name. Carola Roland — bet you anything you like she didn't start that way, whoever she is."

She was sitting up now, leaning away from him against the arm of the chair, looking into his face, her grey eyes wide and dark, her face quite drained of colour.

"She says her name isn't Roland at all."

"Darling, did anyone ever suppose it was?"

"She says it's Armitage."

"*What!*"

"She says you married her."

Giles put his hands on her shoulders. They were heavy enough to hurt, and they gripped her so hard that there were bruises afterwards.

"Have you gone out of your mind?"

Meade felt a little better. He was furious — he was hurting her. She felt better. She said in rather a stronger voice, "No. That's what she says. She showed me a letter —"

"From whom?"

100

"From you. It was your writing. It said you would give her four hundred a year."

The grip held, but the anger was gone from his face. His eyes were intent, hard, and very blue.

"Four hundred a year? Somebody's mad, my sweet — I hope it isn't you or me."

"That's what the letter said. And it said she was to drop the name of Armitage. It said of course she had a perfect legal right to the name, but she wouldn't get the four hundred a year unless she dropped it. And was it worth all that? And that was your last word. And you called her 'My dear Carola'."

"It's a plant," said Giles.

He let go of her so suddenly that she felt giddy. Then he got to his feet, pulling her up with him.

"Giles — what are you going to do?"

"I'm going to see Miss Carola Roland."

It was she who was holding him now.

"Giles — wait! You can't go like this. Oh, Giles — are you sure?"

"Of course I'm sure. I tell you it's a plant. She's heard I've lost my memory and she's trying it on."

Meade was trembling so much that he had to put his arm about her.

"Giles — suppose it was true. I wouldn't have believed anything she said, but it was your letter — not only the writing — it was like hearing you talk. And there was a photograph —"

"What sort of photograph?"

"A big one — of you — head and shoulders — with 'Giles' written across the corner."

He gave a quick angry laugh. The hard blue eyes had a fighting glint in them.

"As long as it wasn't a wedding group! You don't have to marry every girl who's got your photograph! Is that all?"

"Isn't it enough? It was your letter — it was. You've forgotten writing it, and you've forgotten her. If you had married her you might have forgotten that too. Giles — you forgot me —"

Her voice wrung his heart.

"Meade, I didn't — not with anything that mattered. I told you so. I loved you at once, that day at Kitty Van Loo's, and I never stopped loving you. You don't know how I had to hold on to myself in that taxi. It seemed the rightest thing in the world for me to kiss you. I did put my arm round you, you know, and I had to hang on like mad not to kiss you. Doesn't that just show? Now stop wobbling and listen to me! The minute you began to talk about that Carola woman I sized her up. She sounds like a gold-digger, and I don't like gold-diggers. And she's probably a synthetic blonde, and I don't like synthetic blondes. I don't pretend I've been a saint, but I'm really not a fool. I can assure you that I should never have dreamed of marrying Miss Carola Roland."

"It might have been a long time ago —"

"Oh, no — it's only the last eighteen months or so that's gone foggy. I don't see myself falling for Carola at any time after I was out of my teens. You haven't been using your head, you know. I was engaged to you, wasn't I? I hadn't lost my memory then. Was I planning a spot of bigamy, or had there been a divorce?"

"No — I asked her that. She said no, you were just all washed-up."

"Then I was going to lure you into a bigamous marriage, I suppose. Wake up, darling! I didn't hint at having a guilty secret, did I?"

"N-no —" Her eyes widened suddenly.

"What's the matter now?"

"I was trying to think — whether you ever really said — anything about getting married. You said you loved me, and you asked me if I loved you, but . . . Of course there was very little time — only three days . . . Oh, Giles, it does seem such a long time ago!"

He picked her up, kissed her hard, and set her down again.

"I shouldn't have talked like that to a girl like you unless I meant business — not my line of country. Now you sit down good and peaceful and keep on telling yourself that everything's going to be all right! If you cry any more, I'll beat you. I'm going to have a heart-to-heart talk with Miss Carola Roland, and I think she's going to be sorry she tried it on."

Meade ran after him into the lobby.

"Giles — you'll be careful, won't you? You won't do anything silly? You won't —"

He turned on the threshold.

"If she gets what she deserves, I shall probably wring her neck!" he said, and banged the door.

CHAPTER
SIXTEEN

Carola Roland opened the door of No. 8. When she saw Giles her eyes lighted up and her lips smiled. Pleasure and amusement coursed through her. She had been bored, bored, bored. Here was entertainment. She had an old score to pay, and here was Giles delivered into her hands for payment. She said in her best Mayfair manner, "How very nice of you! Do come in."

Giles' response lacked polish. He was plainly an angry man. He stalked into the sitting-room, and then turned to confront her.

"Miss Roland?"

The enormous blue eyes widened.

"Oh, no."

"I understand that you are making some preposterous claim."

The scarlet lips smiled widely.

"There's nothing preposterous about it. You know as well as I do that I am Mrs Armitage."

Giles stood and stared at her. She wore a long white dress, with a string of pearls about an admirably white neck. The bright hair rose above her forehead in a high wave and then fell curling about her neck. She had a perfect figure, a fine skin, and eyes which reminded him

104

of the nursery and his cousin Barbara's favourite baby doll — that wide cool gaze, the size, the darkened lashes. As far as he could remember he had never seen her before. She was to his every sense strange and unknown. He could not believe in any contact, any relationship between them.

And then his eyes went past her and he saw his photograph upon the mantelpiece with the signature black across the corner. It was a plain-clothes photograph, head and shoulders, done just before the war. He remembered having it done — a cold day with a wind, and he had met Barbara afterwards and taken her out to lunch. She was going out to join her husband in Palestine and frightfully pleased about it. He could remember all this, but he couldn't for the life of him remember a single thing about Carola Roland who said she was Carola Armitage.

He went over to the hearth, picked the photograph up, and turned it over. Bare, blank cardboard. He set it down again.

Carola's laugh met him as he turned.

"Giles, darling — how unbelieving! And what a rotten memory you've got! Not very flattering, are you?"

The anger in his eyes delighted her.

"Are you claiming to be my wife?"

"Giles — *darling*!"

"Because if you are, you must prove it. When were we married — and where — and who were the witnesses?"

She arched her brows. The blue eyes opened a little wider. The likeness to Barbara's doll was intensified.

105

"Let me see — it was in March — March 17th 1940 — just eighteen months ago. And we were married in a register office, and it's no use your asking me which one, because you took me there in a taxi and I wasn't noticing about addresses — neither of us was. And the witnesses were the clerk and a man he brought in from the street. I'm sure I haven't any idea what their names were."

"Where's the marriage certificate?"

"Darling, I don't carry it about with me. You see, it wasn't a great success, so we agreed to wash it out — only of course you were going to make me an allowance."

Giles laughed angrily.

"Oh, I was, was I? Now we're getting somewhere! I think you told Miss Underwood that you had a letter of mine. Perhaps you'll let me see it."

Her lids dropped a little, the darkened lashes came down, the blue eyes narrowed.

"Well, I don't know, darling — you're pretty strong, and you're in a horrible temper. If I show it to you, will you promise not to snatch?"

"I'm not trying to suppress evidence — I'm trying to get at the truth. I say you're bluffing, and I'm calling your bluff."

Carola burst out laughing.

"All right, darling, here we go! I'll hold the letter up like I did for your Meade Underwood, and you shall see for yourself. Only no touching, no snatching — word of honour and all that sort of thing."

"I don't want to touch anything — I want to see for myself. You say you've got a letter of mine — well, show it to me!"

"Swear you won't touch — you haven't sworn."

Giles drove his hands deep into his pockets.

"And I'm not going to. I've told you I don't want to touch the thing. If that isn't enough for you, I'm walking out. If you've got anything to show me, get on with it!"

"Always the gentleman — aren't you, darling? Really, you know, it's almost as good as a certificate. People aren't as rude as that except in the family circle."

Something opened and shut in Giles' mind. It opened, and then it shut again — like a door. There wasn't time to see what lay behind the door.

Carola was coming towards him with the letter in her hand.

"Well, here it is, and you can see for yourself. And then perhaps you'll apologise, darling. Keep your hands in your pockets, and then you won't be tempted to do anything you shouldn't with them. There's nothing like keeping out of temptation's way, is there? Here you are!"

She held up the sheet of paper just as she had held it up in front of Meade. He saw his own writing running across it on an upward slant. The pen had driven furiously. Here and there it had grazed the paper. He had been angry when he had driven his pen like that. His eyes went down the sheet and read what Meade had read. They came upon his own name. "I will allow you four hundred a year provided you will undertake to

107

stop using the name of Armitage. If I find that you are breaking this condition I shall have no hesitation in cutting off supplies. You have, as you say, a perfect legal right to the name. It's a good name, but I hardly think it is worth four hundred a year to you. And that, my dear Carola, is my last word." That he had written these words, he could not have the slightest doubt. They confronted him, black and authentic, in what was certainly his own handwriting. He had written them. And it was quite incredible that he should have written them. He had offered Carola Roland four hundred a year to stop using his name.

He turned his eyes from the evidence of his own words and saw, as Meade had seen, Carola's hand holding the letter up for him to read, the long fingers with their scarlet nails, and the diamond ring with its one bright shining stone. His face changed so suddenly that she stepped back, folding the letter and pushing it down the front of her dress.

Giles' hands came out of his pockets. He made a step forward.

"Where did you get that ring?"

So that was it. How very amusing. The whole thing was going with a bang. First-class entertainment from start to finish. And had she been bored! She smiled a wide, decorative smile and held out the hand with the diamond on it.

"This ring?"

"Yes. Where did you get it?"

"Why, darling, you gave it to me of course. Fancy forgetting that!"

His mother's ring — on Carola Roland's hand. The shock struck hard against every sense which declared her a stranger. It was the ring which he had intended to give to Meade. But it had been given already — to Carola Roland — to a stranger. You do not give your mother's ring to a stranger. You give it only when you give her name as well. He said in a stiff, strained voice,

"May I look at it? I'll give it back again. I want to be sure."

Without any hesitation at all she slipped it off and put it into his hand.

Half turning from her, he held it up for the light to strike upon the inner circle. If it was his mother's ring her initials would be there, and a date — the date of her engagement to his father. It was her engagement ring. The light struck on a faint M.B. and a date too worn to read. M.B. for Mary Ballantyne. And the date should be June 1910. It was the hardest thing in the world to give back Mary Armitage's ring to the hand with the scarlet nails. When he had done it he knew that he could do no more. The thing was beyond him. His words, the ring, declared this woman his wife. Heart and flesh denied her. Every instinct slammed the door against the evidence. If there was a marriage, she must prove it. He said so.

"This goes for nothing. You are taking advantage of the fact that I have lost my memory. If there was a marriage, you can jog yours and let my solicitors know where it took place. I don't believe that there was a marriage, or that you can prove it."

CHAPTER
SEVENTEEN

Meade had scarcely shut the door upon Giles, when Ivy Lord put her head round the kitchen door.

"If you please, Miss Meade, I'd like to go out to the post."

"All right, Ivy."

"Will you be going out, miss?"

"No, I don't think so — not tonight."

Ivy hesitated.

"Mrs Underwood said she wouldn't be back till half past seven. If you wouldn't mind lighting the gas under the steamer at seven — full till the water's hot, and then down to a point —"

Meade found a smile. It took exactly five minutes to reach the pillar-box at the corner and return. The post was most undoubtedly a young man. She said, "Of course I will."

She went back into the sitting-room to wait for Giles. She heard Ivy come running out of her room in a hurry to be off. The door of the flat opened and shut. She tried to think what sort of young man Ivy would have. She was such a funny little bit of a thing. But something nice about her too — queerness and niceness in layers, like streaky bacon . . . What a thing to think of. Anything was better than thinking about Giles and Carola Roland. Thoughts didn't ask whether you wanted them or not, they came in — some of them like visitors tapping at the door, and when you opened it, instead of a friend on the doorstep you found an enemy there; some of them like ghosts tapping at the windows and calling strangely in words which you couldn't understand; some of them like thieves creeping in to steal; and some breaking in with violence like a plundering army. A shiver went over her. People kept saying how mild the weather was, but she was cold.

She looked at her watch and wondered when Giles would come. It was between twenty and a quarter to seven. She mustn't forget to light the gas under the steamer, or Ivy would get into trouble. Giles had been gone nearly a quarter of an hour —

The front door bell rang, and she ran. But it wasn't Giles. It was Agnes Lemming with a big dress box. She had set it down to ring the bell; now she picked it up and came into the little hall with her head up and a flush on her cheeks. She was in her old purple coat and skirt again, but somehow she looked different — younger, and with something taut and purposeful about her.

"Are you alone? Can I speak to you? I mustn't stay. I've only got a moment."

With her ears straining for Giles' return, Meade could only be thankful for this. But it wasn't in her to be unwelcoming. She said, "Aunt Mabel is out, and Ivy has gone to the post. What is it? Won't you come in?"

She had shut the door, but Agnes did not move away from it. She said in a difficult voice, "I mustn't stop — my mother will be back at any moment. Will you do something for me? Will you keep this box until the day after tomorrow and not say anything about it to anyone?"

It sounded so strange coming from Agnes Lemming that Meade could not make her voice quite as ordinary as she wanted to. She said, "Yes, of course I will."

Agnes faltered a little.

"It must seem — strange to you. I can't ask anyone else, and you have always been kind —" She paused, and found herself saying what she had not meant to say. "My cousin Julia Mason sent me some very nice clothes. I want to wear them the day after tomorrow. You see, I am going to be married."

Meade was so much surprised that she very nearly cried out. And then, flooding right over the surprise and blotting it out, came a tide of warmth and kindness. She reached up to put her arms round Agnes' neck and kiss her.

"Oh, Agnes — how nice! I'm so glad — I'm so very, very glad!"

"You mustn't tell anyone. Nobody knows — my mother doesn't know. I can't tell her until afterwards. I didn't mean to tell anyone."

"I won't tell — you know I won't. Who is it? And are you very happy?"

Agnes smiled down at her. It was her old nice smile, but with something added. She said in quite a young voice, "It is Mr Drake, and I am very happy. We both are. I mustn't stop." And with that she kissed Meade on the cheek, and was gone.

Meade was left in the middle of the hall with the dress-box. Of all the extraordinary things — Agnes Lemming and Mr Drake! But how nice. And he looked as if he would be able to cope with Mrs Lemming. That was what Agnes wanted — someone to rescue her and bang the door in Mrs Lemming's face. Agnes could never have done it by herself, it just wasn't in her. She put the box away in her wardrobe and had just shut the door on it, when she heard the bell again.

This time it was Giles. He came in, and she said at once, "Ivy's out. Oh, Giles — what's happened? It's been like years!" But even as she spoke, her heart shrank. There was no comfort in his look — angry eyes, and a face set like a flint. He walked past her into the sitting-room.

"I mustn't stop. What's the time? Ten minutes to seven — is that clock right? Your aunt will be coming back. I don't want to meet her. I'm not fit to meet anyone. I must go back and see if I can get on to Maitland. He's my solicitor, and if there's anything in this four hundred a year business, he'll probably know something about it. I believe he's moved out to the country, but I expect I can get a line on him. The sooner he's on to it the better. She needn't think she's going to have it all her own way!"

Meade was appalled. He might have been talking to himself — she mightn't have been there at all. She had never seen him like this — the angry, fighting male who wants to get on with his job and hasn't any time for

113

women. She was appalled but oddly reassured. If there was no softness for her, there was certainly none for Carola. And he meant to fight.

He hardly looked at her as he put a hand on her shoulder for a moment and said, "I'll ring you."

Then he was gone, and the door well and truly slammed behind him.

CHAPTER
EIGHTEEN

From this point onwards the sequence of events becomes of the first importance.

Giles slammed the door of Mrs Underwood's flat at five minutes to seven, and at about the same time Mrs Willard confronted her husband with two pencilled notes and a flood of reproachful tears. The first of the notes has already been in evidence. It ran:

All right, Willie darling, lunch at one as usual.

Carola.

The second had been discovered only this afternoon after an exhaustive search of Mr Willard's effects. It was very short, but it had brought poor Mrs Willard to the point of open accusation.

All right — what about tomorrow night?

C.R.

The dreadful thing about this note was that it wasn't dated. Tomorrow night might already have come and gone. It might be this present Wednesday night, or it might really be tomorrow. Mrs Willard had reached the

115

end of her tether. She had been a mild and submissive wife for twenty years, but this was too much. She looked a good deal like a stout motherly sheep at bay as she produced the note.

It was a most annoying situation for Mr Willard. Throughout their married life he had maintained a masterly discipline in his household. His word had been law, and his foot had been permanently down. Now he was being forced into a position of defence. His word was in question, and the foot was required to save his balance. He cleared his throat and said, "Really, Amelia —"

Mrs Willard burst into tears and stamped her foot.

"Don't you Amelia me, Alfred, for I won't stand it! Running after a bad girl like that at your time of life!"

"Really —"

"Yes, your time of life, Alfred! Fifty you are, and look every day of your age! What do you think a girl like that wants out of you except to pass the time because she's bored, and to get your money, and to b-break my heart —"

Here Mrs Willard's voice broke too. She subsided on to the couch, large and untidy, her face red and puffed with crying, and her grey hair coming down.

Mr Willard took off his glasses and polished them. He tried for the voice of authority but fell short.

"Amelia, I must insist —"

Mrs Willard interrupted him. She had no longer to rely upon her own shaking legs. The sofa gave her confidence.

"Haven't I been a good wife to you? Haven't I done everything I could?"

"That's not the question —" He cleared his throat again. "About these notes —"

"Yes, Alfred — what about them?"

Mr Willard's neat features took on an unbecoming flush.

"There's nothing in them," he said. "And I'm surprised at you, Amelia — more than surprised. And I may say at once that I wouldn't have believed you would do such a thing as to go looking through my pockets."

This was a little better. Too familiar, too colloquial, but it was putting Amelia in her place. It was she who would be on the defensive now.

The vigour of her counter-attack surprised and pained him.

"And if I'd left your saccharine tablets in the pocket of the blue coat you told me to send to the cleaners, what would you have said then, I'd like to know! That's where the first note was, and it just shows how that girl has upset you and got you all played-up, or you'd never have left it there for me to find. And if you'll show me a woman that doesn't read that sort of note when she's got it in her hand, I'll tell you straight out to your face that's she's no proper woman at all, and no feelings like a man expects his wife to have!"

Mr Willard was thrown off his balance again. He said, "Really!" several times in varying tones of protest and annoyance, whilst Mrs Willard attempted to stanch

117

a fresh access of tears with a handkerchief which was nothing but a sodden rag.

"Really, Amelia! Anyone would think that it was a crime to take a neighbour out to lunch!"

"A neighbour!"

"Well, she is, isn't she? And she wanted to consult me about a matter of business, if you want to know."

"Business!" said Mrs Willard with a rending sniff.

"And why not, Amelia? If you must know, it was about her income tax."

"Income tax?"

"Yes, income tax."

"I don't believe a word of it!" said Mrs Willard. "And I'm ashamed of you, Alfred, standing there and telling me lies — bringing them out like peas out of a pod and expecting me to believe them, which I don't and never will! And if she had lunch with you to talk about her income tax, what were you going to talk about 'tomorrow night' — and which night was it to be? Is that where you were on Saturday when you told me you'd been down to see Mr Corner? Or was it tonight you were going to make up an excuse and off upstairs to her? Haven't you got anything to say?"

Mr Willard hadn't. He had never suspected Amelia of so uncomfortable a talent for putting him in the wrong. And after all, what had he done? Run upstairs for a neighbourly chat, changed an electric bulb, unbent in a little friendly badinage, and fibbed about Mr Corner. She hadn't even let him kiss her, only called him "Funny little man" and bundled him out — he dwelt regretfully on this. And here was Amelia behaving as if he had given her grounds for divorce. Such a suspicious mind. And complete lack of self-control.

He achieved a voice of marital authority.

"I must refuse to listen to any more of these — these recriminations. They are unjustified, and I must decline to listen to them. I am surprised at you, Amelia, and I hope and expect that you will before long be surprised at yourself. You have quite lost your self-control and your sense of proportion, and I intend to leave you alone in the hope that you may recover them. In the meantime I should like you to know that *I* am very much displeased."

This time it came off. The voice was once more his own. Large rolling words came flowing out. He turned to the door with the strutting dignity of a bantam.

Mrs Willard had shot her bolt. She called after him with a lamentable sob.

"Where are you going? Oh, Alfred — you're not going to *her!*"

Mr Willard was himself again. Let Amelia cry — it would do her good. On his return he would find her repentant and submissive.

He went out of the flat and shut the door.

CHAPTER
NINETEEN

About ten minutes before Mr Willard left his flat, that is to say at seven o'clock, a young woman in an imitation astrakhan coat came in at the front door of Vandeleur House and took the lift to the top floor. She bore the same kind of resemblance to Carola Roland that an under-exposed photograph bears to its original. The features were the same, but the skin was sallow, the eyes greyish, and the hair plain mouse. Her clothes were neat but without style — mole-coloured coat, brown shoes and stockings, and a dark brown hat with a brown and green ribbon.

Bell saw her passing through the hall and said good-evening in his cheerful way. It wasn't the first time she had dropped in like this after business hours — Miss Roland's sister that was married to Mr Jackson the jeweller. Not a big shop, but old-established and very respectable. Bell knew all about them. The business had belonged to Mrs Jackson's father — Miss Roland's father too for the matter of that. Ella had married her cousin and carried on the name and the shop, but Carrie had run away and gone on the stage. She needn't think he didn't know who she was when she come back here with her hair shined up, and her face painted, and a fine new name. He knew her all right, and thought the better of her for wanting to be near her sister, and it wasn't his business what she called herself or what she did to her face and her hair. Mrs Smollett would like to turn and twist it about on that tongue of hers no doubt, but she wouldn't hear anything about the Jackson girls from him. He could keep his mouth shut. Why, he'd bought his Mary's wedding-ring in Mr Jackson's shop a matter of forty years ago. Well, Mr Jackson was gone ten years, and Mary a matter of thirty-five. Bell could hold his tongue.

Ella Jackson stayed with her sister for a short twenty minutes. Then they came down in the lift together, Carola bare-headed, with a fur coat thrown over her white dress.

As the lift went down, Miss Garside stood at her half open door and watched it go. She had reached the stage when you do things without quite knowing why. Her body was starved, and her mind, like some restless creature in a cage, thrust this way and that, seeking a way out. She had had no food all day. She had no money to buy food. She did not know quite why she had opened her door — some half formed thought of going over to the Underwoods' flat to ask if they could spare her some bread and a little milk — she could say she had run out —

As soon as the door was open she knew that she could not do it. That common, pushing Mrs Underwood — she couldn't do it. She must hold on till tomorrow and get the Auction Stores to take some more of her furniture. The good things were all gone.

They would give her next to nothing for what was left. It couldn't pay the rent, but it would buy her food for a little time longer.

She stood with the door in her hand and watched the lift go down. The landing light shone upon Carola's hair, her fur coat, a glimpse of her white dress. She thought bitterly, "She's going out. She'll be out all the evening now. She'll be meeting some man. They will go to a restaurant and pay as much for a meal as I should need for a week."

She watched the lift pass out of sight and went back into her cold empty room. Carola would be out for the evening, her flat upstairs would be empty. She seemed to see it standing there empty, and, somewhere in one of those empty rooms, the ring which was so like her own. The idea that Carola might be wearing the ring presented itself and was rejected. She didn't always wear it. In fact yesterday in the lift was the only time that Miss Garside had seen it on her hand. They had met perhaps a dozen times in the lift, and always there had been those white, useless hands sparkling with rings. If the girl was going out she carried her gloves until she reached the street. If she was coming in she pulled them off in the lift. Long white fingers, scarlet nails, an emerald on one hand, a ruby and a diamond on the other. But not the diamond solitaire which was the twin of hers — never that until yesterday. So why should she be wearing it tonight?

Miss Garside made up her mind that she would not be wearing it. It would be there, in the empty flat,

122

thrown down carelessly no doubt upon the dressing-table.

"If I had the key of the flat, it would be quite easy to change the rings —"

A voice which was Miss Garside's own inner voice said this very distinctly. It said,

"She will never know the difference — never. It is life and death to me, and nothing at all to her. Mine shines just as brightly. It will look as well on her hand as it has done on mine. It won't make any difference to her at all. Why should I starve so that she may have something which makes no difference to her? If I had a key I could change the rings —"

Bell had a key. Mrs Smollett went down into the old basement kitchen every morning at eight o'clock and took the key of No. 8 off its hook. Then she went up, let herself in, made Miss Roland an early cup of tea, and cleaned the flat. No one who had the slightest contact with Mrs Smollett could avoid hearing all about Miss Carola Roland and her flat.

"Lovely curtains, Miss Garside. And what they must have cost! I got a niece in the upholstery, and what those brocades cost — well, it's wicked."

You might turn your back and take no notice, but it didn't stop Mrs Smollett's tongue.

The key of No. 8 would be hanging now on its hook on the old kitchen dresser. In about twelve hours' time Mrs Smollett would fetch it and go upstairs and let herself in.

Anyone could fetch it now.

No, not now, because Bell would be about. But later, between half past eight and half past nine, when he would have "stepped out" to have a pint of beer and play a game of darts at the Hand and Glove. At half past eight, rain or fine, snow or fog, Bell "stepped out". Between half past nine and ten he returned. There was a whole hour during which it would be as safe to get the key as it was to sit here and think about it.

Between half past eight and half past nine —

CHAPTER
TWENTY

It was twenty-seven minutes past seven when Meade Underwood opened the door to a scared Ivy.

"Ivy, you *are* late! Lucky for you Mrs Underwood isn't back."

Ivy's eyes stared out of her peaked face.

"But, Miss Meade, she come in in front of me — I see her go up in the lift. Oh lor — I must hurry! Did you put on the gas for the steamer, miss?"

Ivy hurried. As it turned out, she had plenty of time. It was twenty minutes to eight before Mrs Underwood entered the flat. She went straight to her room and shut the door. Ivy came sidling in to Meade.

"That's a queer start, Miss Meade. I see her in front of me all the way from the corner. If it had been a bit darker, I'd have tried to get past, but I didn't like to chance it. I thought maybe she'd go to her room and I'd have time to slip me coat off."

Meade looked up, shaking her head.

"No, Ivy — *really!*"

She got a street-child grin.

"All right, all right — but my boy friend was late — we only had five minutes. And he's very good-looking, and lots of girls after 'im, so I had to wait. But when I see Mrs Underwood just in front of me, and Miss Roland —"

"Do you mean they were together?"

Ivy giggled.

"Not likely! Miss Roland, she was on in front — I see her white dress. She was in and gone before I come up, and Mrs Underwood standing there in the hall waiting for the lift to come down, so I'd to wait too — see? Kept back in the porch till I see the lift come down and Mrs Underwood go up. Wonder where she went to though."

Meade looked up with a faint smile.

"Perhaps you'd like to ask her, Ivy," she said.

At half past eight Bell "stepped out", punctual to the minute as he always was, and with the consciousness of a good day's work behind him. As he came into the hall from the basement stair, the front door was shutting. Someone had just gone out, but he couldn't see who it was, for they were already on the other side of that closing door. But when he got out on the steps he could just distinguish the figure of a man disappearing in the direction of the right-hand gate. There were the two gates, one to the right and one to the left as you came out of the house, and the gravel sweep and shrubbery between.

The man went off to the right, and Bell took the left-hand gate, which was nearer the town. Just as he got to it he heard a car start up, and saw it coming sliding past him down the slope of the road. He was to be very much pressed about this brief appearance of a man in the darkness, but all that he could ever say about it was that he took the man who had started the car to be the man he had seen going away from the house in the direction of the right-hand gate, but as to identifying him — "Well, I ask you!"

Bell took his way to the Hand and Glove, where he met his brother-in-law Mr William Barker and played a friendly game of darts. Mary Bell had been Mary Barker in the days when Bell had bought a wedding ring in old Mr Jackson's shop. William Barker was now a widower like himself, living with his daughter Ada and her husband, a master butcher and a very warm man. From the bottom of his heart Bell pitied poor William. "Can't call his soul his own 'cept of an evening when he steps out to the Hand — and she'd stop him doing that if it didn't take him out of the way of an evening." But then Bell had no use for his niece Ada. Purse-proud was what he called her in his own mind, and uppity — "a purseproud female with uppity notions."

In the intervals of play and refreshment they discussed Ada and her notions. It was a very great relief to Mr Barker and enabled him to support a comfortable but enslaved existence in which his daughter made him wear a stiff white collar every day — "And if it was possible to wear two on Sundays, she'd make me do that."

"Give 'em an inch, and they'll take an ell — that's women all over," said Bell.

Mr Barker gloomed.

"Her mother was just such another. Ah — she was a good wife was Annie, but a terrible one for keeping things up before the neighbours, That's where Ada gets it from. I remember Annie giving me a pair of blue vases for me birthday — saved out of the housekeeping money. Very showy they was on the parlour mantelpiece, with gilt 'andles and bunches of flowers painted on the front. And when I took and said to her how I'd rather she'd put good food in my stomach than blue vases on the parlour shelf, she up and told me they was my present and I had ought to be ashamed of myself not to be grateful about it." Mr Barker took a pull at his beer. "Ah," he said — "that's where Ada gets it from. We had words about them vases, but she got the better of me."

"Women always do," said Bell with a twinkle in his eye.

Mr Barker heaved a reminiscent sigh.

"Ada's very like her," he said.

At half past nine Bell took his way back to Vandeleur House. At ten he shut the outside door and adjourned to the basement, where he had a final look round before going to bed. Everything was neat and clean, everything was in order. On the old kitchen dresser eight keys hung in a row, each from its own brass hook. They were all there. Miss Underwood had brought back Mrs Spooner's key. She must have come down with it whilst he was out. All the keys were there. Bell went to bed, and slept until his alarm-clock went off at half past six on Thursday morning.

In due course all except three of the inhabitants of Vandeleur House went to bed, and some of them slept. Those who did not go to bed were Miss Carola Roland,

Mrs Willard, and Miss Garside. Mr Willard did not go to bed either — at least not to his own bed in his own flat. But, as it turned out afterwards, he was not in Vandeleur House at all, which is one of the reasons why Mrs Willard sat up all night.

Meade Underwood went to bed and to sleep. She went to bed because she wanted to be alone, and she slept because she was too exhausted to stay awake. It was a troubled sleep, vexed by dreams which cast a shadow on her thoughts but never came to sight.

She woke suddenly to the sound of the telephone bell. It rang again before she could lift the receiver. Giles' voice came urgently to her ear.

"Meade — Meade — is that you?"

She said, "Yes," and as she said it, the pink enamel clock on the mantelpiece began to strike twelve.

Giles said, "What's that?" and she said, "It's only the clock striking." And then he said, "Never mind about the clock. It's all right, darling. I can't tell you about it now, but it's all right — she won't bother us any more. I can't tell you over the telephone, but there won't be any more trouble. I'll be round in the morning."

The line went dead. The clock had finished striking. Meade lay awake a long time, but her waking thoughts were happier than her sleeping ones had been.

The first thing she heard in the morning was that Carola Roland had been found dead in her flat.

CHAPTER
TWENTY-ONE

It was Mrs Smollett who found her. Eight o'clock was her time for going up to No. 8, and she was punctual to the minute. Afterwards she produced a dramatic version in which as soon as she took the key from its hook she had a kind of sinking in her inside — "Felt cold in my hand that key did — not like it ought to have done — cold and kind of heavy, if you take my meaning. And all the way up those stairs — which is enough to break any woman's heart, but I wouldn't get in that lift, not if you paid me — all the way up I kept thinking to myself, 'There's something wrong. I don't feel like this for nothing.' And when I saw the door was on the jar, well —"

Actually, Mrs Smollett had felt nothing at all except the stairs, which were an old story and a standing grievance. She came out on the top landing, turned to face the door of No. 8, and found that she would not need to use her key. Even then it did not occur to her that there was anything wrong. She thought Miss Roland must be up and had unlatched the door for her. She put the key in her apron pocket and walked in. The light was on in the hall, but there was nothing remarkable about that, these entrances being lighted only by way of glass transoms over the doors which opened upon them. If the curtains were still drawn in these rooms, there would be no light at all. She went into the kitchenette, took down the black-out curtains, drew up the blind, and put on a kettle. Then she opened the sitting-room door.

Under the shaded light of an ornamental bowl which hung from the ceiling she saw Carola Roland lying face downwards on the pale blue carpet. She was still in her white dress. Her face was hidden, but she lay as the living do not lie. Here Mrs Smollett's version coincides with the facts. It never occurred to her for a moment to doubt that Miss Roland was dead. The light showed a horrible dark stain on the carpet and on that bright synthetic hair. The colour of the stain was a reddish brown.

Mrs Smollett backed away from the door with her hand at her side — backed right out of the flat and across the landing, and ran helter-skelter down the stairs for Bell.

Old Jimmy Bell behaved with great presence of mind. He told Mrs Smollett to stay where she was and went up in the lift. Outer and inner doors of No. 8 stood wide. There was no need to touch them, and he took care not to do so. Well, it was murder and no mistake about it. Little Carrie Jackson that he had seen going to school with her hair in a plait — old Mr Jackson's little Carrie that he'd been mortal proud of until she broke his heart. Spoiled, that's what she was — spoiled. Spare the rod and spoil the child. Not that he held with beatings and suchlike for children, but they did ought to be checked. Carrie had never been checked. His crumpled cheeks lost their rosy apple-colour as he stood looking down at her. He had served through the last war and seen plenty of dead men in his day, but you got out of the way of it, and a girl was different. This was murder — a girl murdered in one of his flats.

He went over to the telephone and called up the police. It was while he was waiting for them that he noticed the tray set out with drinks. It stood on a low stool between two armchairs in front of the electric fire. Both bars of the fire were on. He started to turn them off, but stopped himself in time. Of course nothing must be touched until the police came.

The tray was of scarlet lacquer with a gilt pattern round the edge, and the glasses very fine and showy with gold rims. There was a bottle of whisky, a syphon of soda, some red wine in a cutglass decanter, and a plate of sweet biscuits. Both the glasses had been used, one for the whisky, and the other, a much smaller glass, for the wine. He could smell the whisky.

The tray was the first thing he noticed. It wasn't until just before the police arrived that something else struck him. The mantelpiece — there was something queer about the mantelpiece. Well, what was it? Difficult to say, but something queer. That there photograph for one thing — photograph of Major Armitage with his name written across it. That was queer if you like. But it wasn't the photograph, it was something else. And then it came to him. It was that gimcrack statue of a dancing girl doing a high kick with next to nothing on, and none too decent by his way of thinking. That was it — the statue was gone from the mantelpiece.

And then he saw it, thrown down on the couch. He went over and looked at it. Because the queerness didn't end with its being there, it only began that way. The dancer lay where she had fallen from somebody's hand. The pointed silver toe was sharp and bright — almost as sharp as a dagger, almost as bright as steel. The whole poised figure was silver-bright and clean, but just where it had fallen there was an ugly stain on the blue and grey brocade, and the colour of the stain was the same as the colour of the stain on the pale blue carpet.

With the tramping of boots and the sound of voices the police arrived. Bell turned away from the couch and went to meet them.

CHAPTER
TWENTY-TWO

Chief Inspector Lamb sat at a table in what had been Carola Roland's sitting-room. It was the most solid of the tables in the flat, but his mind condemned it as gimcrack. He himself was on the massive side, a stout man with a small, shrewd eye and a heavy jowl. His hair was thin on the top, but even his promotion had brought no grey to it — very strong black hair.

The routine which waits on murder had run its course. The photographer and the fingerprint man had done their jobs. The body had been removed and the blue carpet rolled up. The figure of the dancing girl had been carefully packed up and taken away for examination.

Lamb looked up as Sergeant Abbott came into the room. Quite a different type — public school and Police College — very fair hair slicked back; tall, light figure; very high bony nose; light eyes a little more blue than grey, and flaxen lashes.

"I'd like to see the woman who found the body," said Lamb.

"Yes, sir. Miss Roland's sister is here."

"Sister? Who is she?"

"Mrs Jackson — wife of a jeweller in the town."

134

"All right, I'll see the other woman first. What's her name?"

"Smollett."

"That's right — Mrs Smollett. Bring her in!"

Mrs Smollett entered with an air of importance. And why not? Hadn't she found the body? And wouldn't she be called — at the inquest for sure, and at the trial if they caught the murderer? "And it's to be hoped they will, or we'll none of us be safe in our beds."

In order to support the dignity of the occasion she had reassumed her outdoor clothes — the black cloth coat with its mangy fur collar, the black felt hat with its frayed and faded ribbon. She gave her name — Eliza Smollett; her state — honourable widowhood; and her avocation — daily help. When a good deal of corroborative details had been got through or cut short, it emerged that she washed down the stairs and "obliged" in some of the flats.

"Mrs Spooner in No. 7 — I do for her regular, but she's gone away to join the A.T.S. Mr Drake in No. 5 — Mr Bell does for him. And Mrs Willard in No. 6 — she has me twice a week, Monday and Thursday, to give the place a good clean up. Mrs Underwood in No. 3 — she's got her own maid, and I don't go there, not without there's extra cleaning to be done. Miss Garside in No. 4 — she used to have me all the time I could spare till she began to get rid of her furniture. Lovely stuff it was, and she said it was gone to be mended but it never come back. But that's neither here nor there, as you might say. Then on the ground floor there's old Mrs Meredith, in No. 1, and I do the scrubbing there.

A maid and a companion she keeps, but I do the floors. And Mrs Lemming in No. 2 — well, most times I go there once a week, but not regular. But Miss Roland that was, poor thing, I did for her regular."

Frank Abbott, in a chair to the right of the table, sometimes made a note, and sometimes allowed his gaze to rest upon that portion of the smoothly painted wall where a cornice might have been if Miss Roland's scheme of decoration had been less modern.

The Inspector listened patiently enough. If you want to know something about people, listen to those who go in and out of their houses and do their work. The listening may be tedious, but the gossipy information sometimes comes in handy.

"Well now, Mrs Smollett," he said, "just tell us how you found the body."

Mrs Smollett gave a recital in which she did full justice to her premonition that all was not well, the horrid feeling which came over her when she found the door of the flat ajar, the manner in which her blood ran cold when she saw the body, and the spasms which had been afflicting her ever since.

"And if I'd a-thought what was going to come of it when I heard what I did hear with my own two ears — well, it's no good saying it mightn't have been any different, and it's no good trying to hush me up like Mr Bell did."

"What did you hear, Mrs Smollett?"

Mrs Smollett's large face was warmly flushed.

On the strength of the spasms she had accepted the offer of brandy from Miss Crane — "We always keep it

136

in case of Mrs Meredith being taken ill, and I'm sure, Mrs Smollett, you'd be the better of a sip." Mrs Smollett had had considerably more than a sip. Her face was flushed, her natural sense of drama heightened, and her tongue a runaway. She embarked with gusto upon a highly decorative narrative of what she had heard when she was washing the top landing on Wednesday morning.

"I been down to fill my pail. The water wasn't hot right up at the top there, the way Mr Bell has to spare the furnace these days, so I been down for a drop from the kettle, and when I come back, there they were at it hammer and tongs, and both doors open so you couldn't help but hear them. I'm not one to listen at doors, I'd have you know, but as I said to Mr Bell, I can't be expected to go putting cotton wool in my ears, and there's never been anyone deaf in our family."

Frank Abbott gazed at the ceiling. This sort of woman went on for hours. Lamb said, "Who was talking?"

Mrs Smollett nodded affably. The brandy was having a levelling effect. She was a star witness — she was hobnobbing with the police — the Chief Inspector hung upon her lightest word.

"*Ah!*" she said. "Who indeed? Miss Roland and Miss Meade Underwood — that's who! 'And what's brought her up here?' I says to myself. And there she was, asking Miss Roland, 'What's this about Giles and you?' — Giles being Major Armitage that Miss Underwood got engaged to in America and that everyone thought was drowned till Monday, when he turned up again, none the worse by all accounts if it wasn't that he'd lost his memory along of getting a crack on the head when his ship was torpedoed."

Frank Abbott's pencil had begun to travel. Lamb said, "Miss Underwood asked Miss Roland what about her and Giles — meaning Major Armitage?"

Mrs Smollett nodded again.

"That's right," she said. "And Miss Roland, she says, 'Didn't he tell you about me? Some people might think he'd mention he'd got a wife already.'"

"*What?*"

"That's what she said — 'You'd think he'd mention there was one Mrs Armitage already.' And when Miss Underwood says she's engaged to him, Miss Roland she flares up and says it isn't her fault if he's lost his memory, and she's got her money to think about. And she says it was four hundred a year Major Armitage was giving her, and she says, 'I'm Mrs Armitage, and don't you forget it.' And Miss Underwood says, 'He don't love you.' And when Miss Roland laughs, she says very loud and angry, 'It's no wonder he hates you!' And with that she comes out and past me, and down the stairs."

CHAPTER
TWENTY-THREE

The door closed upon Mrs Smollett. Frank Abbott returned and cocked an eyebrow at his Chief Inspector. Lamb frowned at him.

"We'll have to see this Armitage, and Miss Underwood."

"What about the sister, sir — Mrs Jackson?"

"She can wait. I'll see Miss Underwood at once. But what I want is a time-table. If this Armitage was here yesterday, I want to know when he came, when he left, and whether anyone saw Miss Roland alive after he left. All these people in all these flats — Curtis was going through them. I'd like the results as soon as he's finished. I want to know who saw her last, and when — and who saw Armitage, and when. Let me see, the Underwoods have got a maid, haven't they? See her yourself — she'll know whether he was about. Get on with it! And send Miss Underwood up!"

Meade Underwood came into the blue and silver room and saw a large man sitting at an inadequate table. Lamb saw a small girl in a grey frock with dark hair curling on her neck, and dark grey eyes with smudges under them. Her pallor and fragility were evident. He found himself hoping that she wasn't the fainting kind. His voice was pleasant enough as he said good-morning and told her to sit down, indicating a spidery chair all chromium tubes and silver leather. Meade was vaguely reminded of going to the dentist's. The tubes were cold against her back. A little shiver went over her.

"Now, Miss Underwood — if you will just answer a few questions. Did you know Miss Roland?"

"I knew her to say good-morning to when we met in the lift or on the stairs."

"No more than that?"

"No."

"But you were in this flat yesterday morning."

A very faint tinge of colour stained the pale cheeks. She said, "Yes, I had come up to the opposite flat to get something for Mrs Spooner, and Miss Roland asked me in."

"It was the first time you had been here?"

"Yes."

"You had some conversation with Miss Roland?"

"Yes."

"Was the conversation a friendly one?"

That faint flush had gone again. She was dreadfully pale as she said, "I hardly knew her. We were not friends."

Lamb's small, shrewd eyes looked straight into hers.

"Miss Underwood, I must tell you that your conversation with Miss Roland was overheard. It was not a friendly one — was it?"

"No —" The word was barely audible.

140

Lamb sat back in his chair and said in a kind, easy voice, "Well now, I want you to look round the room and tell me whether there's anything here that you recognise. That photograph on the mantelpiece for instance — do you recognise that?"

"Yes."

"Did you recognise it when you came into the flat yesterday morning?"

"Yes."

"Will you tell me who it is?"

"It's Giles Armitage — Major Armitage."

"And you are engaged to him?"

"Yes."

Every single one of those monosyllables was like a drop of blood dripping from her heart, draining her strength and her courage away. The voice that sounded kind but was quite unrelenting went on.

"It must have been a shock to you to see your fiancé's photograph on Miss Roland's mantelpiece."

Meade sat up straight. If she couldn't fight for herself she could fight for Giles. She said in a much stronger voice, "Oh, no, it wasn't a shock at all. You see, I hadn't known Major Armitage very long. We met in America. Of course he must have had heaps of friends before he met me."

Was that the right thing to say? She didn't know. Perhaps it was, perhaps it wasn't.

Lamb said gravely, "Is it true that Miss Roland claimed to be Mrs Armitage?"

Meade sat silent. It was so dreadful to hear it like that. She heard Lamb repeat his question, "Is it true?"

and in a faltering, stumbling way she forced herself to words.

"She said — her name — was Armitage —"

"And did you believe her?"

"I didn't know — what to believe —"

"Did you say, 'But he doesn't love you'?"

Meade couldn't answer that. She fixed piteous eyes on the Inspector's face and very slightly moved her head in assent. When she saw him frown she looked away. She wasn't to know that old Lamb had a soft spot in his heart for a girl in trouble. He had three girls of his own, one in the A.T.S., one in the W.A.A.F.S., and one in the W.R.N.S., and they did what they liked with him. He said rather gruffly, "Well now, Miss Underwood, did you see Major Armitage after all this took place?"

Meade nodded again.

"Can you tell me what time that was?"

"A little after six o'clock. He had been at the War Office all day."

"And you told him about your interview with Miss Roland?"

It was quite dreadful. He meant to go on asking question after question until he knew just what she had said to Giles and Giles had said to her. If she said "Yes", she might be harming Giles, and if she said "No", he wouldn't believe her — nobody would.

"What did he say when you told him, Miss Underwood?"

That was easier. She relaxed a little.

"He said it was a plant."

"He was angry?"

"Anyone would be."

"Just so. Did he suggest going up to see Miss Roland? Did he in fact go and see her?"

Meade's gaze widened. What could she say? She said nothing.

Lamb went on speaking.

"He went up to see her, didn't he? What time was that?"

Meade said, "Half past six."

"And he came down again?"

"It was ten minutes to seven."

"You were watching the clock for him? . . . Well, I expect you were. What did he say when he came back?"

Meade roused herself.

"He said he must get into touch with his solicitor at once. He had lost his memory — did they tell you that? He can't remember things that have happened in the last eighteen months — it's all a kind of fog. Carola Roland knew that, and we were both quite sure that she was trying it on."

"She didn't produce any documentary evidence? Come, Miss Underwood, I think she did. I think she showed you this letter. I am quite sure that she must have shown it to Major Armitage."

He lifted a paper on his right and took from under it the sheet which Carola Roland's hand had held up for Meade to read — long white fingers, scarlet nails, and a diamond ring with one clear shining stone — Giles' writing in a furious slope across the page: "My dear Carola . . . four hundred a year . . . a perfect legal right

143

to the name of Armitage . . ." She looked at it until it seemed to float away from her and disappear into a mist.

Behind her the door was opened with energy and Giles walked into the room.

CHAPTER
TWENTY-FOUR

Sergeant Abbott came in behind him. There was a slip of paper in his hand. He came over to the Inspector, laid it down in front of him, and stood away again. Lamb, whose frowning gaze had been fixed upon the abrupt and unauthorised intruder, was saying in the measured voice of the man who knows that his authority is not his own but is very sure that it will back him up, "Major Armitage?"

Giles, with a hand on Meade's shoulder, finished what he was saying to her — something like, "It's all right, darling" — but the voice had been pitched for her ear and no one could have sworn to the words. He straightened himself now and came up to the table, his face set and rather pale under the tan.

"I beg your pardon, Inspector. I have only just heard. It's a horrid business."

Lamb said, "Yes" — a single ponderous word. And then, "Will you sit down. I should very much like to talk to you, Major Armitage."

Giles sat down.

Frank Abbott found a chair and his notebook. Lamb dropped his eyes to the sheet which had been laid before him. The ball had been set rolling now. Where was it going to stop?

When the pause had lasted long enough to be left, Lamb looked up and spoke.

"I must begin by telling you, Major Armitage, that a conversation which took place yesterday morning in this room between Miss Underwood and Miss Roland was overheard. I suppose Miss Underwood told you about that conversation. She has in fact admitted that she did so, and that you then came up here to see Miss Roland. You confirm this?"

"Certainly."

He looked at Meade when he spoke, and looked away again. She was quite dreadfully pale. Her eyes were fixed. Her whole face was fixed.

"That was at half past six yesterday evening. Mrs Underwood's maid agrees with Miss Underwood about this." He glanced fleetingly at the paper before him. "She was watching the clock because she wanted to go out and meet her young man, which she did as soon as you were gone. Is that right, Miss Underwood?"

Meade said, "Yes."

The word barely carried. What were they doing to Giles? What had she done to him? What had he done to himself? What was happening to them all? It wasn't true — it couldn't possibly be true. She held on to that.

Lamb was speaking again.

"Now, Major Armitage — would you care to tell us about this conversation you had with Miss Roland? Was it a friendly one?"

He got a faint grim smile.

"What do you expect me to say to that? We were not on friendly terms."

"Did you quarrel?"

The smile went. The grimness was intensified.

"I don't think you could call it a quarrel."

The Inspector held out the letter which he had already shown to Meade.

"You are wondering how much I know — aren't you? Well, I don't mind telling you. This letter was found on Miss Roland's body. She had already shown it to Miss Underwood. I imagine that she showed it to you."

Giles nodded.

"Yes — she did."

"To substantiate a claim that she was your wife?"

"Not quite that." He reached over to touch Meade on the arm and say, "It's all right, darling — don't look like that."

Lamb was frowning over the letter.

"Is this your writing?"

"Certainly it is. I wrote the letter, and as you will have read for yourself, I offered Carola an allowance on condition that she dropped the name of Armitage to which she had a legal right. The letter is more than a year old. To the best of my recollection it was written in August '40."

"The thirteenth of August."

"Yes, that would be it. If I hadn't been suffering from loss of memory I could have explained the whole thing right away." He gave a short laugh. "In point of fact, if it hadn't been for that, the thing would never have come up at all. It was a pure try-on. She wanted to score me off, and she took a chance that I wouldn't remember."

Meade was looking at him now. They were all looking at him. Lamb said quietly, "And can you remember, Major Armitage?"

He gave a most emphatic nod.

"Yes, I can. It would have saved a lot of trouble if I could have done it before, but I suppose it was really the shock of this business that brought my memory back. They all said a shock might do it, and by gum it did. Not at the time, you know, but afterwards. I went to bed and I went to sleep, and I woke up just short of midnight with everything as clear as daylight. I rang Miss Underwood up then and told her not to worry."

Colour came to Meade's cheeks. She said, "Oh, yes — he did!"

Frank Abbott cocked a quizzical, cold eye. What was the chap handing them? The shock — what shock? The shock of murdering Carola Roland?

Lamb put the question in his slow, heavy voice.

"What shock do you refer to, Major Armitage? Miss Roland's death?"

The fair brows drew together with a jerk. They were oddly light against the brown skin. The blue eyes brightened, angrily, warily.

"No, of course not! I didn't know she was dead."

"What shock were you referring to then?"

Giles gave that short laugh again.

"The shock of having a perfectly strange young woman trying to make me believe I'd married her in a fit of temporary insanity or something. And now

148

perhaps you'll let me explain who she was, and how I came to write that letter."

Frank Abbott bent to his notes. Well, well, *well!* Nice chap — impetuous chap. Wonder if he came back and did her in before he remembered whatever it was he did remember. She was getting between him and his girl. Murders have been done for less than that. And he'd had a crump on the head . . . He heard Giles Armitage say in a quiet, level voice, "She was my brother's widow."

Meade said, "Oh!" Everything in her relaxed — the tight straining muscles, the tight straining thoughts. A kind of happy weakness came over her. She leaned back as far as she could against the chromium tubes and shut her eyes. Warm drops welled up behind her lashes and rolled down slowly one by one until her face was wet. She let them fall. It didn't matter at all — nothing mattered. She heard Lamb say something, but the words didn't reach her. Then Giles again:

"Yes, my brother Jack's widow. He was killed at Dunkirk. He had married her in the previous March — March 17th 1940, at the Marylebone register office. But I didn't know anything about it till after he was killed — no one did. I was at Dunkirk myself, but I was lucky. After I got home Carola came to see me. She plonked her marriage certificate down in front of me and said what was I going to do about it. Jack hadn't left her a sou — he hadn't anything to leave. He was only twenty-one when he was killed, and all he'd ever had was an allowance from me. It was a good allowance, because I always thought it was unfair that I should have all the money. Jack was eight years younger, and I inherited from my father under an old will made before my brother was born. He must have meant to alter it, but he crashed in the hunting-field when Jack was only six months old. I always meant to square things up, but I wasn't prepared to hand over to Carola. That's where I piled up the grudge she was trying to pay off. Finally I wrote the letter you've got there, and she agreed to my terms."

"May I ask why you wanted her to drop the name of Armitage?"

There was no answer for a moment. Then Giles said, "I had my reasons. It's nothing to do with this case."

"I'm sorry, Major Armitage, but it might be. You must see that Miss Roland's character might have quite a lot to do with her being murdered."

He got a shrug of the shoulders.

"I'm afraid you'll have to find that out for yourself. I can't help you."

There was a pause. Then Lamb said pleasantly, "Well, Major Armitage, I won't press you. But I'm sure you will want to give us any help you can. You were here for about twenty minutes, and you have said that there was nothing that you could call a quarrel. Did you have a drink with Miss Roland?"

Giles stared.

"Certainly not."

"Were there drinks in the room?"

"I didn't notice any."

Lamb turned in his chair. He indicated a stool set before the hearth between two chairs in blue and grey

150

brocade, a spindly thing with twisted chromium legs and a silver leather top.

"If there had been a tray on that stool, you would have noticed it?"

"I might have — yes, as a matter of fact I should. I went over to the mantelpiece and picked up that photograph. If the stool had been where it is now it would have been in the way. It wasn't there."

"You went over to the mantelpiece to look at the photograph. Did you touch it?"

"Yes, I picked it up. It must be the one I gave my brother. I certainly never gave one to Carola."

"Did you notice anything else on the mantelpiece — anything that isn't there now?"

Giles looked. Except for his photograph the silver shelf was empty. His eyes narrowed for an instant. Then he said, "There was some kind of a statuette — a girl dancing. It isn't there now."

Lamb said drily, "No, it isn't there now. Did you take it in your hand or touch it at all?"

Giles looked surprised.

"Oh, no."

The Inspector turned back to the table.

"I suppose you will have no objection to letting us have your fingerprints? Just routine procedure. We would like to eliminate the prints of anyone whom we know to have been in this room."

Giles gave that slight grim smile. He got up, came over to the table, and held out his hands.

"Here you are! A little crude though, isn't it? I thought one was handed a letter to look at after cross-examination had produced the right degree of clamminess."

Lamb allowed himself to smile. He had good teeth.

"Thank you, Major Armitage, we haven't always time to go round about when there's a short, straight way. And now, just to finish up. You left Miss Underwood at about ten minutes to seven. Do you mind telling me what you did after that?"

"Not at all. I went back to my rooms in Jermyn Street and tried to get a line on my solicitor, who was out of town. I got an address, but when I got on to it he had left. They said he'd be in office by ten o'clock this morning, so I decided to see him then. I went over to the club to have something to eat, and then I went out for a walk."

There was a flicker behind Frank Abbott's light eye-lashes. The chap was either a damned fool, or else he was innocent. He didn't look like a fool, but of course you never could tell. He didn't look like a murderer either — but then murderers didn't — not unless they were crazy. This chap wasn't crazy — just impetuous, and mortal fond of that little white-faced girl. Well, he'd just made them a present of a nice long walk in the dark which might very well have brought him back to Putney in time to do Carola Roland in. He made a note of this, and Lamb put the question.

"Did your walk by any chance bring you out in this direction?"

Giles stared, said "No", and then suddenly stiffened. The word conveys a little too much. Only very sharp eyes would have noticed that the muscle between cheek and jaw had tautened. Frank Abbott's eyes were very sharp indeed. He thought, "He's just tumbled to the fact that he's made a damaging admission. Good control — his hand didn't move. I wonder if he did come back."

Lamb said affably, "Thank you, Major Armitage — we needn't keep you or Miss Underwood any longer."

CHAPTER
TWENTY-FIVE

Mrs Smollett went downstairs in a very glorified state. She met Mr Willard coming up. He looked as if he had been up all night, and he looked as if he had been drinking — two things so extraordinary in so proper a gentleman that Mrs Smollett, who had usually no difficulty in believing anything about anyone, really did feel some difficulty about stretching her mind to take them in.

As she passed through the hall, Miss Crane popped out of No. 1 with an alacrity which suggested that she had been on the look-out and had no intention of letting a possible source of information pass her by.

"Oh, Mrs Smollett, do come in for a minute! Such an unpleasant experience! How did you get on? I thought perhaps a cup of tea — and perhaps a dash of brandy in it just to steady your nerves —"

Mrs Smollett responded graciously. She wasn't making herself cheap. She had become an important personage and she knew it. Reporters would question her, her photograph would be in all the papers, but she had no objection to a rehearsal. Miss Crane was an audience. Hot tea and brandy were a lure. She pressed a hand to a massive side and said the spasms were something cruel and she didn't mind if she did.

Miss Crane was most appreciative. She didn't know how Mrs Smollett bore up as well as she did. And as for going into the witness-box and having to take an oath and swear to things, well, she always hoped she would never have to do anything of the sort, for she was quite sure she would never survive it.

"There was a young man here just now wanting to know when any of us saw Miss Roland last, and whether we'd seen Major Armitage. Such a handsome soldierly-looking man. Major Armitage, not the detective, though he was quite a nice-looking young man too. And of course I was able to say that we hadn't. Such a comfort, because one doesn't want to get anyone into trouble. But as I told him, none of us actually went outside the flat yesterday except just down to the post in the evening. And then I didn't see anyone at all except Miss Garside coming up from the basement. And I wondered what she'd been doing there, though of course no business of mine. And as I said to him, I can't be too thankful, because anything like being dragged into a murder case would have a very bad effect indeed on Mrs Meredith's state of health, and that must always be my first consideration. She was quite poorly yesterday — that's why we didn't go out. Packer and I were quite anxious. But I'm glad to say she had a good night and is a great deal more like herself this morning."

Packer, happening to pass through the room at this moment, was called upon to confirm the happy improvement. She was a tall, lanky woman with hard features and a sour expression. There was no softening of either as she jerked head and shoulder in something which might be construed as assent and went out again, shutting the door with what was not quite a bang.

Miss Crane sighed and said in a deprecating manner, "That's the worst of a murder — it's so very upsetting. Packer is quite upset. Now, Mrs Smollett, another cup of tea — and a dash, just a dash of brandy —"

Mr Willard had passed Mrs Smollett on the landing without seeing her. He used his key to let himself into No. 6 and, crossing the lobby, pushed open the sitting-room door. The curtains were still drawn and the electric light blazing. At any other time this sinful extravagance would have called forth a well-phrased and pertinent rebuke. The state of Mr Willard's mind is indicated by the fact that he hardly noticed it. He came just inside the door and stood there staring at his wife.

Mrs Willard was sitting at the fumed-oak writing-table. She was still in the dress she had worn the night before, an artificial silk patterned in red and green. It looked as clothes look when they have been up all night. Mrs Willard looked that way too. She had stopped crying hours ago. The handkerchief which had been a soaked rag at midnight lay forgotten in the corner of the couch. It was almost dry. It was nearly ten hours since she had left it there and gone up the last flight of stairs to the top landing, her usually placid mind in a state of conflagration at the thought that Alfred was behind that right hand door, the door of No.

8. It was these flames which had dried her tears. Afterwards she had been too cold to cry. She had come back to her room and sat down upon the couch again, and the time had gone slowly by.

It was not until nine o'clock that she went over to the writing-table and rang up Alfred's brother. The Ernest Willards lived in Ealing. Ernest was a clerk in the Admiralty. She had come very slowly and stiffly to the conclusion that Alfred might be at The Limes. She dialled the number, and was answered immediately by a click and Ernest's voice. Very like Alfred's, but a little lower in tone. The resemblance was strengthened by a note of displeasure.

"Yes, Alfred is here. We are just about to start — in fact we should have started already. You had better ring him at his office."

Mrs Willard said in a cold, dull tone, "I can't, Ernest. He will have to come home. Something has happened here. Will you tell him that Miss Roland was murdered last night." She rang off, letting the receiver fall clattering back upon its stand.

After that she didn't move, just sat there in her crumpled dress, her hair fallen untidily about her neck. The flush which had covered her face changed to a heavy waxen pallor.

Mr Willard stood and stared at her. For a moment she was someone he had never seen before. And then his own sense of shock and misery blotted that out and she was Amelia again — Amelia who was always kind, Amelia who nursed him when he was ill, Amelia to whom he had been married for twenty years. He came over to her at a stumbling run, dropped down, put his head in her lap, and burst out crying like a child who has lost a glittering toy. His dry precision gone, he found simple phrases, broken by sobs.

"She was — so beautiful. There wasn't anything — in it, Amelia. It was just — that she was — so beautiful. I didn't even — kiss her — she wouldn't let me. She laughed at me — and called me — a funny little man. Perhaps I am — but she was — so beautiful —"

After a moment Amelia Willard put her arms round him. No child had ever called to her in vain. It was the child in Alfred that she loved. For the sake of that child she had for twenty years put up with his tidiness, his fault-finding, his dictatorial ways. When he was tired, when he was unhappy, when he was ill, the child would cling to her. The agony of last night had been the agony of believing that the child was dead.

She held him now, rocking him, and saying foolish, loving things. After a while he lifted a tear-stained face. His glasses were crooked and smudged. He took them off, dried and polished them, wiped his eyes, blew his nose, put the glasses on again, and gazed at Amelia. When he had drawn away from her she had rested her right elbow on the table, lifting the hand to prop her head.

Alfred Willard's gaze became fixed and horrified. The sleeve which fell away from that lifted hand was stained and dabbed with blood.

CHAPTER
TWENTY-SIX

Mrs Underwood sat in the tubular chair. She thought how uncomfortable it was, and tried to remember that she was a Wing Commander's wife, and that the stout man facing her was, after all, just a plain-clothes policeman, not so very far removed from the constable who stops the traffic for you and helps you on your way in the blackout. She had put on a smart hat and taken pains with her face, but none of these things prevented her from feeling as if more than twenty years had been rolled away and she was Mabel Peabody again, dreadfully frightened and wishing that the ground would open and swallow her up. Old Lamb, country born and bred, was reminded of any scared animal. Fear is fear, and you can't hide it. Cows in a burning shed — he'd seen that when he was a boy and never forgotten it — a rat in a trap, sheep when a dog has been worrying them, a badly startled horse, and this fine lady in her smart London clothes — frightened creatures, the lot of them. He didn't wonder what Mrs Underwood had to be frightened about, because he knew. That is to say, he knew enough to be going on with. There might be more to it. There might even be a great deal more, but this would do for a start.

He began in his pleasant manner.

"I believe you were out for a good part of yesterday afternoon and evening, Mrs Underwood. We are making a time-table of the comings and goings of everyone in the flats. It will help us to find out at what times it would have been possible for a stranger to have visited Miss Roland without being seen. Have you any objection to giving us your times?"

This was quite reassuring. Mabel Peabody faded — Mabel Underwood produced the required information.

"I went out to lunch, and then on to take my niece's place at Miss Middleton's centre. They pack parcels for people who have been bombed out, and for necessitous evacuees, and I'm sure it's all very useful, but I couldn't work under her myself. Well, of course that won't interest you, and I mustn't take up your time. Let me see, where was I? Oh, yes — I packed parcels till five o'clock, and then I went on to play bridge at the Soames', and I suppose I got back here about half past seven."

"You came straight back?"

Mrs Underwood looked surprised.

"Oh, yes."

"Straight back to your own flat, Mrs Underwood?"

She was frightened again now. She hadn't enough breath to answer. She looked at the window — at the fireplace — anywhere except at Chief Inspector Lamb.

"I don't know what you mean. Of course I came back to my flat."

"Yes, of course you did. But you didn't come straight back — did you? Your maid, Ivy Lord, says you were in front of her all the way along from the corner, and that Miss Roland was in front of you. There would be quite enough light at half past seven for her to recognise two people whom she knew. She says Miss Roland was not in sight when she came in, but that you were standing by the lift shaft waiting for the lift to come down again. She waited in the porch until you had gone up in the lift. Miss Underwood had given her leave to go out, but she had overstayed her time. She hoped you would go straight to your room and not realise that she was out, but when she entered the flat she found to her surprise that you had not come in. It was then a minute or two before the half hour. She says she looked at the clock in the hall as she came in, and at the kitchen clock in the hall as she came in, and at the kitchen clock as soon as she had taken her coat off. It was then exactly half past seven. She says that it was not until ten minutes later that you came into the flat. Do you dispute this statement?"

That unbecoming mauve flush had risen to the roots of the tinted chestnut hair. The high bust lifted and fell.

"No — no — of course not."

Lamb leaned forward a little.

"Miss Roland was in front of you all the way from the corner?"

"Yes. She was seeing someone off by the bus in front of mine."

"You didn't speak to her?"

"Oh, no. She had started back before I got off my bus."

"You mean that you waited purposely to give her a start — you didn't very much want to catch her up?"

"Well, something like that. I had only met her once. The Willards had her in to make a four at bridge on Monday. I didn't want to get too intimate — I had my niece to consider."

"Just so. Well now, Mrs Underwood, would you like to account for that time between half past seven and twenty to eight? Ivy Lord saw you go up in the lift. Where did you go to?"

The flush deepened almost to purple. Mrs Underwood gripped the tubular arms of the chair. The metal was cold against her sweating palms. She drew a long breath, and lost control of it. Her words came unevenly, catching and stumbling.

"I went up — to the top floor. There was — something I thought of — something I wanted to — say to Miss Roland. It wasn't anything at all — I just thought — I would speak about it — if I could catch her. It wasn't really anything — but I thought — it might be — a good opportunity —"

"And was it?" said Lamb.

She didn't look at him.

"Oh, I didn't see her. I changed my mind."

"You just went up to the top floor and came down again? But that wouldn't take ten minutes, would it?"

Mrs Underwood took another of those long breaths.

"Well, no — but I didn't come down at once. I expect it sounds very silly, but I just couldn't make up my mind. I got out of the lift, and there was the flat but the door was shut, and I thought, 'Well, it's getting late.' And then I thought I might as well see her and be done with it. I got right up to the door, and I was going to ring the bell but I didn't. I walked down the stairs nearly as far as the next landing. And then I thought I was being stupid and I went back, but in the end I just came down again. I suppose that's how the time went."

It sounded a very lame and unconvincing tale. Sergeant Abbott, sitting a little to Mrs Underwood's rear, permitted himself to raise an unbelieving eyebrow. Lamb had a frown as he said, "You didn't see Miss Roland then?"

"Oh, no, I didn't."

He allowed a pause to weigh upon them all before he said with an abrupt change of manner, "What did you want to see her about?"

"Oh — nothing special —"

"It wasn't by any chance about a letter?"

Lamb rummaged among the papers before him and leaned towards her with a folded sheet in his hand. One of the corners had been torn off. She stared at it, holding on to the arms of the chair.

Lamb unfolded the sheet.

"This letter is signed Mabel Underwood. You wrote it, didn't you? There is only a small piece missing. It starts without anybody's name and says, 'I really cannot do what you ask me. It is quite impossible. I ought not to have sent you anything the first time, but you said that would settle everything. It is quite impossible for me to give you any more money without my husband knowing about it.' Your signature follows. Then there's

163

this piece that's been torn off — was there anything written on that?"

She gave a sort of nod.

"Do you remember what it was?"

She spoke with a gasp.

"I said — I had no money to give."

Lamb leaned over the table, resting his arms upon it.

"Miss Roland was blackmailing you?"

"I — don't know."

"How do you mean you don't know?"

"I didn't know it was Miss Roland. I posted the letter."

"Will you give me the address?"

Frank Abbott took it down.

"Was it the same address to which you sent the first letter — the one with the money in it?"

"No — that was another address."

"Will you give me that too?"

She gave it, unable to do anything except answer whatever they asked her. Her first desperate fear had slipped into lethargy. It was no use — they had her letter — she must answer them. She did not see the quick look which passed between Lamb and Abbott as she gave the second address.

Lamb said quickly, "Can you give me the date of this first letter? I take it it was the first — the one with the money in it?"

There was some additional distress. She answered with difficulty.

"Yes — I don't know — I sent the money — I don't remember the date — it was about six months ago — in the spring —"

"And how much money did you send?"

"Fifty pounds."

"And you heard no more for a time?"

"No — not till the other day — last week."

She told them about writing the letter and posting it.

Then Lamb said, "How did you know that Miss Roland had your letter?"

It was no use — she had to answer them.

"I saw it — in her bag."

"Will you explain that a little, Mrs Underwood."

Another long breath.

"It was on Monday evening — when we were playing bridge at the Willards'. She opened her bag to get a cigarette, and I saw my letter."

"You recognised it — like that?"

"I wasn't sure. I thought it was my letter — I wasn't sure."

"Then you went to see Miss Roland with the idea of finding out whether she had your letter?"

"Yes. But I didn't see her — I changed my mind."

"Why?"

Mrs Underwood pulled herself together. She hadn't told about finding the torn-off corner of the letter on her bedroom floor, and this small circumstance helped her back to self-control. It was as if she had managed to keep her feet for a moment, and the fact that she had done so steadied her. She said, "Because I wasn't sure. Coming up in the lift, I thought I was, but when I got out on the landing I wasn't any more, and I thought how awkward it would be if I went in and said a thing like that and then it wasn't my letter after all. That's

165

when I began to go downstairs, and when I got a bit of the way down it came over me that it really was my letter and that I ought to go back and ask about it. But I just couldn't make up my mind, and that's the truth."

They pressed her, but she stuck to it. She had had her finger on the bell, but she hadn't rung it. She hadn't entered the flat. She hadn't seen Carola Roland or spoken to her.

In the end Lamb let her go. She went back to her flat a badly frightened woman and rang up Miss Maud Silver.

A prim little cough and a kind, decided voice:

"Miss Silver speaking."

"Oh, Miss Silver — I'm in such trouble — such dreadful trouble! I don't know what to do. You said you'd help me — you remember — Mrs Underwood — and I said I didn't see how I could manage it — but now I must. It would be so dreadfully bad for Godfrey — if I got mixed up — in this case — and I could see they didn't believe me — though I swear I was telling the truth —"

Miss Silver's voice cut in sharply.

"What case, Mrs Underwood?"

Mabel Underwood lowered her voice to a shaking whisper.

"She — has been — murdered. Oh, Miss Silver!"

Miss Silver said, "Who?"

"The girl I told you about — the one who had my letter — Carola Roland."

"Dear me!"

Mrs Underwood began to pour it all out, but was presently stopped.

"I think it is inadvisable to say any more. I will come and see you."

CHAPTER
TWENTY-SEVEN

Upstairs Lamb frowned over Sergeant Abbott's notes.

"Fishy story," he said. "And she was frightened —
badly frightened. Wonder what she was being
blackmailed about. It might be that — she might be
afraid of its coming out — there's always that."

Frank Abbott said without any expression at all,
"The letter was in the bag where she said she had seen
it. If she killed Carola Roland to get it back, why did
she leave it there?"

Lamb nodded. Frank was sharp — there was a time
when he had thought he was going to be too sharp —
but he was shaping well — a good boy, if a little
inclined to think a step ahead of his superiors. Wind in
the head — that's what he had to watch out against —
wind in the head, and being too clever. He'd seen a lot
of good men spoilt that way — up with the rocket and
down with the stick. When necessary, he did not
hesitate to point the moral. At the moment he was too
busy.

"Oh, I don't think she did it. But there's no denying
that she'd motive and opportunity — not a great deal
of either, but some. To my mind Major Armitage is the
more likely of the two."

168

"She was alive fifty minutes after Armitage left. Of course he may have come back."

"Bell saw a man going away from the house at eight-thirty. Those were a man's prints on the larger of the two glasses — the one with the whisky and soda in it. She had a man here some time before she was killed, and it may have been the man Bell saw going away — it probably was. Someone else may have seen him come in or go out. He may have been the murderer, and he may have been Major Armitage — he's engaged to Miss Underwood. Carola Roland was trying to blackmail him, and it looks as though she had been blackmailing Mrs Underwood. That brings the Underwood family right into the case, doesn't it?"

Frank Abbott nodded.

"That address Mrs Underwood gave — the one to which she sent the money, sir — I saw you noticed that."

Lamb nodded again.

"It's the one that was being used in the Mayfair blackmail case. Accommodation address of course. We only got Smithson, worse luck, and I'll eat my hat if he was alone on the job. He hadn't the education for it, or the brains. No, to my mind the principal got away and left him to take the rap. Let me see — that would be about six months ago, which corresponds very nicely with the date when Mrs Underwood sent her fifty pounds. Of course two separate blackmailers may have been using the same address, but I'd want good jury-proof evidence to make me believe it. Now I wonder whether Miss Roland was the principal who slipped through our fingers. Looks as if she might have been."

Frank Abbott looked over his Chief Inspector's head.

"In which case a good many people may have had a motive for murdering her," he observed.

At this point there was a knock on the door and Sergeant Curtis came in — a dark young man with horn-rimmed spectacles and an air of polite efficiency. He had seen everyone in the flats he had been sent to cover, and proceeded to detail the results.

"Flat No. 1, sir: — Mrs Meredith — very old lady — deaf — partially helpless. Companion, Miss Crane. Maid, Ellen Packer. Both middle-aged. They say none of them went out all day, except Miss Crane to the pillarbox at the corner. She puts this at between 8.30 and 8.45. Says she saw no one except Miss Garside, tenant of No. 4, who was coming up from the basement. Did not speak to her.

"Flat No. 2: — Mrs and Miss Lemming. Mrs Lemming out with friends until just after 7.00. Miss Lemming out until about 6.20, when she returned to flat, but left it again at 6.35 to pay a short call on Miss Underwood in No. 3.

"Flat No. 3: — Covered by Sergeant Abbott.

"Flat No. 4: — Miss Garside. I could get no reply on my first visit, but returned after covering 5 and 6. Miss Garside had then come in. Said she had been out shopping. I thought this strange, as she appeared to be having breakfast. Said she had not been out all the previous day and could shed no light on Miss Roland's movements or those of anybody else. When I

170

mentioned Miss Crane having seen her come up from the basement between 8.30 and 8.45p.m. she said, 'Oh, *that?* I didn't see Miss Crane or anyone else. I went down to tell Bell that there was a faulty washer on one of my taps.'

"Flat No. 5: — Mr Drake. He waited in to see me, and has now gone to business. Says he was out as usual all day yesterday. Returned about 9.15. Says he met no one.

"Flat No. 6: — Mr and Mrs Willard. Some disturbance going on there — possibly a quarrel. Mr Willard left flat at a little after 7.00p.m. and did not return until about 9.30 this morning. Says he went to see his brother at Ealing and stayed the night. Agitated — signs of tears. Mrs Willard — face puffed with crying — eyes red. Looked as if she had been up all night. Crumpled handkerchief in corner of sofa. Says she didn't leave flat and saw no one. Considerable evidence of strain."

"She had a row with her husband, and he stayed out all night. She kept hoping he'd come home, and he didn't, so she cried her eyes out and forgot to go to bed. That's about the size of it, my boy."

The efficient Curtis disciplined a sensation of annoyance and returned to the charge.

"It might have been like that, sir. But there was more than an ordinary quarrel would account for — definitely. If there was a quarrel, it must have been a very bad one."

Lamb gave his deep chuckle. He liked getting a rise out of Ted.

"Wait till you're married, my boy!" he said, and heard Frank Abbott murmur, "I wonder what they quarrelled about."

Lamb chuckled again.

"What *do* husbands and wives quarrel about? Perhaps you'd like to ask 'em."

"I wonder if it was about Miss Roland," said Frank Abbott in the gentle voice which Curtis found irritating.

Lamb looked up sharply.

"Any grounds for that?"

Curtis said, "No, sir."

Frank Abbott slid a hand over his already immaculate hair.

"First-class row between husband and wife suggests other man or woman. The lady in this case, is, I gather, middle-aged."

"They're never too old to get into mischief," said Lamb a little grimly.

"Not if they're that sort, sir. I took the opportunity of asking Miss Underwood about the people in the other flats, and she described Mrs Willard to me as a perfect pet — rather like a hen without any chickens."

Lamb chuckled.

"Well, I don't like hens myself and shouldn't want to make a pet of one. But it doesn't sound as if Mrs W. was one of the gay deceiving kind — I grant you that. What about it, Ted?"

Sergeant Curtis agreed, a touch stiffly.

"Not that sort at all, sir. Good housewife and all that. Everything as clean as a new pin — polished up to the nines. She only has Mrs Smollett twice a week, so she must do most of it herself. That sort hasn't got time for carrying on."

"A world-beating cook according to Miss Underwood," said Frank Abbott. "Lucky Willard! You wouldn't think he'd risk all that — would you? Did he strike you as a gay deceiver, Ted?"

Curtis frowned.

"He struck me as a man who had just had a pretty bad shock. I don't really think a quarrel would account for the state he was in. He'd been crying — actually crying, and he was as nervous as a cat on hot bricks."

Lamb swung round in his chair.

"Well, if he'd been flirting with her a bit he'd be bound to be upset. That's the worst of police work — it makes you forget about people being human. If you come to think of it, Ted — there's a pretty girl living next door to you, and you see her going up and down. Perhaps you pass the time of day, perhaps you flirt with her a bit, perhaps you only think you'd like to. Perhaps you have a row with your wife about her, perhaps you don't. I don't know. But if you've got any human feelings, what are you going to feel like when you hear that girl has been murdered? It's bound to be a shock, isn't it? Human feelings are things you're bound to take into consideration. That's where a lot of these detective novels go wrong — there aren't any human feelings in them. They're clever the same way a game of chess is clever, or a problem in mathematics, and nobody with any more feeling than one of the chessmen or the plus and minus signs. It isn't natural, and it don't do to go jumping to the conclusion that a man's a criminal because he's got his feelings and they've been too much for him. All the same you'd better see if you can dig up anything about Willard and Miss Roland. Find out where he goes to lunch and dine. See what you can get. And now I'd better see Mrs Jackson."

CHAPTER
TWENTY-EIGHT

In The Willards' flat husband and wife looked at each other. Sergeant Curtis had come and gone. His brisk, efficient manner, his notebook with its carefully sharpened pencil, his dark tweed suit and horn-rimmed glasses, were interposed between the moment when Mr Willard had seen the blood on Mrs Willard's sleeve and the moment when the door had been briskly and efficiently shut and they were alone again.

Alone with the width of the room between them. Mr Willard had receded until he stood against the sitting-room door. Mrs Willard sat by the writing-table with her hands in her lap. In this position the stain on her sleeve was hidden, but Alfred Willard knew that it was there. He was shaking from head to foot as he leaned against the door and said, "Take off that dress, Amelia!"

Mrs Willard said, "Why?"

"Don't you know why?"

"No, Alfred."

His shaking increased. How she could sit there and look at him — how she could sit there at all! That the stained sleeve had been touching him when he knelt before her with his head in her lap made him feel actually and physically sick. He said in a desperate whisper, "It's stained, Amelia — it's stained — it's got blood on it — didn't you know?"

Mrs Willard didn't speak or move for a moment. Then she turned her arm and looked at the stain with an expression of distaste. After about half a minute had gone by she got up and began to walk slowly in the direction of the bedroom.

Still in that whispering voice, Mr Willard said, "Where are you going?"

"To change my dress."

"Is that all — you've got to say?"

There was a door between the bedroom and the sitting-room. Mrs Willard stopped on the threshold and said without turning round, "Yes, I think so. I'm too tired to talk."

The door shut behind her. Mr Willard sat down on the couch and burst into tears.

Presently when he went into the bathroom to wash his face he saw that Mrs Willard had left her dress soaking in the basin. The water was horribly tinged. With an extreme effort he overcame the nausea which threatened him and pulled out the plug. The stained water ran away, the dress settled in a sodden mass.

He ran in more water, and rinsed the dress. When the water ran clear he wrung it out and folded it in the small cupboard through which the hot water pipe ran, removing his own and his wife's towels in order to make room for it.

When he had finished he opened the bedroom door and looked in. The pink curtains were drawn. By the

176

light that came in through the door he could see that Mrs Willard was lying on her bed. She had pulled back the coverlet, which lay trailing on the floor, but she had not troubled to turn down the bedclothes or to undress herself. She lay outside the bed, covered by the rosy eiderdown, her grey hair tumbled on the pillow, her hands tucked together under her chin, her eyelids closed, her breathing deep and natural.

Mr Willard stood and looked at her with an extraordinary mixture of feelings, trivial and profound. She had done murder for him. Few husbands are as dearly loved as that. She shouldn't let the coverlet trail on the floor. It was careless, very careless. Pink was a delicate colour. Recollection of the tinged water flooded his mind and sickened it. She was a murderess — Amelia. He had never been in a room with a murderess before. He had been married to Amelia for twenty years. Suppose the police found out and took her away . . . Suppose . . .

Mrs Willard slept peacefully.

CHAPTER
TWENTY-NINE

Mrs Jackson was a young woman of decision. Rejecting the tubular chair, she had picked one out for herself and set it at the angle which she preferred. Old Lamb contemplated her with relief. He never got over his dislike of interviewing the near relations of what his report would presently call the deceased. Mrs Jackson had obviously been crying, but she wasn't crying now, and she had a businesslike air. He judged her to be the elder sister, and thought she might easily be a mine of information. One- or two-and-thirty, and a plain likeness of the murdered girl, was what he put her at.

He began by being sorry for having kept her waiting. And then, "I'm afraid, Mrs Jackson, I must ask you some questions about your sister's private life. She was on the stage?"

Ella Jackson sniffed. It might have been the aftermath of the tears, or it might not.

"Chorus parts, pantomime, and now and again a travelling company," she said.

"And her last engagement?"

"Six months ago, at the Trivia Theatre. She was in the chorus there."

"And since then?"

"Resting," said Mrs Jackson laconically.

Sergeant Abbott bent over his notebook. This was the sort of witness who didn't give anything away. If you thought of the right question you'd get the right answer — perhaps.

Lamb went on.

"Was your sister married or single?"

"She was a widow."

"Can you tell me her married name?"

Ella Jackson hesitated. Then she said, "Well, she wasn't using it, but I suppose it doesn't matter now. It was Armitage."

Lamb's voice was at its pleasantest as he leaned towards her and said, "Will you tell us a little more about your sister's marriage, Mrs Jackson? It has a definite bearing on the case."

She looked startled, but she answered at once.

"Oh, there's nothing to hide. She wasn't married to him for very long. He was a nice young fellow a good bit younger than her, and I don't know how it would have turned out. Let me see — they were married in March last year, and he got killed at Dunkirk in May."

"Did he leave your sister provided for?"

She had that startled look again.

"Well no — he didn't. Carrie thought there was money, that's a fact, but it turned out he only got an allowance from his brother."

"Major Giles Armitage?"

"That's right."

"Did Major Armitage continue the allowance after his brother's death?"

"He gave her four hundred a year."

"Did you know that he was supposed to have been drowned, but that he recently turned up again, and that he had an interview with your sister yesterday?"

Mrs Jackson coloured and said, "Yes."

Lamb went on.

"He was suffering from loss of memory — I suppose your sister told you that?"

"Yes."

"Did she tell you that she took advantage of this fact to try and make him believe that she was his wife?"

Ella Jackson looked distressed.

"Yes, she told me. And I told her it was right down wicked and she'd be getting herself into trouble if she didn't look out."

"And what did she say to that?"

"She laughed and said it was only a joke. And when I said that sort of joke could make a lot of trouble, she said she'd been wanting to score him off and it was much too good a chance to be missed."

"She didn't give you the impression that it was a serious attempt to get money out of Major Armitage?"

"Oh, no, nothing like that, or she wouldn't have told me about it — she knew what I'd say. It was nothing in the world but a joke."

Lamb said, "I see —" and then, "You came to see your sister last night, didn't you? Bell saw you come in. What time would you say that was?"

"Seven o'clock," said Mrs Jackson. "I looked at my watch because I'd got a bus to catch."

"Yes — that agrees with Bell. And when did you leave?"

"Twenty past. Carrie came to the corner with me and saw me on my bus. I only just caught it."

"How was she dressed, Mrs Jackson?"

For the first time Ella Jackson faltered. She dropped her voice to keep it steady.

"A white dress and a fur coat — a long white dress."

"She had changed for the evening?"

"Yes."

"Do you know if she was expecting anyone?"

"I don't know — she didn't tell me."

"Would she have changed if she hadn't been expecting someone?"

"She might have done. She had pretty clothes and she liked wearing them."

Lamb shifted in his chair.

"Did your sister offer you any refreshment?"

Mrs Jackson looked surprised.

"Oh, no. She knew I couldn't stay."

"You didn't have drinks together?"

"Oh no."

"Mrs Jackson — was there a tray set out with drinks in the room whilst you were here?"

She shook her head.

"Oh, no."

"Quite sure about that? It's important."

"Oh, yes, I'm quite sure. There wasn't any tray."

Frank Abbott wrote. Lamb shifted again.

"Because that tray was here on the stool in front of the fire when she was found. She'd been drinking with someone — both glasses had been used."

Ella Jackson coloured up. Just for a moment she was very like her sister.

"Carrie didn't drink."

Lamb hastened to pacify her.

"Well, I didn't mean that in the way you've taken it — only that she'd been having a drink with a friend. There was a little red wine in the glass she had used — port wine."

Ella nodded.

"Yes, it would be port if it was anything. But it wouldn't be more than a thimbleful. I wouldn't like you to think she was one of those drinking girls, because she wasn't."

"That's all right, Mrs Jackson. Now would you mind taking a look at this letter? It was in your sister's blotter, and as you will see, it was written on Tuesday and left unfinished."

Ella ran her eyes over the lines in which Carola Roland had told the gentleman whom she addressed as Toots how much she missed him, and what a nun-like existence she was leading at Vandeleur House. "Missing my Toots so dreadfully." The words swam for a moment before Ella's eyes, but she blinked them back into focus.

"Do you know the name of this gentleman she was writing to?"

Ella blinked again.

"She was going to marry him," she said.

182

"After he'd got his divorce — that's what the letter implies, doesn't it?"

Ella nodded.

"That's the reason she came down here — to be quiet."

"Whilst the divorce was going through?"

She nodded.

"What brought her to Vandeleur House?"

"Mr Bell told me there was a flat to let. Carrie wanted to be near me."

"I see. And now, Mrs Jackson, what about the gentleman's name? I think you know it."

She looked distressed.

"Yes, I do, but —"

Lamb shook his head.

"That won't do, I'm afraid. We've got to have it. Things can't be kept private in a murder case, Mrs Jackson. You'll have to give it to us."

"Well, it's Mr Maundersley-Smith — *the* Mr Maundersley-Smith."

Frank Abbott's eyebrows went up as far as they would go. Old Lamb stared and frowned. Maundersley-Smith! By gum! No wonder the girl thought it was worth while to bury herself in Vandeleur House and live like a nun, for Mr Maundersley-Smith was a hub of the Empire, a prince of the shipping world, a household word for success and wealth. Miss Carola Roland had played high, and if the fingerprints on the larger glass proved to be his, Mr Maundersley-Smith might be called on to foot a heavier bill than even

183

he could afford. Well, well, that was as might be. Meanwhile —

He addressed himself again to Ella Jackson.

"Did you see anyone besides Bell, either coming or going?"

There were signs of definite relief at the change of subject. For the first time information was volunteered.

"Well, not exactly coming or going, because it was while I was up here with Carrie. He came and rang the bell, and she sent him away — laughed at him, and called him a silly little man, and said she hadn't got time for him."

"Who was it?"

"Oh, just Mr Willard from the flat downstairs. There wasn't anything in it, you know — she only laughed at him. But I told her she oughtn't to encourage him because of his wife — even if it didn't mean anything at all, his wife would have her feelings."

Over her head Frank Abbott looked at Lamb and Lamb looked back. So the Willards' row probably had been about Carola Roland. And Alfred Willard had come straight from it up the stair to try and see her, for it was soon after seven that he had left his flat, and he had not returned to it until this morning.

After a minute Lamb spoke.

"Was Mr Willard the only other person you saw besides Bell?"

Ella Jackson hesitated.

"Well, I don't know about *saw*," she said, "but when we were going down in the lift the door of one of the flats opened and someone looked out. I couldn't see

184

who it was myself, but Carrie laughed and said, 'Hope she'll know me again — she had a good look at me.' And I said, 'Who?' and she said, 'Miss Garside — prying old maid.'"

CHAPTER
THIRTY

As Ella Jackson was coming away from Vandeleur House she met a small, dowdy-looking woman coming in — curled fringe under a close net, small neat features under a black hat with a bunch of mignonette and pansies pinned on one side and two old-fashioned hatpins keeping it in place, black cloth jacket with the shoulder line and waist of a bygone day, laced shoes very neatly blacked, thick grey stockings, and a fur tie which had probably been at its best round about the time of King George V's accession to the throne. Black gloved hands carried a small case and a tidily rolled umbrella. A black handbag depended from the left wrist.

The encounter took place upon the steps. Miss Silver enquired if this was Vandeleur House, and receiving an affirmative reply, passed on and took the lift to the first floor, where Mrs Underwood welcomed her with relief.

Miss Silver let her talk until she had said everything she wanted to say and said it twice over. She listened with admirable patience to an account of Giles Armitage's loss of memory, his engagement to her niece, and her determination that there should be no shilly-shallying about it. She heard what Mrs Underwood herself knew

186

or had gathered about the murder — a narrative derived mainly from Mrs Smollett — and she received an almost verbatim account of Mrs Underwood's own interview with Chief Inspector Lamb, at the end of which Mabel Underwood burst into tears and said, "I know they think I did it!"

They were in Mrs Underwood's bedroom, a cheerful flowery room with a good deal of the same pink as in Meade's room next door — rose chintzes, pink and green chushions heaped on the bed and smothering a comfortable deep sofa, moss-green carpet, and pink lampshades. Miss Silver thought it was all very pretty. She looked at Mrs Underwood, who was gulping and dabbing with her handkerchief, and said briskly, "Dry your eyes and stop crying. I cannot help you if you give way like this. Naturally it has been a shock, but you must control yourself. Now, Mrs Underwood, if I am to help you I must know what really happened last night. Did you see Miss Roland?"

Mabel Underwood gave a faint sob.

"No — I didn't —"

Miss Silver coughed.

"If that is not correct, it would be better to admit it at once. If you did see Miss Roland last night, some evidence of your visit may be in the possession of the police. It is difficult to be in a room without touching anything, and you may have left fingerprints."

Mrs Underwood flushed.

"I didn't take my gloves off. But I didn't go in — I swear I didn't. I didn't even ring the bell. I was going to, but when it came to the point I hadn't the nerve, and that's the fact. I never had more than half a look at that letter in her bag, and every time I got up to the bell I thought what I'd look like if she showed it to me and it wasn't my letter at all."

Miss Silver nodded, and asked who was in charge of the case. On being informed, she nodded again approvingly.

"A most excellent man — very sound indeed. I know him. Mrs Underwood, can you put me up? I would like to be on the spot."

Mabel Underwood looked rather blank.

"We've only got two bedrooms — and Ivy's room. But Mrs Spooner did say to make any use of her flat if my husband was coming on leave or I wanted to invite a friend. I could send Ivy up there to sleep —"

"I hardly think that would be advisable. She would be afraid to be alone up there after there had been a murder in the house. But if I might occupy one of the rooms, that would be a great deal more suitable. Could you not telephone and get Mrs Spooner's permission? I think you said she was in Sussex. Perhaps Miss Meade could ring her up at lunch-time. Then after lunch — if I might make a few suggestions —"

Miss Silver's suggestions resulted in Ivy being sent out to shop whilst Mrs Smollett obliged with the washing-up. In the next three-quarters of an hour Miss Silver acquired a mass of information about everyone in Vandeleur House. She was an excellent listener, the best Mrs Smollett had ever had, not wanting to hold forth herself, but always ready with the encouraging monosyllable and the attentive glance.

188

"Mind you," said Mrs Smollett, "I'm not one to talk."

As she gave a hand with the washing-up Miss Silver learned that Mrs Spooner was pleasant enough and very bright about the house but not what Mrs Smollett would call a lady, and that Mr Spooner liked his glass and didn't always come home the way he should. That Miss Roland had a deal too much jewellery to be what Mrs Smollett would call out and out respectable, but of course her sister's husband being in the trade she might have got a good bit off the price, and no use saying anything about the poor thing now she's dead. That Mr Drake was a nice enough gentleman for those who liked a gentleman to be what Mrs Smollett called *secreative*.

"Two years he've had his flat, and off in the morning and back at night and not a word to anyone where he goes or what he does, and it he's got friends he doesn't bring them here — never seen him with anyone if it wasn't with Miss Lemming yesterday, and I couldn't hardly believe my eyes when I see them going into Parkinson's together and set down to have tea. I'd just looked in to see if they'd any of their sausage rolls, but they hadn't. Very scarce and difficult to get they are now, and I'm sure —"

Miss Silver recalled her gently.

"You must have a very interesting life, Mrs Smollett, going in and out of so many people's homes. Do you help Mrs Willard at all — in No. 6? Mrs Underwood was telling me —"

"Twice a week regular," said Mrs Smollett. "And very nice to work for, I must say — likes everything shined up proper but lets you alone to do it your own

189

way and no fuss about where everything goes. Now I put it to you, when you go in and out of arf a dozen places, how can you be expected to remember what goes where? Miss Garside in No. 4, she's dreadful that way — a place for everything and everything in its place. A proper old maid if you don't mind my saying so. But Mrs Willard don't care where anything goes so long as it's clean."

"Do you help Miss Garside also?"

Mrs Smollett tossed her head in a majestic manner.

"Used to be there every day. But she don't have anyone now — come down in the world if you take my meaning." She clattered plates into a rack and started to scrape a saucepan. "Well, miss, if you really want to, there's that soft cloth and the silver to polish. My word, Ivy hasn't half let this pan catch! Girls don't trouble these days, and that's a fact. She'd have found out what's what if she'd worked for Miss Garside and no mistake about it. You'd got to see your face in everything there, and the floor fit to take your dinner off any time of the day. Lovely furniture she'd got too before she took and sold it. Gone to be mended, she says, but there wasn't nothing wrong with it, and it never come back. And if you ask me, things have been pretty bad over there, for I was in Talbot's Tuesday and the girl in the groceries says to me, 'What's come to Miss Garside up at Vandeleur House? We haven't had an order from her this last three weeks, butter, nor margarine, nor tea, nor fats, and she haven't been in for her bacon neither. Is she all right?' And I says, 'So far as I know' — not being one to talk. If ever I see anyone starving on her feet it's been Miss Garside this last week, poor thing, white as a sheet and her cheeks regular drawn in, but this morning I see her come in with her shopping basket all piled up, butter and marge and tea and all — you could see the packets sticking out over, and a nice tin loaf right across the bag. And I thought to myself, 'Well, that's a funny time to go out shopping, right on the top of someone being murdered,' so I up and says, 'This is 'orrible news, Miss Garside, isn't it?' And she says, 'What news?' just as if she hadn't took my meaning, and I says, 'Oh, Miss Garside, haven't you heard — Miss Roland's been murdered.' She looks at me and she says, 'Oh, that?' as if it wasn't nothing at all, and then she says, 'I'm going to have my breakfast,' and she goes into her flat and shuts the door. Funny — wasn't it?"

Miss Silver laid down the spoon she had been polishing and agreed.

"You have such a graphic way of telling things, Mrs Smollett. I am sure you quite make me feel I know all these people. Do pray go on. It is most absorbing. What about the two ground-floor flats? Do you know the people in them?"

Mrs Smollett preened herself.

"Old Mrs Meredith in No. 1, I'm there regular twice a week — have been ever since they come. The beginning of the summer it was, if you can call it a summer."

"They are newcomers?"

"They and Mrs Underwood and Miss Roland, they all come round about the spring. Spooners, they've been here since Christmas. Mr Drake, and the Willards a matter of two years, Miss Garside and the Lemmings nearer five. You see, Mrs Meredith's got to be on a ground floor because of going out in her chair — and awkward enough getting it up and down the steps, but there's two of them and Mr Bell gives a hand."

"Two of them?"

Mrs Smollett nodded.

"Miss Crane — she's the companion. And Packer — she's the maid."

"I hope they look after the old lady well. It is very sad to be dependent upon strangers."

Mrs Smollett heaved a sigh.

"That's right, miss, and if it was that Packer, I wouldn't like to be the one that depended on her. Mind you, I don't say but what she's good at her work. Give everyone their due, she keeps the place and the old lady well enough with me going in twice a week, but not a word out of her half the time and sour enough to turn the milk. I don't know how Miss Crane puts up with it. Quite a different kind of person she is, and devoted to the old lady — well, you wouldn't credit it. Only yesterday she says to me, 'Mrs Smollett,' she says, 'I don't know what I should do if anything happened to Mrs Meredith.' "

Miss Silver took up another spoon.

"Has she been with her long?"

"Bound to have been," said Mrs Smollett, wringing out a dishcloth. "She's not the changing sort Miss Crane isn't. Come to think of it, there was Mrs Meredith's nephew that come to say good-bye before

192

he went off to Palestine, and I heard him say when he come in, 'Well, Miss Crane, it must be a matter of ten years since I saw my poor aunt. I'm afraid I'll see a great change in her.' And Miss Crane she says, 'I'm afraid you will, Colonel Meredith. There's changes in us all in ten years,' she says, 'and I don't suppose you'd have reckernised me if you'd a-met me in the street,' and he laughs and says, 'I'd a-known you anywhere.' A very jolly, laughing gentleman, but I thought he was having her on, for the hall was that dark you could hardly see your way let alone reckernising anyone you hadn't seen for ten years. Seems he'd been in Ireland and India and all over the place, and about the only relation the poor old lady's got by all accounts. Funny the way things turn out, isn't it? There's Miss Garside and poor old Mrs Meredith with next to no relations at all, and Miss Lemming in No. 2 that's got one too many, poor thing."

Miss Silver said "Indeed?" in an interested voice.

Mrs Smollett stood the washing-up bowl on end and hung the dishcloth over it to dry.

"Well you may say so!" she said. "If ever there was a poor trampled slave it's Miss Agnes Lemming. Day nor night her mother don't give her no peace. It's 'Do this!' and 'Do that!' and 'Come here!' and 'Go there!' and 'Why did you do this?' and 'Why didn't you do that?' till you'd wonder how any 'uman woman could put up with it. She don't do it to me, Mrs Lemming don't, for I wouldn't take it not from her nor from nobody, not if I was a heathen black I wouldn't. And why Miss Agnes don't walk out and leave her passes me. Her spirit's broke, poor thing, that's what it is, and a crool shame, for she's as nice a lady as you could find, and a very feeling heart — too feeling, if you was to ask me."

Miss Silver went on asking her.

CHAPTER
THIRTY-ONE

It was a little later that Sergeant Abbott came in on his Chief Inspector and said, "Guess who is here."

Lamb removed his gaze from Sergeant Curtis' report and said, "What's that?"

Sergeant Abbott permitted himself a faint malicious smile.

"I said, 'Guess who is here.'"

"Haven't time for guessing."

"Well, then, I'll tell you — Miss Silver."

"*What!*"

"The one and only Maud Silver. In the character of visiting friend to Mrs Underwood."

"Oh, good lor!"

"You've said it, sir."

"What's brought her here?"

"Mrs Underwood — obviously. She's rattled — wants someone to hold her hand. Enter Maudie as the discreet friend."

Lamb gave a long soft whistle and tilted back his chair.

"She's discreet enough. I wonder what she's up to."

Frank Abbott sat down on the arm of one of the big chairs.

"What are you going to do about it — let her in?"
Then, as Lamb frowned and made no answer, "She's
lucky, you know. Every time she touches a case the
police come out of it in a blaze of glory. Maudie the
Mascot. The Policeman's Joy — Promotion waits upon
her Path."

Lamb nodded.

"It isn't all luck either," he said. "Remember the first
time we ran up against her? I don't mind saying I put
her down as a harmless old maid and I handed her off
— politely, you know, because you don't want to be
hard on a lady. Well, as often as I handed her off, there
she was back again, and the next thing I knew, it was,
'May I have a word with you, Inspector?' and she was
giving me the answers as neat as a crossword puzzle
and no fuss about it. I've got a respect for Miss Silver."

Frank Abbott laughed.

"Oh, so have I. She makes me feel like the bottom of
the infant class in a kindergarten. That's why I call her
Maudie — it's just whistling to keep my courage up.
Are you going to let her in on this?"

"You can't keep her out," said Lamb — "and I don't
know that I want to. This is the sort of case where she
could be useful. She'll be watching Mrs Underwood's
interests over the blackmailing, I take it. Mrs U. may
have been in touch with her before the murder —
probably was. That would account for her coming in at
once like this. Yes, she might be useful, and I'll tell you
why. People — that's her strong suit — she knows
people. Learnt it in the schoolroom teaching kids — I
don't know — but she's got it. She sizes people up

quicker than anyone I've known, and she don't make mistakes. Remember the Poisoned Caterpillars case — March told us about that — and the Chinese Shawl? If she's got a line on this blackmailing business — and I suspect she has, or Mrs Underwood wouldn't have called her in — then we want whatever it is she's got. There hasn't been time for Mrs U. to make a new contact, but if she had already been to Miss Silver about the blackmailing, then she'd have done exactly what she has done — gone straight out of this room to the telephone and called Miss Silver in. You see, the blackmail may be at the bottom of the whole business, and we want to know all about it. The girl may have been mixed up with the Mayfair people — may even have been a principal. If it weren't for that accommodation address, I'd think she'd only been having a kind of private flutter with Mrs Underwood, and that the Armitage business was just what her sister says, a nasty spiteful joke. But the address sticks in my throat. It was the one the Mayfair people used, and Mrs Underwood sent her first letter there — the one with the money in it. Then the Mayfair business blows up, and Mrs Underwood gets a different address next time, and the answer she sends there turns up in Carola Roland's bag. There's something there, and I'd like to know what Miss Silver knows about it. Of course the girl may have been murdered by the man she had drinks with. Mr Maundersley-Smith will have to account for his movements. He may have been the man Bell saw going away at half past eight. If he's got an alibi, the man may have been Major Armitage — he had plenty of time to come back and kill her. It's no good saying she was just having a joke with him, because he didn't know that until after she was dead. She certainly upset Miss Underwood very much indeed, and the letter she showed her and Major Armitage must have looked uncommonly like proof that there had been a marriage. And he didn't remember that she was his brother's widow until midnight, when she had probably been dead for an hour or two. You remember he accounted for the sudden recovery of his memory by saying he supposed it was due to the shock, and he explained that by saying he meant the shock of having Miss Roland claim to be his wife. But it might quite easily have been the shock of having killed her. I don't say he did, and I don't say he didn't, but he might have done . . . Then there's Mrs Willard. I don't think a lot about her, but she's there. Mr Willard seems to have been dangling after Miss Roland, and it looks as if he and his wife had had a fair-sized row, or he wouldn't have stayed out all night. But husbands and wives quarrel a lot more than anyone thinks, and it's oftener about little things than big ones, so it mayn't have had anything to do with Miss Roland at all. I don't give much for their being upset this morning. If he liked the girl he would be upset, and the more he showed it, the more upset Mrs W. would be — that's human nature. Well, I'm expecting the fingerprints and the surgeon's report along any time now, and then we'll know where we are. I think Curtis got prints from most of the people in the house, so we'll be able to see whether any of them were up here or not. Major

Armitage and Miss Underwood were, we know, but I'm curious about whether Mrs U. was telling the truth when she said she didn't come in."

Frank Abbott sat on the arm of the chair and listened. Old Lamb holding forth. Awfully sound, the old boy. No frills. Apotheosis of plain common sense. Damned fair — no bias. Backbone of the nation and all that sort of thing. The plain man speaking out of a plain, honest mind. He admired his Chief Inspector quite a lot.

"Mrs Jackson's coming back, isn't she?" he said.

Lamb nodded.

"Going to check up on her sister's jewellery. There's a good deal of it, and it looks valuable to me."

Frank Abbott's left eyebrow went up.

"Probably is if it came from Maundersley-Smith."

Lamb nodded again.

"That's what I thought. Mrs Jackson says her husband's got a list of it — he was seeing about getting it insured for her —so I said she'd better bring it along and check up."

"The girl wasn't wearing much jewellery, was she?"

"Pearl and diamond earrings — diamond brooch. Three rings left beside the wash-basin in the bathroom. Funny what a lot of women forget their rings when they go to wash their hands."

CHAPTER
THIRTY-TWO

Ella Jackson sat at her sister's dressing-table checking the dead girl's jewellery. There was, as Chief Inspector Lamb had said, a good deal of it, and some of the things had cost a lot of money. Every now and then it came over Ella that Carrie would never wear them any more, and when that happened the diamonds swam before her eyes and she had to stop what she was doing and have a quiet cry. Carrie had always been a trouble right away from the time when their mother died and left a serious little girl of ten to look after a pert little girl of five. Pert and pretty — that was Carrie. And Dad encouraged her. All the men encouraged Carrie. They led her on until you couldn't do anything with her. No use for Ella to talk. She remembered Carrie saying, "You're jealous — that's what you are. Men like me, and they don't so much as look at you and never will." The part about the men was quite true, but the part about being jealous wasn't true. Ella didn't want men. She only wanted Ernie, and in the end she got him. But that was after Carrie had run away and Dad was dead of a broken heart. Ten years ago and nothing to cry about, but the old trouble seemed to come welling up until she couldn't tell it from the new one.

In the sitting-room Miss Silver held converse with Inspector Lamb. Compliments had passed, and a due exchange of courtesies.

"I hope Mrs Lamb is well. And your three daughters . . . Really — how very interesting — one in each of the services! You must be very proud of them. Have you photographs — in uniform? I should be so much interested."

A cynical but admiring gleam was in Frank Abbott's eye. Humbug? No, something cleverer than that. Humbug wouldn't go an inch with old Lamb, not even about his daughters. This was the real thing — genuine interest. And it was going down like butter — the best butter. From this by tactful transition to the case — simple sincerity of manner, due deference towards the law and its immediate embodiment, all the old-fashioned politenesses one had observed in one's great-aunts.

"I am afraid I cannot tell you very much more than Mrs Underwood herself has done. I can only assure you that I believe her to be telling the truth when she asserts that she did not in fact enter this flat last night or see Miss Roland. I am doing my best to persuade her that since she is innocent she should co-operate with the law to the fullest possible extent. As dear Lord Tennyson so wisely says, 'Pure law commeasures perfect freedom.' So true, and so beautifully put. Do you not think so?"

Lamb cleared his throat and said he wasn't much of a hand at poetry, but people couldn't be free to break the law, only to keep it, and if that was what was meant, he agreed with her and with Lord Tennyson.

"And now I'm going to tell you some things in confidence. I'm not making any bargains, but I'm telling you just about where we stand at the moment, and if there's anything you know that we don't, or anything you get to know, well, fair's fair, and I hope you'll do as much for me as I'm going to do for you. No bargains, but what they call a gentleman's agreement — how's that, Miss Silver?"

Miss Silver gave her little dry cough.

"Indeed, that is exactly what I had in mind. I can assure you that at the moment I know very little. Mrs Underwood consulted me. I advised her to go to the police, and she burst into tears and said that she could not. There are a few small circumstances which I hope I shall be in a position to communicate to you before very long. The information will be of more use when I have been able to complete it. There are points which require delicate handling, and any premature intervention of an official kind would be very undesirable. I should be glad if for the moment you would refrain from pressing me upon these points."

Lamb cleared his throat again.

"Well, if you were anyone else, I should say you had better let me be the judge of what course to take when it comes to handling a witness who knows something and doesn't want to talk. That's what you mean, I take it."

Miss Silver gave him the gracious smile with which in her schoolroom days she would have received a

202

correct answer from a deserving pupil. She inclined her head and said, "You put it so well, Inspector."

Lamb laughed.

"Almost as well as Lord Tennyson? Well then, I won't press you, but the sooner I have all the threads in my hand the better pleased I shall be, so don't hold out on me too long. Now this is where we've got to. I've just had the surgeon's report and the fingerprints. She was killed somewhere around about three-quarters of an hour to an hour after she had a light meal — if you can call it a meal — of wine and biscuits. We don't know when she had this meal, but it wasn't before half past seven, when she returned to her flat after seeing her sister off by the seven-twenty-five bus at the corner. When Mrs Smollett found the body at eight o'clock next morning there was a tray with drinks and biscuits set out on that stool in front of the fire. Miss Roland's finger-prints were found on the smaller glass, which contained port wine, and those of an unknown man upon a tumbler which had been used for whisky and soda. I don't mind saying I was quite prepared to find that the tumbler prints had been left by Major Armitage. Well, they weren't — they're not his, or Mr Drake's, or Mr Willard's, or Bell's. So we get the certainty that some man from outside this house was here in the flat within an hour before the murder. Miss Roland had been living here very quietly indeed, because she was going to be married. We shall expect the man who was going to marry her to account for his movements during those evening hours. Now as to the crime itself. It looks as if it had not been premeditated,

203

because the weapon used was undoubtedly this metal statuette."

Miss Silver looked at the dancer's silver figure with the pointing, upflung toe.

"Where was it found?"

Lamb indicated the couch.

"Flung down there where you see the stain. She must have been struck from behind, and the weapon dropped on to the couch. According to how the body was found, the murderer would have been standing just right for that. But here's the queer part — the stain was like you see it. It hadn't been touched, but the statue was as clean as a whistle — not a mark on it except where the back of the figure had come into contact with the stain whilst it was still wet. The sharp pointed foot which undoubtedly inflicted the wound hadn't a mark on it — nothing for the microscope to pick up, nothing for a chemical test. They got a faint trace of soap in the folds of this sort of scarf." He indicated the wisp of drapery which fell in a slender twist from the dancer's naked waist.

"It had been washed?"

"Very thoroughly," said Lamb. "But the extraordinary thing is that whoever took the trouble to do that shouldn't have put the figure back on the mantelpiece. I don't know that I ever came across anything like it before. The murderer throws it down on the couch and makes that stain, and then he or she picks it up, washes it with soap and water, and puts it back on the stain again. It doesn't make sense."

Miss Silver coughed.

204

"Dear me — were there no fingerprints on the figure?"

Lamb shook his head.

"Not a trace. Clean as a whistle. Looks as if gloves had been worn, but unless they were rubber gloves that soaping and scrubbing would come a bit difficult, wouldn't it?"

"Rubber gloves would mean premeditation," said Miss Silver briskly. "And premeditation in connection with the use of this statuette as a weapon would mean that the murderer was familiar with the room and with this particular ornament. I suppose a man might have held it under the tap and washed it whilst wearing, let us say, heavy motoring gloves, but I do not believe that any woman wearing an ordinary pair of gloves would have done so. I am inclined to believe that no gloves were used. The washing of the statuette seems to me to be one of those instinctive and unpremeditated actions — something done whilst under the influence of shock — which puzzle the investigator just because they are in fact meaningless, except as an index of character. I put forward the suggestion with diffidence, Inspector, but I imagine that no fingerprints would be left if the statuette and the hand holding it were wet at the time of contact."

Both men looked up sharply. Lamb struck his knee and exclaimed, "By gum — yes! You're right!"

Miss Silver rose to her feet and walked over to the couch.

"The heat of the room would quickly dry any surface damp, but I should expect some slight spreading of the stain. It should, I think, be paler at the edges if the statuette had been wet enough not to take fingerprints. Yes — look here, Inspector — the stain has definitely been spread. Here — and here. Look how pale it is at the edges."

The three of them stood there looking at the spoiled blue and grey brocade. Lamb said, "Yes, you're right — that's the way it was. Though why on earth it was done at all beats me. If it was to puzzle us about the weapon, the figure should have been put back on the mantelpiece. If it was to remove fingerprints, it might just as well have been left in the bathroom. It don't make sense."

CHAPTER
THIRTY-THREE

He had got as far as that, when the door was opened and Mrs Jackson appeared on the threshold. She held a typewritten list in one hand and a solitaire diamond ring in the other. She crossed the room in an agitated manner, laid both these things in front of the Inspector, and said in a hurrying voice, "This isn't my sister's ring."

Everybody looked at her and then at the ring. Lamb said, "What do you mean?"

She swallowed quickly and repeated what she had said before.

"This isn't my sister's ring."

Lamb swung his chair round to face her.

"Just a minute, Mrs Jackson. When you say this isn't your sister's ring, do you mean that it isn't on the list of her jewellery, or that you hadn't seen it before, or what?"

Ella Jackson made an effort. She was a controlled young woman, but the discovery which she had just made, coming on the top of everything else, had knocked her off her balance. She regained it now.

"No, I don't mean that, Inspector. Look at the list and you will see 'Solitaire diamond ring' half way down the page. This is a solitaire diamond ring, but it isn't the one on the list. It isn't my sister's ring. The stone isn't a diamond — it's paste."

There was a queer electric thrill in the room. Each of the four people present was aware of it. Each felt a heightening of interest, a sense of anticipation. One of them had also a faint sick instant of recoil.

Lamb, frowning, picked up the ring.

"This is the ring Miss Roland had been wearing. It's one of the three that were found in the bathroom by the side of the wash-basin."

Ella Jackson's colour had risen. She was quite calm now.

"It isn't Carrie's ring."

Lamb looked up at her.

"She might have had the stone changed herself, Mrs Jackson."

"She wouldn't — not without telling me. My husband was going to arrange the insurance. She knows how careful he is — he'd never have done it without checking up on the things. Besides she'd no reason — she wasn't short of money."

He turned the ring this way and that. The rainbow colours flashed.

"Looks all right to me. What makes you think it's paste?"

Ella Jackson had a very decided look as she said, "I don't have to think about it — I *know* it's paste. I was brought up in the trade. I knew it wasn't Carrie's ring the minute I took it in my hand. You can show it to anyone in London and they'll say the same as I do — it's paste."

"She might have had the stone changed — you can't be sure she didn't."

"Well then, I can," said Mrs Jackson, "Because it's not just the stone — it's the ring. It isn't Carrie's ring. She got hers from the boy she was married to, Jack Armitage, and he told her it was his mother's, and it had her initials in it. Carrie was a bit put out about that — said she didn't want to go wearing a ring with another woman's initials."

Lamb turned the ring to the light. There was no mark at all on the inner surface of the gold.

"Perhaps she had the initials taken out."

Ella shook her head.

"Well then, she didn't, for when she told me about the trick she was playing on Major Armitage she told me she showed him the ring, and what he looked like when he saw it. Seems he remembered it, though he didn't remember her. She said he turned it over at once to see if the initials were there, and looked as vexed as vexed to think she had his mother's ring."

Miss Silver said, "Dear me!" She turned to the Inspector with a deprecatory cough.

"Major Armitage was expected when I left Mrs Underwood's flat. He will, I am sure, have arrived by now. Do you think —"

Lamb nodded, and Frank Abbott got up and went out.

"It isn't Carrie's ring," said Ella Jackson. "Major Armitage will tell you the same as I do. But if it's not Carrie's — and it *isn't* — well, I've got an idea that I know whose it may be. It was only last night when she was telling me about showing it to Major Armitage she said, 'Funny there should be two rings like this in Vandeleur House. Dead spit and image of each other too. I saw her look at mine the other day going down in the lift. She might have thought I'd been pinching hers if she hadn't had it on. She's that sort.' "

"Miss Roland said that?"

"Yes, she did."

"Who was she talking about — who had the other ring?"

"Miss Garside in No. 4. Mind you, I'm not saying anything against her."

Miss Silver was watching the Inspector's face. She saw his eyes go to the papers on his right. He half put out a hand and drew it back again. Then he said in a slow, meditative way, "Miss Garside . . . Did your sister know her?"

"No, she didn't. Very stiff and stand-offish, Carrie said. Not so much as a good-morning if you met her in the lift."

"Not a chance that the rings might have got mixed up — when they were washing their hands — anything like that?"

"Not an earthly."

Lamb said, "H'm!"

There was a brief silence, and then Giles Armitage came in, followed by Sergeant Abbott. He came right up to the table and said, "What is it, Inspector? I'm told you want to see me."

Lamb said, "H'm!" again. Then he held out the ring.

"I want to know whether you can identify this ring."

210

Giles frowned and said, "Yes — it was my mother's. My brother gave it to Carola."

"When did you see it last?"

His frown deepened.

"She was wearing it yesterday."

"She showed it to you?"

"Yes."

"Did you examine it?"

"Yes."

"Was there any mark by which you could be certain of identifying it?"

"My mother's initials were in it — M.B. for Mary Ballantyne. It was her engagement ring."

"You actually saw those initials yesterday when you handled the ring?"

"Yes."

Lamb reached across the table. The diamond took the light.

"Do you see them now?"

Giles put out his hand for the ring, turned it about, and stared incredulously.

"No. But —" He broke off, looked up and down again, and came out bluntly with, "This isn't the ring."

Lamb sat back in his chair.

"Sure of that, Major Armitage?"

"Yes, quite sure. It hasn't got the initials. It isn't the ring I saw yesterday." He went to the light switch and pulled it down, then came back to the middle of the room. "She had the light on yesterday when I was here. I stood where I am standing now. This stone isn't such a good one, the ring is a little lighter in the hand — at least that's my impression — I can't be sure. But I'm quite sure about the initials."

Lamb said, "Thank you, Major Armitage — we needn't keep you." He turned to Ella. "We'll look into the matter, Mrs Jackson. Perhaps you would just go through the rest of your sister's things and let us know if anything else is missing."

When the bedroom door had closed upon her, and the outer door of the flat upon Giles Armitage, Frank Abbott came back into the room and shut that door too.

Miss Silver looked from him to the Inspector. Her small, neat features wore a look of mild but inflexible obstinacy. She coughed and said, "I really do not see how it could have been Miss Garside."

Lamb looked at her with the indulgence of a man who holds the winning card.

"If this is her ring she'll have to explain how it got into Carola Roland's bathroom on the night of the murder. If it isn't her ring, she'll have to prove that by producing her own. And when she's done all that, she'll still have to explain how she came to leave her fingerprints pretty well all over this flat."

"Dear me!" said Miss Silver in a tone of distress. "Did she do that?"

Lamb nodded.

"On the outer door, both inside and out — on the bathroom door and on the ledge where the rings were found — on the bedroom door — and on the door of this room."

"Dear me!" said Miss Silver.

CHAPTER
THIRTY-FOUR

Miss Silver sat in front of a gas fire in Mrs Spooner's sitting-room and studied the neatly written time-table with which Sergeant Abbott had furnished her. The privacy of No. 7 was a boon, the room a most comfortable one. The carpet, it is true, was a little too modern in design to appeal to her old-fashioned taste, but the colours were nice and bright, and the suite with its large deep couch and two well-cushioned chairs upholstered in moss-green velvet was, she considered, most tasteful and luxurious. She studied the time-table with attention.

6.15 — Major Armitage arrives No. 3 (Mrs Underwood's flat).

6.30 to 6.50 — Armitage at No. 8 (Miss Roland's).

6.30 or so — Ivy Lord leaves No. 3.

6.35 — Miss Lemming short call at No. 3.

6.50 — Armitage returns to No. 3.

6.55 — Armitage leaves No. 3.
About this time Mr and Mrs Willard in No. 6 appear to have been having a row.

7.00 — Mrs Jackson to No. 8 to see her sister.

7.10 — Willard to No. 8. Refused admittance. Goes to his brother at Ealing for the night.

7.20 — Mrs Jackson leaves to catch 7.25 bus at corner accompanied by Miss Roland. Miss Garside in No. 4 sees them go.

7.28 — Miss Roland returns, followed from bus stop by Mrs Underwood. Ivy Lord close behind. Roland by lift to No. 8. Underwood waits for lift, and is seen going up in it by Ivy.

7.30 — Ivy to No. 3. Finds Mrs Underwood has not returned.

7.40 — Mrs Underwood to No. 3. She explains this ten minute hiatus by saying she went up to top floor with intention of seeing Miss Roland but changed her mind.

8.30 — Bell to Hand and Glove. Nightly habit. Punctual to the dot. Sees man going away from house to farther gate. Cannot identify or describe. Car starts up and passes him.

8.35 — Miss Garside seen coming up from basement (Miss Crane). Says she went to get Bell to change faulty washer.

N.B. Bell's punctual habits matter of common knowledge. Duplicate keys of flat hang on dresser in old kitchen. Miss Underwood borrowed key of No. 7 earlier in day. Replaced it some time during afternoon, Bell doesn't know when. Did

Miss Garside go down to borrow key of No. 8? She had reason to think Roland was out, having seen her leave with her sister.

9.30 — Return to Bell. Keys all present and correct.

12.00 midnight — Armitage telephones Miss Underwood to say everything is all right.

8.00a.m. — Mrs Smollett discovers body.

9.45 — Willard returns No. 6. Interviewed by Curtis, he and Mrs Willard appear to be in considerable distress — Willard has been crying, Mrs Willard has apparently been up all night.

This leaves the time between 7.40 and 8.30p.m. for the unknown male visitor who had drinks with Miss Roland. They may have had a row — he may have killed her. He may have been the man Roland was expecting to marry, or he may have been Armitage — he had time to come back. Or he may have been someone we don't know anything about. On the other hand, Roland may have been killed by Miss Garside, who had procured key of No. 8 and believed flat to be empty. If she had the bright idea of changing her paste ring for Roland's diamond, and if Roland caught her in the act, she might have snatched up the statuette and struck when Roland's back was turned, as it might have been if she was going to call up the police. Telephone fixture on table a yard or two to the left of where body was found.

Fingerprints — Miss Garside's, as the Chief said, pretty well everywhere. Other fingerprints — Mrs Smollett's faintish, accounted for by the fact that she works everywhere. Other fingerprints — Mrs Smollett's daily at No. 8. Miss Underwood and Armitage one each, accounted for by visits yesterday admitted by them. Prints of unknown man on tumbler but not anywhere else, suggesting that he may have worn gloves when he arrived. No other prints except Miss Roland's own. No prints from Mrs Underwood. N.B. She was wearing gloves when she went up in the lift.

Miss Silver studied this time-table and Sergeant Abbott's notes with the deepest attention. Sometimes she nodded, sometimes she shook her head. Presently she picked up her knitting. The Air Force sock revolved, the needles clicked. Her thoughts were busy.

216

CHAPTER
THIRTY-FIVE

At the sound of the electric buzzer Miss Silver roused herself and went to the door of the flat. She found Sergeant Abbott on the threshold and invited him in.

He said, "I thought we might have a talk," and received an approving smile.

Arrived in the sitting-room, he agreed with her that the weather was very cold for the time of year — such a sudden change — and that really a gas fire was a great convenience. When they were both seated and she had resumed her knitting, he said, "We've had Mrs Smollett up again. She has been working both for Miss Roland and for Miss Garside. She said straight off that the ring was Miss Garside's. She knew all about the initials in the other one. A nosy female."

Miss Silver sighed.

"These women are always very inquisitive. They spend their lives in other people's houses, and it is really only natural that they should take an interest in what goes on there. Their own lives are often sadly drab." She looked at him across the clicking needles. "I hope the Chief Inspector will not do anything precipitate in the matter of arresting Miss Garside."

A faint satirical smile appeared for a moment on Sergeant Abbott's face.

"Do you see him being precipitate about anything?" he murmured.

Miss Silver's glance reproved him.

"Caution is a virtue when you are dealing with other people's lives," she observed. "I feel bound to say that I do not consider the exchange of the rings at all conclusive. It is one of those pieces of evidence which at first sight appear convincing, but which can often be explained in quite a natural manner. It is, of course, quite possible that Miss Garside procured the key of Miss Roland's flat and entered it for the purpose of exchanging the rings, that she was surprised, and that she struck Miss Roland with the statuette in order to prevent her calling in the police. It is also possible that she paid Miss Roland an ordinary visit, in the course of which some occasion for washing her hands may have arisen. Miss Roland's rings were found beside the wash-basin. The exchange may have been quite accidental. This would at any rate be a possible line of defence. Of one thing I am tolerably certain, whoever washed the statuette and put it back on the sofa, it was not Miss Garside."

Frank Abbott displayed a lively interest.

"And how do you arrive at that?"

Miss Silver regarded him with an indulgent eye. He was of about the same age as her nephew Howard, at present somewhere in the Middle East. Howard was of course a great deal better looking.

"Mrs Smollett has given me a very good idea of Miss Garside's character. Like so many single women who live alone, she is neat and orderly in the highest degree. Mrs Smollett is not, I think, a very neat person herself. She complains of Miss Garside being so particular about everything being put back in exactly the right place, contrasting her unfavourably with Mrs Willard who, she says, will have everything clean but doesn't care where it goes."

Frank Abbott gave a low whistle.

"So that's it!"

Miss Silver coughed.

"I feel sure that anyone so particular as Miss Garside is said to be would have replaced the statuette upon the mantelpiece after washing it."

"But Mrs Willard doesn't care where anything goes, though she likes things clean?"

Miss Silver's needles clicked.

"According to Mrs Smollett," she said.

Frank Abbott lay back in his chair and looked at her, a spark of malice in his light blue eyes.

"May I ask when you received these interesting confidences?"

He got a smile which he had done nothing to deserve.

"When I was helping her with the washing-up after lunch at Mrs Underwood's."

He smiled back at her.

"That's where you take the bread out of the poor policeman's mouth. I can't very well drop in and help with the washing-up. Did she tell you anything else?"

"Yes, a great deal, but not all of it pertinent. I must tell you that Miss Garside is believed to be in great financial straits. She has been doing without any household help for some time. She has sold her furniture, and Mrs Smollett declares that she had bought no food for a week until this morning, when she came back with a full shopping-basket."

"So that's why she was having breakfast after she came back from the town. Curtis found her out the first time he went, and when he did get her she was just going to have breakfast. He thought it odd at the time. I wonder if she had been selling the ring. The Chief's going to see her when he gets back. He's gone off to interview the man Carola Roland was going to marry — thought he'd like to get that cleared up straight away. If those were his fingerprints on the tumbler, and he was having drinks with the girl within an hour of the murder, he was probably the last person to see her alive — or the last but one if someone else killed her. If the Chief counts him out he'll go for Miss Garside. Unless anything else turns up. Have you really got anything about Mrs Willard, or was that just a red herring?"

Miss Silver put a shade of reproof into her cough.

"It would be in Mrs Willard's character as described by Mrs Smollett to wash the statuette and then leave it lying about. Mrs Smollett had been in the Willards' flat this morning. It was her regular day. Mrs Willard admitted her, and told her she could not go into the bedroom as Mrs Willard was asleep. He appeared a good deal distressed, and when she spoke of Miss Roland's death he said, 'Don't talk of it!' and went out of the flat. She found the dress which Mrs Willard was wearing yesterday in a wet heap inside the bathroom cupboard. She said, 'It was a new dress and quite clean — why did she want to wash it?' She also said Mr Willard was running after Miss Roland. She is of course a gossip, and will make the most of any material she has picked up."

Frank Abbott whistled again.

"How many more people may have killed the girl, do you suppose? At the moment we have Armitage, Mrs Underwood, an opulent City gent, Miss Garside, and Mrs Willard. *Embarras de richesse*. I suppose they didn't all have a stab at it?"

"I'm not suggesting that any of them killed her, Mr Abbott. I think that both Miss Garside and Mrs Willard should be questioned, and that this dress, which seems to have been somewhat unaccountably washed, should be examined for bloodstains. If the washing were not extremely thorough, there might be some traces left. Also, I think, it would be as well to look into the antecedents of all the tenants of these flats. The Lemmings and Miss Garside have been here some time. The Willards have been here for two years. So has Mr Drake, but nothing seems to be known about him. He is considered to be something of a mystery. The Spooners are recent tenants, but they are away. Other recent tenants are Mrs Underwood and the old lady on the ground floor, Mrs Meredith. As regards Mrs Underwood, I met her at the house of friends of my own who are well acquainted with her and her husband, Wing Commander Underwood. As regards

Major Armitage, the War Office can be referred to, and I would suggest an enquiry as to Mrs Meredith's previous address and the length of time she has had her staff. I imagine that the Chief Inspector will have all this in hand. He is extremely thorough."

"In fact," said Frank Abbott in his most casual voice, "we can't at the moment see the wood for the trees. And I'd very much like to know what sort of wood you think it is. Not officially of course, but just between ourselves — *unter vier Augen*, as the Hun has it. Very illustrative idiom, don't you think — under four eyes. Suggests two patient professors at the microscope being distressingly thorough about a new germ. But to get back to the point. You called me Mr Abbott just now. Well, I'm not — I'm Sergeant Abbott. But if you could go on forgetting that for a bit, I should be interested to know what you do think about that wood — as between two private individuals gossiping over a gas fire."

Miss Silver primmed her mouth, but her eyes were kind. This was undoubtedly an impudent young man, but like most elderly spinsters she had a soft corner for the impudent and young. After a short pause she said, "Well, Mr Abbott, there is the gas fire. As for the gossip, I am not so sure. I have, perhaps, already repeated more to you than I should have done. In order to arrive at a just conclusion we need the whole of the evidence. It is made up of an indefinite number of words and actions which act and react upon each other, combining, separating, and joining up again. Gossip picks out some of these words and actions, focusses a strong light on them, and puts them under the microscope, with the result that the balance is destroyed and a distorted picture obtained. This is undoubtedly what Lord Tennyson had in mind when he wrote that 'A lie which is all a lie may be met and fought with outright, But a lie which is part a truth is a harder matter to fight.' " She turned the Air Force sock and gazed mildly across it.

Frank Abbott smiled. If there was a faint flavour of satire in his appreciation, it was nevertheless perfectly sincere. He said, "You know, you haven't answered my question. I suppose you didn't mean to, or perhaps it just slipped out of your mind. I did say that we couldn't see the wood for the trees, and I did ask you what sort of wood you thought it was. In other words, is there anything behind all this, and if so, what? Is this just a casual murder which happened because someone was jealous or didn't keep his temper, or is there something behind it — something that makes the murder just a symptom?"

Miss Silver looked up.

"Do you feel that, Mr Abbott?"

He met the look, his light eyes narrowed and intent.

"I think I do."

She nodded gravely.

"Yes."

"Are you going to tell me what you think it is?"

She nodded again.

"I think it is blackmail, Mr Abbott."

CHAPTER
THIRTY-SIX

Mrs Smollett dropped in at No. 1 at about the same time that Sergeant Abbott was pressing the bell at No. 7. Ostensibly she came to enquire whether Miss Crane had ordered the primrose soap, "because if not, I could just as easy drop in and get it on my way home and bring it along in the morning," but actually she was bursting with importance at having been called in a second time by the Chief Inspector and she wanted to talk about it.

Miss Crane, with her old lady resting for the afternoon, was all ears and attention.

"And of course they told me not to talk. The p'lice always do, and I wonder what they think you are — mummies in a museum or what? After all, yuman beings, are yuman beings, and if they've got tongues I suppose they were meant to use them. Not to say nothing to nobody was what the Inspector says — and of course I wouldn't, not to anyone that matters — I'm not one to talk, as you know."

"Oh, no," Miss Crane agreed. "And of course I shouldn't dream of letting it go any farther."

Mrs Smollett nodded.

"I know that. Well, between you and me it's Miss Garside they've got their eye on, and I'll tell you why. You know that ring she wears — the one with the big diamond?"

Miss Crane looked disappointed.

"No — I don't think so —"

They were in the kitchenette, Mrs Smollett leaning against the dresser, the kettle just beginning to sing on the stove, and Miss Crane fussing with the teacups.

"Well, you wouldn't," said Mrs Smollett indulgently. "She's one of the particular ones, Miss Garside — always puts on her gloves before she comes out of the flat and doesn't take them off again until she gets back. Well, this ring has got just the one diamond in it, a big one, and she wears it all the time. First thing I noticed when Miss Roland come she'd got just such another, and so I told her when I was doing her room. 'Funny thing, isn't it,' I says, 'you and Miss Garside having these two rings as like as two peas?' And about a week later she told me she had seen Miss Garside's ring and I was quite right. It was the time Miss Garside's furniture was took away, and she was out on the landing and Miss Roland come past and seen the ring on her hand. Well, the Inspector, he has me in, and he hands me a ring and says, 'Ever seen that before, Mrs Smollett?' And I says, 'Every day of my life.' And then he says, 'Whose ring is it?' and I tell him it's Miss Garside's. Well, he says how do I know that, and I tell him, well, I ought to, seeing I've had it under my nose every day for a good five years. And he asks if I know Miss Roland's got one like it, and I says of course. And,

225

'Would you know them apart?' he says, and I tells him, 'Of course! Many's the time I've had Miss Roland's ring in my hand, and it's got initials in it — an M and a B. Some kind of a family ring, she told me it was.' And then he said I could go, and not to talk about it."

Miss Crane had been listening with her hands clasped and her mouth open.

"Oh!" she breathed. "Oh, Mrs Smollett — what do you think it means — about the rings? It seems so strange —"

Mrs Smollett tossed her head.

"Don't ask me to say what it means, Miss Crane. Least said soonest mended to my way of thinking. I'm not saying anything nor suspecting anyone, but if it was my ring that was in a murdered person's flat instead of the one that ought by rights to be there, well, I wouldn't be feeling too comfortable in my inside. And there's something I can tell you, Miss Crane, only don't you let it go any further. When Miss Garside come in with her shopping-basket this morning, there was Mrs Lemming coming out of her flat. You know they're a bit friendly, her and Miss Garside, so they stopped and talked and I could hear what was said. And Mrs Lemming, she asks Miss Garside, 'What was you doing last night?' she says. 'Three times I tried to get you on the telephone between half past eight and nine, and no reply,' she says. And Miss Garside — well, I thought she looked funny, and she said she'd been down to see Bell about a washer. And Mrs Lemming laughs — and not what I'd call a very pleasant laugh neither — and she says, 'You'd have to go a bit further than the basement to find Bell if it was after half past eight. Down at that pub of his, that's where you'd have to go to find him anywhere between half past eight and half past nine. And unless that's what you *did*, it wouldn't take you the best part of half an hour, my dear.' And Miss Garside says quick, 'Half an hour? What do you mean?' And Mrs Lemming says, 'Well, I rang you at five-and-twenty to nine, and at twenty to, and soon after the quarter, and I couldn't get any answer.' And Miss Garside she says the bell couldn't have rung, and off up the stairs without waiting for the lift. Funny, wasn't it? 'Tisn't as if she might have run down to the post either, because everyone knows she wouldn't put her foot outside in the black-out, not if it was ever so. But there — it doesn't do to go saying things, does it, Miss Crane?"

"No, *indeed*." Miss Crane was earnest in agreement.

"And I haven't mentioned it to anyone but you, if it wasn't for the little governess person that's staying with Mrs Underwood. Very friendly kind of person she is — give me a hand with the washing up after lunch and we got talking. And she says just what you and me's been saying — you've to be careful how you talk with the police about. But you can't help what you think — can you?"

Miss Crane looked distressed.

"Appearances are often so misleading —"

"Let's us 'ope so," said Mrs Smollett, and departed.

It being Packer's afternoon out, Miss Crane went on making tea for her old lady.

CHAPTER
THIRTY-SEVEN

All over Vandeleur House tea was being prepared. Mrs Willard, refreshed by several hours of sleep, made herself a nice strong pot and partook of it with some thinly buttered toast. Mr Willard had not returned, but as he never was at home to tea except on a Saturday or a Sunday, that did not disturb her. She felt as if she had emerged from a nightmare. Alfred had been foolish, but he was her own again. He had knelt at her feet and wept. Carola Roland was dead. She had had a nice long sleep, and she was enjoying her tea.

Ivy Lord had returned from the town. She had seen her boy friend in the distance and had a wave of the hand and a smile, so she was feeling better. Mrs Underwood had retired to her room directly after lunch and could be presumed to be resting. Giles and Meade had the drawing-room to themselves. Meade had stopped thinking. She felt as one feels after an anaesthetic which has blotted out pain. Consciousness has come back, but it is a state in which one is afraid to move lest the pain should return. She was content to feel Giles' arm about her, to lean her cheek against his, and to let him talk.

Presently Ivy came in with the tray, and after that the front door of the flat opened and shut. Mrs Underwood came in. She said in a complaining voice, "I can't think what Miss Silver is doing. She's been up in the Spooners' flat all the afternoon. I've just looked out to see if she was coming, and there isn't a sign of her. Ring her up, Meade, and say tea is ready. You know the number." She plumped into a chair, and as Meade went over to the telephone, she said, "Miss Garside has had a visitor — wonders will never cease! I saw her getting into the lift."

Miss Garside had just poured the boiling water from the kettle into the small brown pot which had replaced a cherished piece of Queen Anne silver, when there was a ring at the bell. She opened the door and saw with surprise that the person who had rung was a stranger — an ultra-fashionable youngish woman, a good deal made up, with fair hair curling on her shoulders, a smart black coat, a ridiculous little tilted hat, and spectacles with rims of very light tortoise-shell. She moved into the lobby and spoke with a mincing accent.

"Miss Garside?"

Miss Garside inclined her head.

"If I could just speak to you for a moment. It is about the ring."

Miss Garside closed the door. Her manner, always very reserved, became more so.

"Are you from Allingham's?" she said.

The conversation which followed was not a very long one. Some time later the visitor came out of the flat and went down in the lift. It was at this moment that she was seen by Mrs Underwood.

The woman in black makes this brief passage and disappears. Her remark about the ring and Miss Garside's response were heard only by themselves. There was therefore nothing to connect her in anybody's mind with Allingham's or with the ring. What passed between her and Miss Garside in the closed flat is, and must remain, a matter of conjecture. The most important thing about her brief appearance is that she was the last person to see Miss Garside alive.

CHAPTER
THIRTY-EIGHT

Miss Silver had enjoyed her tea. Such a bright, comfortable room. Damp and misty outside, but so cosy in Mrs Underwood's sitting-room with the light switched on and a small bright fire. Ivy had made some very good scones, and Wing Commander Underwood had sent his wife some honey from the north. Of course everyone was rather quiet. That was only to be expected. So recent and so shocking a fatality, and though not in any case a personal loss, poor Miss Roland was, after all, Major Armitage's sister-in-law. It was only natural that he should appear grave and preoccupied, and that his fiancée should look white and shaken. Not a pleasant experience for a young girl — not at all. Mrs Underwood too — it was quite clear that she had a great deal on her mind. It would do them all good to be taken out of themselves.

In pursuance of this laudable object Miss Silver produced a constant stream of small talk interspersed with so many questions about everything and everybody in all the flats that the others were kept busy answering her. She took a most particular interest in Mr Drake, of whom she had caught just a glimpse on her arrival.

"Such a fine man — quite romantic-looking really. And he reminds me of someone. Now, I wonder if you can help me —"

Meade achieved a smile and said, "Is it Mephistopheles?"

Miss Silver beamed.

"Of course! How very stupid of me! Really a most remarkable likeness. I hope it does not extend to his character. What did you say his business was?"

Meade said in a hesitating voice, "I don't know —"

"Nobody does," said Mrs Underwood. She put a disagreeable emphasis on the words.

Giles raised his eyebrows, and Miss Silver said mildly, "Dear me — that sounds very intriguing."

Mrs Underwood tossed her head. Its auburn waves were in perfect order, but her face sagged and seemed to have another ten years of lines upon it. She said in a hard, accusing voice, "No one knows anything about him at all, and if Agnes Lemming isn't careful she'll find herself in a mess."

For the next five minutes Miss Silver was regaled with all the things Mrs Underwood had not said to Agnes Lemming.

"I've seen them walking up from the town. I suppose she knows when his train gets in, and happens to be shopping then. What he can possibly see in her, I can't imagine, and I must say if I were her mother I should want to know a good deal more about him . . ."

Meade looked distressed and said nothing. Miss Silver presently switched the conversation to another flat.

"Mrs Meredith — such a dear old lady, Mrs Smollett tells me, but sadly deaf. Do you know her at all? She seems to have a very devoted companion in Miss Crane, but the maid appears to be a very uncommunicative person. I am wondering if there is any connection with some Merediths of whom I used to hear from a dear friend of mine. Do you know where this old lady lived before she came here?"

Meade was so relieved at the change of subject that she was quite glad to have something to say.

"Bell says —" she began, and then hesitated.

"*Bell?*" said Mrs Underwood sharply.

"Yes. He told me that when she first came here Mrs Meredith used to ask every time she went out in her chair whether they were going to the Pantiles, and once she said she wanted to go to the Toad Rock. And she told Bell she used to live on Mount Pleasant — he has to help to get her chair down the steps, you know — but she doesn't talk so much now, poor old thing."

"Very sad," said Miss Silver in a kind, brisk voice. "And now tell me something about Miss Garside. I have not met her yet, but she interests me. Do you know at all what her tastes and connections have been?"

Mrs Underwood tossed her head in an even more marked manner than before.

"She thinks herself better than anyone else — we all know that — but I don't know that anyone knows why. She used to keep house for a brother who was a professor, I believe, and they used to travel a great deal

— France, Germany, Italy — all that kind of thing. I suppose that's how she got her stuck-up ideas."

"The Lemmings know her," said Meade. "Agnes says she is very proud and reserved. She came here after her brother died, and I'm afraid she isn't at all well off now. Agnes isn't very happy about her."

Miss Silver said, "I see —" and began to ask a great many questions about Mr and Mrs Willard and the Lemmings.

CHAPTER
THIRTY-NINE

When tea was over she proceeded helpfully to the kitchen.

"We are such a party that I am sure you would like a little assistance with the washing-up, Ivy. I was drying for Mrs Smollett after lunch, and we got along so quickly."

Ivy looked doubtful. She wasn't sure that she wanted a visitor in her kitchen. If Miss Meade had thought of giving a hand — but she didn't hardly look fit, and there was Major Armitage there and all. She received such a pleasant smile that she changed her mind. Company was company when all was said and done, and after what had happened you didn't want to be alone no more than you could help. She said, "It's very kind of you, I'm sure."

"Such pretty china," said Miss Silver brightly. "Roses are great favourites of mine. Ah, I see that you have a good hot water supply. Such a comfort."

Ivy had turned on the tap and was piling the tea things in a papier maché bowl. Miss Silver continued to talk. The girl looked as if she had cried her eyes out — she had noticed that as she arrived this morning. It had been a good idea to send her out after lunch. She was looking all the better for it. She said aloud, "You are very quick and clever with your hands, Ivy. I expect that would be your training as an acrobat. Miss Meade was telling me about it. Such a fascinating life. I read a very interesting book about a year ago about circus life called *Luke's Circus* — really most charming, and of absorbing interest. Domestic work must be a great change for you, is it not?"

Ivy found herself telling the visitor all about Glad, and the accident, and how the doctors didn't think she'd ever be much good at walking again.

"But I'm as good as ever as far as that goes. I wouldn't like to go on the wire again. I'm awful out of practice, and I wouldn't like to anyhow, not without Glad. I miss her bad enough as it is, and it'd be worse if I went back. We wasn't reelly circus people, you know — not reelly. We were on the halls most of the time. Glad and Ivy — that was us. I've got some old bills with the names on. Seems a long time ago."

"Was that where you knew Miss Roland?" said Miss Silver gently.

Ivy dropped one of the rose-flowered cups. It fell into the sink and broke. She gave a queer half-smothered cry.

"Don't be frightened," said Miss Silver — "and never mind about the cup. It was when you were on the halls that you met Miss Roland, was it not?"

Ivy blinked.

"She didn't want anyone to know," she said.

Miss Silver said, "No, I suppose not." She looked at Ivy very kindly. "But it does not matter now."

236

Ivy stood with her back to the sink, gripping the edge of it with her strong bony hands.

"What's it got to do with you? I never said a word — I swear I didn't. I never told no one. She was kind to Glad and me when we were kids. She used to let us watch her dress — help her on with her wings. She was in an act called The Fairy Butterfly, and she looked lovely. She didn't want no one to know about us knowing each other. What does it matter now anyhow? She's dead."

Miss Silver said in her kindest voice, "No, it doesn't matter now. I think you had better tell me about it. She got you to come here to Mrs Underwood, didn't she?"

Ivy stared. She would have backed away if there had been anywhere to go, but the sink held her.

"How do you know?" she said in a frightened whisper.

Miss Silver took the success of a chance shot equably.

"You met her. Was it by accident? It is always pleasant when one runs up against an old friend like that. And she told you she had taken a flat here, and suggested that you should apply for Mrs Underwood's place?"

Ivy nodded. It was like being at the dentist's, only worse. All the things she wouldn't have told anyone were being pulled out of her one by one. Her thoughts raced to and fro, looking for a place to hide themselves. Her sharp Cockney mind came to the rescue. "Tell her something — quick! She won't stop till you do. Tell her enough to make her stop, and she'll think she's got

237

the lot. Coo — she's a one!" She blinked again and said in a breathless voice, "You didn't arf give me a start, miss. However did you know?"

Miss Silver made no answer to that. She asked a question instead.

"Do you really walk in your sleep?"

This was awful. It took the rest of Ivy's breath away. She began to feel as if she hadn't any clothes on and Miss Silver's eyes were looking right through her to her bones. She gasped and said, "I did when I was a kid."

"Have you walked in your sleep since you came here?"

"I might ha' done."

Miss Silver shook her head in slight but kind reproof.

"I think not. Mrs Underwood locks the front door and takes the key into her room at night, does she not? I think you have been getting out of your window and walking along the ledge that runs round the house until you came to the fire-escape. Only someone who had had an acrobat's training would have attempted such a thing, but it would not be difficult for you. I expect you rather enjoyed it. I notice that a ledge runs round the house on a level with the windows of each floor, so you had only to go up the fire-escape in order to reach Miss Roland's flat. I see that the escape comes up beside the sitting-room window. In this way you could pay her a visit without anyone knowing about it. That is what you used to do, is it not?"

"How did you know?"

"Because you dropped a piece of paper inside Mrs Underwood's bedroom window on your return from one of these visits. I do not know whether you meant to drop it there or not. I think not. I think you had it in your hand, and that you dropped it as you were steadying yourself by the sash whilst passing the window. Now this piece of paper was the corner of a letter which Mrs Underwood had written. The rest of the letter was found in Miss Roland's bag. So, you see, it was quite clear to me that you must have passed Mrs Underwood's window on a return journey from Miss Roland's flat. There was really no other way in which that particular piece of paper could have reached the spot where Mrs Underwood found it. Her bedroom door and the door of the flat were both locked. There was no other way."

Ivy stared. Then she moistened her lips with her tongue and said, "That's right."

"How did the letter get torn?"

Miss Silver had hardly asked the question before she was aware of having made a mistake. Ivy's immediate reaction was that after all Miss Silver didn't know everything. Quite visibly she rallied to the defence of what she was determined to hide. Something uncommonly like impudence looked sideways out of the reddened eyes.

"Coo! Don't you know?"

Miss Silver's manner became gently repressive.

"I think you tried to snatch it."

Impudence ran away in a fright. Ivy gaped.

"It wasn't hers — she didn't ought to have had it — I told her so. Mind you, it wasn't a row. She only

239

laughed, but I thought I was going to lose my temper, so I came away."

"How did she get the letter?" said Miss Silver.

Sharp and quick, Ivy's Cockney wit prompted her. "Here's your chance. Take it, you fool!" Easy — easy — easy — She opened her eyes in a blank stare.

"How do I know how she got it? Same way we all do. Postman comes reg'lar, doesn't he?"

"How did you know she had it?"

No way out after all. And your heart coming right up into your throat by the feel of it. What could you do?

She did the only thing that was any good. It happened also to be the easiest thing in the world. She gave a rending sob and burst into tears.

"What are you getting at? What's it got to do with me? And what's it got to do with you? I don't know nothing about it, and I wish I was dead!" Upon which she ran out of the kitchen and banged the door.

Miss Silver, listening with an air of sober attention, heard the slam of the bedroom door and the sound of the key clicking round in the lock.

CHAPTER
FORTY

Miss Silver sighed, smiled resignedly, and went in search of Mrs Underwood, whom she found in her bedroom, and apparently without occupation. She was sitting in a chintz-covered easy chair beside a small gas fire turned low. There was plenty of daylight outside, but it was of a cold and cheerless nature.

Miss Silver was pleased to observe the fire. She considered the fumed-oak mantelpiece and the surround of rose-coloured tiles very tasteful. Drawing a smaller chair up to the hearth, she sat down and came to the point.

"Ivy and Miss Roland were old friends. I was convinced that this must be so, and she made no attempt to deny it. She has been in the habit of walking along the ledge outside your window and climbing up the fire-escape to visit her friend."

"That narrow ledge? *Impossible!*"

"For you or me, yes, but not for a girl who had been trained as an acrobat. I felt sure from the beginning that she was not walking in her sleep. Her possession of a piece torn from your letter to the person who was blackmailing you would have been too much of a coincidence. I was sure that there was some connection between her and the person who had your letter, but when you discovered that this person was Miss Roland, I was not altogether convinced that it was she who was the blackmailer. It seemed unlikely that she would in that case have been so careless as to carry your letter in her bag, and to allow you to catch sight of it there. When she was murdered, I felt tolerably sure that it was not she who was blackmailing you. It also became evident that the affair was extremely serious, and that the blackmailer was a dangerous person who would stick at nothing. You have not been entirely frank with me, but I now urge you in your own interest and from a sense of public duty to tell me what I want to know."

"What is it?" Mabel Underwood was breathing quickly. Her eyes were fixed on Miss Silver's face.

Miss Silver coughed.

"Pray do not be alarmed. Remember that I am trying to help you. I cannot do so while you keep me in ignorance. The matter is urgent. I want to know whether it was only money that was demanded of you."

All the colour dropped away from the plump cheeks, leaving them pale under two rouged patches. A fumbling hand went up to the throat.

"How did you know?"

"You told me that you could not raise the money. I did not think that the amounts you could manage would be worth the blackmailer's risk. Remembering your husband's position, it struck me that money might not have been the chief object. You had paid one sum. The fact that you had done so was enough to compromise you. I wondered whether the next demand had been for information."

Mrs Underwood nodded.

"The letter said they wouldn't insist on a money payment if I liked to help them with some facts for a book about the Air Force."

"And what did you say to that?"

"I didn't say anything. I just put what was on the torn piece of paper — that I hadn't any money to give."

Miss Silver nodded approval.

"That was very wise of you. Now, Mrs Underwood, I have to ask you why you were being blackmailed. I cannot work for you in the dark. I have to discover the blackmailer's identity. You must help me to do this. You have a secret. If you will tell me what it is, it will narrow the field of my search. I beg of you to remember that this is a murder case, and that the murderer is at large. Suspicion is bound to rest on innocent people. You yourself are not exempt. Pray be frank with me."

Mrs Underwood got out her pocket-handkerchief and began to cry.

"If I knew what to do —"

"You had better tell me all about it."

"It will get into the papers —"

"I think I can promise you that it will not."

Mrs Underwood gave a great gulping sob.

"I was only seventeen," she said, "and Father brought us up so strict. Mother'd been dead two years, and he had his sister to keep his house. A good hand with the dairy work she was, but we hated her. She was stricter than Father. We'd a farm ten miles out of

Ledlington, but I'd never so much as been in to see the shops, she was so strict. I'd never been into a shop in my life, only the little general store at Penfold Corner, till I went to stay with my cousins the winter I was seventeen. I'd been poorly, and the doctor said I ought to have a change, so I went into Ledlington to the Tanners that were Mother's second cousins. Minnie was about a year older than me, and the next one, Lizzie, was twenty-three. They took me shopping with them. It was just before Christmas. I'd never seen anything like it in my life. I didn't tumble to it as first, but those two girls — well, they came home with more than they paid for. What with the crowds and the Christmas shopping, it was easy enough — a pair of stockings here and a bunch of artificial flowers there, and no one any the wiser. They weren't a bit ashamed either when I began to notice it — only laughed and boasted about how smart they were." Mrs Underwood dropped her handkerchief into her lap and gazed at Miss Silver with the tears running down her face. "I don't know what came over me, but I took a pair of stockings. There was going to be a party, and I hadn't any to wear, only thick hand-knitted wool, and not a penny in my pocket. I don't remember meaning to do it — I don't believe I did — but the next minute I was putting the stockings into the pocket of my coat and the shop-walker had me by the wrist. I don't know what I felt like. I wanted to die, but you can't just because you want to." She wasn't sobbing now, but the tears kept running down. Her voice and her words were the voice and words of Mabel Peabody — a low, horrified voice

244

and simple words. "He gave me in charge. They brought me up in court and I was bound over because of being only seventeen and nothing against me. But there was a headline in the *Sun* — Farmer's Daughter Charged, and my name. And Father wouldn't have me in the house again. He sent me down to his cousin Ellen Sparks that kept a boarding-house at Southsea and told her to keep me strict. Oh lord — and didn't she! Up early and down late, working my hands off, and never a penny in my pocket. Six years that went on — six years hard labour. And then Godfrey came and stayed, and took ill — some kind of a low fever he'd got abroad — and I looked after him. Well, he fell in love with me and we were married. And that's all. Only if anything was ever to hurt him through me, what do you suppose I'd feel like? I was like a slave in prison and he took me out. What do you think I'd feel like if I was to hurt him?"

Miss Silver said in a very gentle voice, "We won't let your husband be hurt, Mrs Underwood. Now please be brave and dry your eyes, for I want your help. All this took place how long ago?"

"We've been married getting on for sixteen years."

"And this occurrence was six years before that —" She thought deeply for a time, whilst Mrs Underwood sniffed and dried her eyes. Then she said, "Twenty-two years ago — that makes the time right. But you were only a visitor in Ledlington, and for a very short while. However there is just the possibility — did your cousins by any chance attend at St Leonard's church?"

Mrs Underwood opened her eyes very widely indeed.

245

"Oh, yes, they did."

"The Vicar was the Reverend Geoffrey Deane?"

"Oh, yes — he was."

"There is often quite a little gossip about a clergyman's family — parishioners take an interest. Mr Deane had a daughter, had he not?"

Mrs Underwood nodded.

"Oh, yes. Lizzie and Min talked a lot about her. She'd been married in the summer to a Mr Simpson. Now what was her name? Why, Maud — that was it — Maud Millicent. Sweetly pretty, we thought it was, but she was a fast sort of girl. There was some story about her dressing up in her brother's clothes and getting the bank to pay her out some of his money. It was passed off as a joke, but it made talk, and Min said if it hadn't been for who her father was she'd have been in trouble. Liz said she was the best mimic you could think of. She could take off anyone she wanted to and you'd think it was them."

Miss Silver coughed and said, "I believe she could."

CHAPTER
FORTY-ONE

A couple of hours later Chief Inspector Lamb looked in. Sergeant Abbott had news for him, but allowed it to wait while his chief talked.

Lamb pushed back his hat, stuck his thumbs in the armholes of his waistcoat, and stretched himself out in Carola Roland's largest chair.

"D'you know, Frank," he said, "human nature is — well, I don't know if I've got the word to describe it, not having had your advantages in the way of a fancy education. The nearest I can get to it is, it's uncommon like a cartload of monkeys — can't tell what it'll be up to next."

Frank Abbott sat on the arm of the other chair in a languid attitude.

"Meaning Maundersley-Smith?"

Lamb nodded.

"A rum go," he pronounced. "He's got the name of being pretty hard-boiled. You don't get from nothing to where he's got to without you're tough, and that's his reputation. Well, this tough nut broke down and cried like a baby when I told him about the girl. Made me feel bad, I tell you — me — and I suppose I'm tough if anyone is."

Frank Abbott failed to suppress a smile — perhaps he didn't try very hard. It made him look much younger.

He got a reproving frown.

"Insubordinate — that's what you are. No respect for your superiors. Why, when I was your age I'd have burst into a cold sweat if a Chief Inspector'd so much as looked at me."

Frank laughed.

"Too hot in here for a cold sweat, sir."

"No discipline left in the Force," said Lamb. "I was telling you about Maundersley-Smith when you interrupted."

"What did he say, sir?"

Lamb shifted in his chair.

"Broke down and cried like I was telling you, and then came out with the whole story. Seems there's a wife he's been separated from for fifteen years, and he never troubled about a divorce because he hadn't any thoughts of getting married again — said it kept the girls off from chasing him. Then he comes across Carola Roland and goes down flat. He started divorce proceedings, got a decree nisi in July, and was going to marry Carola in January as soon as the decree was made absolute. That's what brought her to Vandeleur House and kept her so quiet — there wasn't to be a breath of scandal in case the King's Proctor took it into his head to intervene. The girl knew which side her bread was buttered. She wrote him smarmy letters like the one we found, and made him stay away. Last night he said he simply couldn't bear it. He got out his car and drove himself here — didn't ring up or anything, but just came along. I fancy he was pretty jealous about her. Anyhow he says he got here about eight o'clock and didn't stay more than half an hour — says she wouldn't let him. She gave him a drink, and she had a glass of wine and a biscuit herself, so we've got that accounted for. And then she said a few kind words and pushed him off — said she'd got her reputation to think about, and what fools they'd be to risk upsetting the divorce. I asked him if there had been any quarrel, and he broke down and said she loved him for himself alone and there had never been a cross word between them — said the last he saw of her she was smiling and kissing her hand to him as he went down in the lift. It must have been him Bell saw going away from the house at half past eight."

"Think he was telling the truth, sir?"

"Well, I do. Of course there's no corroboration. There might have been a quarrel, he might have killed her, and he might have been putting on an act for me, but I don't think so. Simple sort of chap once you got under his skin, and mortal fond of the girl. I think he was telling the truth. Now what have you got for me — anything?"

Frank Abbott stretched his long legs and then sat up.

"Plenty, sir. To begin with, I spent an hour with Maudie. She was kind and instructive. She suggests amongst other things that the Willards would bear investigation. Mr Willard was dangling after Carola, and Mrs Willard washed a perfectly new dress some time between last night and ten o'clock this morning —

don't know what she was wearing when Curtis saw her. Possibility that the dress was stained, and that traces of the stain still remain. She is also very insistent on the antecedents of all flat-holders being dug up. Furthermore, there was quite a piece about Miss Garside being on the rocks. No groceries for a week — all that kind of thing."

Lamb looked up with his eyes round and bulging.

"As bad as that, was it? We knew she was hard up. Here — where did Miss Silver get all this?"

"She helped Mrs Smollett wash up, sir." A smile flickered and was gone. "Well, then, after all that I went round the jewellers — I got a list from Mrs Jackson — and the second place I went to had the ring. Big shop in the High Street — Allingham's. Miss Garside brought it in this morning at half past nine, and they bought it. Mr Allingham said she was an old customer and they never dreamed of there being anything wrong. They had bought other things from her — a couple of diamond brooches and a fine Queen Anne teapot. He showed me the ring, and there were the initials all right — M.B. It looks bad."

Lamb frowned.

"Looks mad to me. Woman must be off her head to go to a shop where she's known, with a murdered woman's ring. I suppose she thought we shouldn't find out that the rings had been changed. The public's got an idea that the police are a lot of thick-headed numskulls who can't see what's under their noses. And that's the fault of all these detective novels — a pack of rubbish! Well, we'll have to go along and see the woman

— arrest her, I suppose. There's a case over the ring anyhow, unless she's got a much better explanation than I can think of."

Frank Abbott got up.

"She might have taken the ring, and yet not have had anything to do with the murder. Have you thought of that, sir?"

Lamb nodded.

"That's on the cards, but not very likely."

"You remember saying what Maudie's strong suit was — that she knew people? You said she didn't make mistakes about them. Well, she says if Miss Garside, who is a very tidy and particular person, had washed the blood off that statuette she would have put it back on the mantelpiece, but that Mrs Willard, who is clean but very untidy, might very easily have washed it and dropped it back on the sofa. If she handled the statuette before the blood was dry she might have stained her dress, and that would account for her having washed it."

Lamb got to his feet.

"Look here, Frank, what are you driving at? They didn't all kill her, did they? I like a case where there aren't so many people who might have done it. All right, all right — we'll take 'em one at a time. Mrs Willard's on the way down anyhow."

CHAPTER
FORTY-TWO

Mrs Willard had plugged in her electric iron and was slipping a damp dress over the ironing-board when the bell rang. She looked surprised to see the Chief Inspector and Sergeant Abbott, but not at all disconcerted. She liked doing her ironing in the sitting-room because two of the chairs there were of just the right height to take the board. Well, she supposed that both the men had seen a woman ironing before now, and it wasn't as if it was underclothes. She led the way into the room and went over to turn the iron off. So easy to forget, and she didn't want a hole in her board and the flat smelling like a fire. When she straightened up, there they were, both of them, looking down at the damp dress. For the first time something touched her like a cold finger.

The large man who was the Chief Inspector looked up from the dress and said, "There are just a few questions we should like to ask you, Mrs Willard."

She managed a hesitating smile and said, "Yes?"

"I think you told Sergeant Curtis that your husband left you soon after seven o'clock last night and did not return until this morning."

Mrs Willard said, "That's right."

She was standing behind one of the big chairs. She put out a hand now and rested it upon the back.

"I'm sorry to put a personal question, but I'm afraid I must ask you if this was in consequence of a quarrel between you."

She took a moment before she said, "Well, it was — but it's all made up now."

"Was the quarrel about Miss Roland?" Lamb's tone was very direct.

Mrs Willard flushed all over her face and made no reply. She stood quite still behind the chair and looked down at her hand.

Lamb said in an authoritative voice, "Then I take it that you did quarrel about Miss Roland. You can correct me if I'm wrong."

Mrs Willard said nothing. She stood there looking down. Her hand had closed on the back of the chair and was gripping hard.

"Mrs Willard, I can't force you to answer — I can only invite you to do so. If you have nothing to conceal on your own account, you know that it is your duty to assist the police. Did you leave your flat at any time last night and go up to No. 8? Did you wash this dress because it became stained whilst you were in Miss Roland's flat?"

Frank Abbott had lifted the right-hand sleeve and turned it over. The stuff was only faintly damp. A red and green pattern straggled over a cream-coloured ground. The colours were fast and had not run at the edges, but on the outside of the sleeve from wrist to elbow the cream was clouded by a stain of brownish red. Frank Abbott exclaimed, "Look here, sir!"

Mrs Willard looked up, and the Chief Inspector down. There was a pause before Lamb said, "A laboratory experiment will prove whether that stain is blood or not. Is there anything you would like to say, Mrs Willard?"

She took her hand off the chair and came up to the ironing-board.

"It ran up my sleeve when I was washing the little statue," she said in a meditative tone. "A stain does spread so on silk. I suppose it was the shock, but I forgot all about it till I saw Alfred looking at it this morning. I don't know what he thought, because I was too tired to talk — I'd been up all night. I just put the dress in to soak and went and lay down —"

Lamb broke in.

"I have to warn you that anything you say will be taken down and may be used in evidence against you."

They were both looking at her. Abbott had his notebook out.

Mrs Willard looked down at the stained sleeve and went on.

"Alfred must have just wrung it out and put it in the cupboard to dry. I never thought of his doing that. The stain hasn't really come out at all — has it?"

Lamb said, "No," and suddenly she looked up at him with a ghost of her pleasant smile.

"You want me to tell you about it, don't you? Shall we sit down?"

254

They sat, the two men on the sofa, Mrs Willard in her own chair facing them, her manner quite easy and unembarrassed now.

"I suppose I ought to have told you this morning, but I was feeling so dreadfully tired. Of course you must be thinking it strange, my dress being stained like that, but it's quite simple really. You see, we've been married for twenty years, and there's never been anyone else with either of us. And then Miss Roland took the flat upstairs, and I couldn't help seeing that Alfred admired her. I don't want to say anything hard about her now she's dead, but she was the sort of girl who lays herself out to catch a gentleman's eye. There wasn't anything in it, but last night — it's no good pretending, is it? — we did have words about her, and Alfred went off to his brother's and stayed away all night."

Mrs Willard sat there in a dark blue dress with the collar pinned crooked, her grey hair rumpled and her eyes fixed on the Inspector's face with the candid gaze of a child. Her hands lay in her lap, and as she talked she fingered her wedding ring. It was impossible for anyone to look less like a murderess. She went on speaking simply and directly, with the least trace of a country accent cropping up here and there.

"He went off, and I didn't know where he had gone. He'd never done such a thing before, and I got fancying things the way you do when anything's happened and you're sitting alone and thinking about it. I kept going to the door and looking out to see if he was coming back. It was stupid of me, but I didn't think about his brother. It kept coming over me that we'd had words, and that perhaps he had gone upstairs to her."

Frank Abbott wrote, his fair sleek hair catching the light as he bent over his notebook. Lamb said, "Did you know that he did in fact go up to Miss Roland's flat soon after seven o'clock?"

She nodded.

"Yes — he told me. She laughed at him and sent him away. She didn't take him seriously, you know. He was very much hurt about it."

"She had her sister with her — that's why she sent him away. Well, you didn't know all this at the time, I take it. He told you afterwards?"

"Yes — when he came back this morning."

"Well, let's get back to last night. You were wondering where your husband had gone —"

"Yes, I was dreadfully unhappy, and it kept on getting worse. When it came to eleven o'clock and Alfred not back, I couldn't bear it any longer. I'd got to know whether he was up there with Miss Roland or not, so I went up."

"Yes, Mrs Willard?"

"I meant to ring the bell. I didn't care whether she was in bed and asleep or not. But when I got up there I didn't have to ring — the door was ajar."

"What!"

She nodded.

"I didn't think anything but that someone had shut it carelessly and it hadn't latched. And I thought that wouldn't be like Alfred, because he's always so particular, but it might have been Miss Roland. And I

256

thought here was my chance of catching them if he was there, so I pushed the door and went in."

"Just a moment, Mrs Willard. How did you push it — with your hand?"

She shook her head.

"No — I don't think so. I wouldn't if it was like that. I'd just give it a push with my shoulder."

"All right — go on."

"Well, the lights were on, so I thought she hadn't gone to bed."

"What lights?"

"Oh, the hall, and the sitting-room. The door was half open and I could see in. I stood in the hall and called, 'Miss Roland!' and no one answered, so I went in."

"Did you touch the sitting-room door?"

Mrs Willard looked faintly surprised.

"Oh, no — the door was half open. I just walked in and saw her. It was a most dreadful shock."

"You mean that she was dead?"

The surprise was in her voice as she responded.

"Oh, yes, she was quite dead, lying there on the floor — I suppose you saw her. I didn't touch her except to feel her pulse, and the minute I took hold of her wrist I knew that she was dead."

"Why didn't you give the alarm, Mrs Willard?"

She looked worried for a moment.

"I suppose I ought to have, but — I expect it was the shock — and I didn't know where Alfred was —"

"You thought he might have done it?"

She actually smiled.

"Oh, not really — he wouldn't, you know. It was just the shock, and not knowing where he was. Why, he was at his brother's by a quarter past eight. I rang up my sister-in-law and asked just now, but of course I didn't know any of that last night."

Lamb sat there grave and solid, a hand on either knee. The overhead light picked out his bald patch and the strong black hair growing round it. He said, "Go on — tell us what you did."

Mrs Willard fingered her wedding ring.

"Well, after I'd felt her wrist I just stood there. I didn't know what to do. It was a shock, you know, seeing her like that, and not knowing where Alfred was. I didn't seem to be able to think properly. I'd never seen anyone murdered before — it was dreadful. It seemed as if I ought to do something, but I didn't know what. There was that silver statue she had on the mantelpiece — a girl dancing — it was lying on the sofa all over blood. I couldn't bear to see it like that. It had made a dreadful stain on the cover — I couldn't bear to see it. Well, the next thing I knew I'd got it in my hand taking it into the bathroom to wash the blood off. There was some nice hot water, and I gave it a good scrubbing with the soapy nailbrush. I suppose that's when I stained my sleeve. The blood had dried and I'd a job to shift it. Why, the basin and the taps and all were stained. I had to go over them with the brush and fresh hot water."

"And then?"

"I put the statue back."

"On the mantelpiece?"

"Oh, no — on the sofa."

"Why did you do that?"

A slightly bewildered expression came over her face.

"I don't know — I found it there. Does it matter?"

He shook his head.

"I just wanted to know — that's all. Now, Mrs Willard — the whole time you were in the flat, did you handle anything except Miss Roland's wrist, and the statuette?"

"There were the taps, and the soap and nailbrush —"

"They would be too wet to take fingerprints, or if there were any on the taps you scrubbed them off. What about the bathroom door?"

"It was open — I didn't have to touch it."

"And the light?"

"I had to turn it on, but I found I'd left a smear there, so I took it off with the brush."

"Did you happen to notice Miss Roland's rings whilst you were in the bathroom?"

"Oh, yes — they were lying by the side of the washbasin. I didn't touch them."

CHAPTER
FORTY-THREE

They came out of the flat and stood for a moment on the landing. Lamb said, "There's another queer start."

"Think she was speaking the truth?"

"If she wasn't she's the best hand at a tale I've ever struck. It all fits in, you see. The statuette — well, the way she told about that, it all seems natural enough. And there being none of her fingerprints in the flat — well, that all fits in too. There's always a place where a patched-up story comes away from the cloth, but this story of hers doesn't. She's either a very clever woman or else she's telling the truth — and she don't look clever to me." Then, with an abrupt change of voice, "Where's Miss Silver?"

"In the Underwoods' flat, I suppose. That's where she told me she'd be."

Lamb gave a sort of grunt.

"Well, go and get her! I'm going to take her along. If this Garside woman hasn't been eating anything for the best part of a week, as likely as not she'll be fainting on our hands — I'd like to have a woman there. Go and get Miss Silver — just say I want to see her. And look out for the door being shut after she comes out. That's

260

the worst of flats — everybody looks into everybody else's front door. Cut along and get her!"

They stood at Miss Garside's door and rang the bell. Frank Abbott could hear the faint buzzing sound of it. He thought the kitchen door must be open. At the third or fourth repetition the sound began to remind him of a fly buzzing on the window pane of a deserted room. Something in Maudie's favourite Lord Tennyson . . . "The blue fly sung in the pane" . . . Mariana in the moated grange — " 'He cometh not,' she said."

Lamb put his thumb on the bell and kept it there. The buzzing was continuous. Nobody came.

The Inspector's hand dropped. He said over his shoulder, "Go and get Bell! He's got a key — tell him to bring it along! And just see where he gets it from. I never heard of such a thing as letting them hang on the dresser! I told him he was to keep them locked up. Just you see if he's done it!"

Miss Silver stood grave and prim beside the door whilst they waited for Abbott and Bell. The Inspector leaned his big shoulder up against the jamb, his face heavy and stern.

Two or three minutes can seem a very long time. A cold draught came up the well of the stairs, bringing with it a smell of cellar-damp and mist. Then the lift shot up and the two men emerged from it, Bell first, with the key, his face puckered, and his hand not quite as steady as usual, because if they couldn't get an answer out of No. 4 there must be something very badly wrong. Miss Garside, she'd never go out at this time in the evening with a fog coming up like it was.

They opened the door and went in.

Two doors faced them. The sitting-room door on the right was open, the bedroom door on the left closed but not latched. They went into the sitting-room and found it empty and full of shadows. It was not dark outside yet, but with the mist hanging like a curtain at the windows there was very little light to see by.

The Inspector pulled down the switch and a ceiling light came on. There was no sign of the tea-tray which had been set two and a half hours before. The tray was back in the kitchen, the teapot washed and put away, the cup and saucer clean and in its place. The biscuits, which had been laid out upon a plate, were back in their airtight tin. Everything was in order, and there was no one in the room.

It was Miss Silver whose eyes picked up a single crumb upon the hearth-rug. She pointed it out to the Inspector. He looked round with some impatience.

"A crumb? Well, I daresay! What of it?"

Miss Silver gave her slight cough.

"She had had her tea. It is a biscuit crumb, and you can see that a stool has stood just here on the hearth-rug. That stool over there by the wall, I should say."

He looked at her sharply, grunted, and went through the hall to the bedroom door. After knocking on it he pushed it open and went in, switching on the light. Abbott and Miss Silver followed him, but old Bell stayed in the hall and said his prayers. He didn't know what things were coming to — he didn't indeed. It wasn't what he was accustomed to, and he didn't know what to do.

Inside the light shone down upon a clean, bare room. What furniture there was stood stiffly in place. The bed with its old-fashioned brass knobs and rails faced the door. The counterpane had been neatly folded back and the faded eiderdown pulled up to cover Miss Garside to the waist. She lay there fully dressed in an attitude of profound repose, her left arm bent with the hand lying across her breast, the right arm stretched out straight.

Lamb stood over her, frowning, and spoke her name. "Miss Garside —"

His deep voice filled the room but did not touch the stillness on the bed. With a sudden ejaculation his big hand went out to the left wrist. His fingers felt for a pulse, and did not find it.

He laid the hand back again, rapped out an order to Abbott, and began to look about him. On a table beside the bed there was a tumbler with a little water in it. Between the tumbler and the edge of the table a small glass bottle with one or two white tablets.

Lamb stooped to read the label and spoke over his shoulder to Miss Silver.

"Foreign stuff," he said — "more in your line than mine. German, isn't it?"

She stooped as he had done.

"Yes, German — morphia tablets. You could get them in Germany up to a few years ago."

"Had she been in Germany, do you happen to know?"

"Yes. I believe she used to travel a good deal. Mrs Lemming will be able to tell you about that. They were friendly."

The pause which followed left the air so still that Frank Abbott's voice came to them from the next room — no words, but just his quiet, unhurried voice speaking to Scotland Yard.

After a minute Lamb said, "The police surgeon will be along, but there isn't anything he can do — she's dead all right. Well, Miss Silver, there's our case, finished and done with."

"You think so?"

He humped a massive shoulder.

"What else is there to think? It happened the way I said, and this proves it. She was on the rocks, didn't know where to turn for money, and went up to No. 8 when she thought Miss Roland was out. She'd seen her go down in the lift with her sister, you'll remember. Well, she went to the basement for the key which that old fool Bell had hanging up where anyone could get at it. Miss Crane saw her coming back."

Miss Silver said in a slow, reluctant voice, "Mrs Smollett says that Mrs Lemming tried to get Miss Garside on the telephone three times between five-and-twenty to nine and some time after the quarter."

Lamb nodded.

"Well, there you are — that's when she went up to No. 8. There's no way of knowing just what happened, but we know that Miss Roland had come back to the flat at half past seven after seeing her sister off. She

264

catches Miss Garside, there's a row, she turns round to go to the telephone and call up the police, and Miss Garside snatches the statuette off the mantelpiece and lays her out. After that she's got to get away, and get away quick. She drops the weapon on the couch, changes the rings — she'd reckoned nobody would spot that — and she makes off, leaving the door ajar behind her, either because she's in a panic or because she's clever enough to see that with the door open it might be anybody's job. First thing this morning she goes out as bold as brass and sells the ring. I don't know when she begins to find out that she hasn't brought it off. Mrs Jackson and Mrs Smollett had both tumbled to the fact that the ring found in Miss Roland's bathroom wasn't the right one. Mrs Smollett recognised it as Miss Garside's. Well, you couldn't keep that woman from talking if you gagged her. I suppose she let on, and here we are. Miss Garside would know very well that she hadn't a chance once we'd spotted the exchange of the rings. It's as clear a case as you want."

Miss Silver's small neat features were set in an obstinate gravity. She gave a very slight cough and said, "You have not thought that she may have been murdered?"

Lamb stared at her.

"No, I haven't," he said bluntly.

"Will you think about it, Inspector? I should like to urge you to do so."

He met her earnest look with a frown.

"On what grounds?"

265

She began to speak in a steady, quiet voice, and in a manner at once firm and deferential.

"I do not feel that the central fact of the case is explained by the theory you have put forward, Inspector. I have all along felt that this central fact was not robbery but blackmail. Your theory leaves this quite untouched. Mrs Underwood was being blackmailed."

Lamb nodded.

"By Carola Roland."

Miss Silver looked at him.

"I am not entirely sure of that."

"Why, Mrs Underwood's letter was in her possession. We found it in her bag."

"Where she had allowed Mrs Underwood to see it on Monday evening whilst they were playing bridge in the Willards' flat. To my mind that makes it impossible that Miss Roland herself was the blackmailer. We have to look deeper than that. If she had been blackmailing Mrs Underwood, everything would depend on her keeping her identity a secret, yet she carried the letter carelessly in her bag and allowed it to be seen. This would be in keeping with the spiteful trait in her character which led her to pay off an old score against Major Armitage by a pretence that she was his wife. She knew very well that such a claim could not cause more than a few hours' annoyance, but she seems to have thought it worth while. In the same way she may have enjoyed upsetting Mrs Underwood, who had shown rather plainly that she did not wish for more than a casual acquaintance."

Lamb wore a good-tempered smile.

"You should write one of these detective novels, Miss Silver. I'm a plain policeman, and facts are good enough for me. Mrs Underwood wrote a letter in reply to a demand for blackmail, and that letter was found in Miss Roland's bag. That's enough for me, and I think it would be enough for a jury. You know, what's wrong with you amateurs is that you can't believe in the plain facts of a plain case — they're not good enough for you. You've got to have a case all tangled up with fancy trimmings before you can believe in it."

Miss Silver smiled politely.

"Perhaps you are right, Inspector. I do not think so, but I should be sorry to appear ungrateful for the courtesy and help which you have given me. I am not very happy about this case. If you will bear with me for a moment, I should like to discharge my conscience by telling you what I suspect. I have no evidence to lay before you. I can only ask you to consider whether Miss Garside may not have been removed because someone whose life and liberty are at stake had come to realise that she must have been in Miss Roland's flat at a time so near the murder as to make her survival dangerous." Without any break or change of expression she went on speaking. "Do you recall the case of Mrs Simpson?"

Lamb, who had turned aside, swung round with a slow rolling movement. He gave a kind of grunt and said, "Well, I should think so!"

"She was a pupil of the Vulture's, I believe. They specialised in blackmail of a political nature, did they not?"

"I think they did. It was a Foreign Office business — the Yard didn't really come into it. There was the Denny case — she set herself up as a medium — called herself —"

"Asphodel," said Miss Silver. "Then there was a case of impersonation. In the end she was arrested for the murder of a Miss Spedding, but she was never brought to trial. I believe she escaped."

Lamb nodded.

"Someone engineered a collision. The driver of the prison van was killed. Maud Millicent disappeared."

Miss Silver frowned in a manner reminiscent of the schoolroom.

"I think we will allude to her as Mrs Simpson. The name of Maud has been given such beautiful associations by the late Lord Tennyson."

Lamb found himself apologising.

"Well now, Miss Silver, I'm sure that's quite true — Mrs Simpson it is. How do you happen to know so much about her? There wasn't much publicity about the cases she was mixed up in. Hush-hush stuff most of it."

Miss Silver gave a small discreet laugh.

"I have had a good many contacts with Ledlington. Mrs Simpson's father was the Vicar of St Leonard's church there. A most estimable man, I believe. I had the pleasure of meeting Colonel Garrett of the Foreign Office Intelligence at my friends the Charles Morays' just after the Spedding case. When he found that I was conversant with Mrs Simpson's early history he told me a good deal more about her. She was never traced, I believe."

"Never heard of again. Must be a matter of three years ago."

"Did you ever suspect that she might be the principal in the Mayfair case?"

He shook his head.

"You're making it too difficult. Blackmailers are as common as dirt — no need to drag Mrs Simpson into it. She's probably dead."

Miss Silver said in a reserved voice, "You would agree that she was a very dangerous woman."

"Well there's no doubt about that."

"I said that I had no evidence to lay before you, but I was wrong — I have one item. It is this. Miss Garside had a visitor this afternoon."

He gave her his attention.

"How do you know that?"

"Mrs Underwood saw her come out. It was just after half past four, and she was looking out to see whether I was coming down to tea."

"Who was it?" said Lamb.

"A stranger. Mrs Underwood had never seen her before, and she only saw her then for a moment — fair hair, hanging down on her shoulders, smart black dress and hat, spectacles with light tortoiseshell rims, light gloves, very thin stockings and smart black shoes."

Lamb allowed himself to laugh.

"She managed to see a good deal in her moment!"

"No more, I think, than any woman would."

"Ah well — there you have me. And what's the suggestion about this visitor? We'll trace her of course. She must have been the last person to see Miss Garside alive. But as for her having any other importance — well, you're not suggesting that she was the notorious Mrs Simpson, are you?"

Miss Silver coughed.

"It is not my province to make suggestions. You would, however, agree that if Mrs Simpson were implicated in this case she would not hesitate to remove any person whose evidence might prove dangerous."

Lamb had a good-humoured smile.

"Now, Miss Silver, you go along and have a rest. You're letting your nerves get the better of you, and we can't have that. Good people are scarce, you know."

Miss Silver took no notice. She came up close to him and put a hand on his arm.

"Will you leave a man here all night, Inspector? I am feeling very apprehensive about the safety of one of the inmates of Mrs Underwood's flat. I shall make an excuse to stay there myself tonight, but I shall be greatly obliged if you will place a man on duty in the hall of the flat."

Lamb looked grave.

"I could place one on the landing outside. I couldn't put one into the flat without bringing a charge or getting Mrs Underwood's consent."

She thought for a moment, and then said, "The landing will do, Inspector."

"And you go and have a nice rest," said Inspector Lamb.

CHAPTER
FORTY-FOUR

Instead of taking the Inspector's kindly meant if somewhat patronising advice, Miss Silver put on her coat and hat and walked briskly to the corner, where she caught a bus into the town.

There was still daylight when she alighted in the High Street. A few enquiries and about five minutes' walk brought her to her destination, a small old-fashioned jeweller's shop with the name of Jackson above it in letters of faded gold. The shutters were up. Miss Silver made her way to what appeared to be a private door and rang the bell. After a few moments' delay Mrs Jackson opened it. Miss Silver at once said, "May I come in? We met this morning in your sister's flat at Vandeleur House. My name is Silver — Miss Maud Silver. I am very anxious indeed to have a talk with you."

As she spoke she was over the threshold.

There was no welcome in Mrs Jackson's manner, but she closed the door and led the way along a dark passage to the back of the house. Here the light was on and red chenille curtains drawn in a pleasant old-fashioned parlour with a table in the middle, chairs round it, a horsehair couch with a carved back, an upright piano, and a mantelpiece crowded with photographs. Under the light Ella Jackson was seen to be pale and tired, her colourless hair disordered, her air very obviously that of a woman who has been caught at a disadvantage. There was quite a pause before she said, "Do sit down."

Miss Silver accepted the proffered chair. She drew it out from the table and seated herself. When Mrs Jackson had followed her example, she said, "I owe you every apology for intruding upon you in this manner. It is very good of you to receive me. I ask you to believe that I should not have troubled you if the matter were less urgent." She paused, and then went on in her gravest voice. "There has been another death at Vandeleur House."

Ella Jackson started.

"Oh, how dreadful!"

"Yes — it is dreadful. It is Miss Garside who has been found dead in her flat. She sold your sister's ring this morning, and this evening she was found dead in her flat. The police regard her death as suicide. They believe that she killed your sister. I do not share that belief. I am of the opinion that she was murdered, and for the same reason that your sister was murdered — she knew too much, or the murderer suspected that this might be the case and was taking no risks. I do not dispute that she effected an exchange of her own ring, which was paste, for your sister's which contained a valuable diamond, but I believe that her presence at or near the time of the murder was accidental, and that she was not a party to it."

272

The reluctance had gone from Mrs Jackson's manner. Her eyes were fixed upon Miss Silver's face. She put up a hand and pushed back a straggling lock of hair, but she did not speak, only moved her head in an almost imperceptible motion of assent.

Miss Silver went on.

"I see that you are inclined to agree with me. I am very glad of that, for I need your help. The murderer is a cunning and dangerous person and is still at large. The matter is extremely urgent, and the greatest care and discretion must be exercised if a further fatality is to be avoided."

Ella Jackson said "Oh!" on a sharp breath of protest.

Miss Silver shook her head.

"I am not exaggerating. I am very deeply concerned. Chief Inspector Lamb is an able and honest man — I have a great respect for him — but I cannot shake his conviction that Miss Garside committed suicide, and that this suicide closes the case. I must have evidence in order to shake this conviction. Enquiries which I shall make tomorrow will, I hope, provide me with some of this evidence. Meanwhile it is in your power to help me. Will you do so?"

Ella Jackson said, "Yes, I will."

Miss Silver beamed upon her.

"That is so very kind. I will not keep you any longer than I can help. I have a question to ask you, and I hope very much that you will be able to answer it. Your sister talked to you about her affairs, did she not?"

"About some of them. She didn't tell me everything."

"Did she tell you that she was being blackmailed?"

273

Ella Jackson took a quick, short breath.

"How did you know?"

"Another person in the house was being blackmailed. Miss Roland was in possession of a letter from this person to the blackmailer. The police regard this as evidence that your sister was herself the blackmailer, but from the fact that she exposed this letter carelessly in her bag and allowed the writer to see it I deduce that she was not a principal in the matter. I believe she merely intended to tease the writer of the letter. I began to wonder whether she herself was being blackmailed, and had come into possession of the letter in an attempt to secure evidence against the blackmailer. If she knew who this person was, it would supply a motive for the murder. Now, Mrs Jackson — can you help me?"

Ella Jackson leaned forward.

"She was being blackmailed — she told me that — and she came down here because she thought she'd got a clue to the person who was blackmailing her. She thought it was someone in Vandeleur House — that's why she took that flat. Of course it suited her in other ways — it was out of the way and quiet, and she wanted to be near me — but that's really why she took it. There was a girl she'd known when she was on the halls — a girl that used to be an acrobat but she had an accident and couldn't carry on. Carrie got her to go into service with Mrs Underwood in No. 3 so that she could help her. The last thing she told me was they were getting on fine and going on fine and going to make someone sit up."

"She didn't tell you who it was?"

Ella shook her head.

"I didn't ask her. To tell you the truth, Miss Silver, I didn't like the sound of it. The fact is she'd got the idea she could turn the tables — get hold of something that would put this blackmailer in the wrong, and use it to make them give up trying to blackmail her. I didn't like the sound of it at all. It seemed right down dangerous to me, and so I told her."

"You were right. She tried to blackmail the blackmailer, and she got the worst of it. That was inevitable. She was dealing with a dangerous and experienced criminal. We still have that criminal to deal with. She gave you no clue as to the person's identity?"

Ella shook her head.

"Not even by the use of a pronoun? She never said *he* or *she*?"

Ella shook her head again.

"No, it was always *they*. 'They think they can do this or that, but I'll show them' — you know how one talks. It isn't grammar, but everyone does it."

Miss Silver nodded in an abstracted manner. Her thoughts were busy. After a little she said, "Mrs Jackson, will you tell me why your sister was being blackmailed?"

Ella started and flushed. Then she said, "Oh, well, I suppose it doesn't matter now. You get past minding, don't you? And it wasn't her fault, poor Carrie — she thought he was dead."

"Bigamy?" said Miss Silver.

Ella flushed again.

"She thought he was dead. She married him when she was only a kid — ran away from home. They were on the halls together. He was a horrid man. Well, in the end he went off with someone else, and she heard he was dead. I suppose she ought to have taken more trouble about finding out if it was true, but she didn't bother. Only after she'd married Jack Armitage and he'd been killed the blackmail began. She paid up once or twice because she was afraid that if Major Armitage found out he'd stop the allowance, and she was getting friendly with the gentleman she was going to marry, Mr Maundersley-Smith — she didn't want him to know. He was the sort that thinks a girl's perfect because she's pretty. I always thought he'd have some shocks if he married Carrie. But there — it never came to that, only you can see why she didn't want him to know."

Miss Silver said, "Yes, indeed." She thought Ella Jackson a very sensible young woman. Fond of her sister too, but not blind to her faults. She coughed and enquired, "Was she being asked for money all the time, or only at first?"

Mrs Jackson had a startled look.

"She hadn't a lot to give," she said.

"She had some valuable jewellery."

"Well, nearly all of it came from Mr Maundersley-Smith — everything except the diamond ring that Jack Armitage gave her. Mr Smith would have noticed if she hadn't worn his presents. Besides she looked upon the jewellery as a kind of nest-egg."

"Then it wasn't money she was asked for?"

276

The startled look was still there. Ella said, "No — it wasn't."

"I think I can guess what it was. Mr Maundersley-Smith is a big man in the shipping world. It might have been supposed that your sister would be able to supply valuable information."

Ella nodded.

"Yes — that was it. And it fairly got her back up. Carrie was my sister, and no one knows her better than me. She'd done a lot of things I didn't like — it's no good pretending she hadn't — but that's a thing she wouldn't do, not with a war on anyhow. So she set herself to find out who was running the show, and to get even with them."

"A very dangerous enterprise," said Miss Silver gravely.

CHAPTER
FORTY-FIVE

The night passed without incident. A young police constable kept solitary vigil on the landing between No. 3 and No. 4. Miss Silver remained at No. 3. A comfortable bed was made up for her on the drawing-room sofa, but she did not occupy it. As soon as the rest of the household had retired and might be supposed to be asleep, she carried a chair to the kitchen and sat there all night with the door wide open to the hall of the flat. At intervals she went to the window and looked out, raising the sash so that she could see right along that side of the house. The window of Ivy's small bedroom was so near that she could have touched it with her hand. She observed with approval that it was closely fastened, and that the curtains were drawn across it on the inside. She could also have touched the ledge which ran all round the house beneath the windows. There was a similar ledge on every floor. She wondered how often Ivy Lord had passed along this one. She meant to make quite certain that neither she nor anyone else should pass along it tonight. The night went slowly by.

As soon as it was light she took a bath — the hot water supply was really most commendable. She dressed herself in her outdoor clothes, partook of a cup of cocoa and a bowl of bread and milk, and went into Mrs Underwood's room to inform her that she would be away for some hours and not to wait tea, though she hoped to be back by then. After which she walked downstairs, bade Bell a cheerful good-morning, and departed upon her errand.

Vandeleur House woke up flat by flat and began to go about its business. Mrs Smollett, arriving to scrub the stairs, was took bad at the news of poor Miss Garside's suicide, and had recourse to the ready hospitality of Miss Crane. A restorative of a most congenial nature was produced. Gossip and horrified speculation ran riot. Mrs Smollett had rarely enjoyed a fatality so much. She was very late indeed in beginning the stairs. She had in fact got no farther than Mrs Underwood's landing, when Miss Lemming came running up to ring the bell and be admitted by Miss Meade Underwood, who seemed to be expecting her.

"Wearing her old purple when she came up, wasn't she, same as she's worn it day in and day out till you're sick sore and weary of seeing it. And Miss Meade kisses her, and in they go and shut the door. And I hadn't got done with the hall not by the half of it before Miss Lemming comes down again. Well, Miss Crane, I give you my word I was that taken aback I dropped my brush. I wouldn't hardly have known her, and nor would you. Real good clothes she'd got on — a kind of sandy mixture tweed with an orangy fleck in it and a jumper to match. Took ten years off her age and that's a fact."

Miss Crane, over an eleven-o'clock cup of tea, displayed the deepest interest.

"How very strange."

"And what's more," said Mrs Smollett, "everything she'd got on was new — shoes, stockings, hat, gloves, and a brand new bag. Wonderful what a difference clothes make. You'd have took her for under thirty. 'Well,' I says to myself, 'if that don't beat the band!' Mind you, she didn't give anyone time or I'd have said something. Short of running I never see anyone go faster."

Just before one o'clock Miss Silver put through a telephone call to Chief Inspector Lamb at Scotland Yard. As her familiar voice and slight hesitant cough fell upon his ear, he looked decidedly cross. For women in general he had a great deal of respect, but one thing he would say, and he defied anyone to disprove it, they never knew when to leave a thing alone. It wasn't just the last word they wanted either — it was all the words, all the time. His voice though perfectly polite informed Miss Silver that she was overstepping the limits of his patience.

In a brisk and businesslike voice she said, "I told you last night that I had no evidence to lay before you. I have some now. I should be glad of an opportunity of talking it over with you. My train arrives at half past three. I can be with you by four o'clock. I should prefer to see you at the Yard."

Lamb cleared his throat.

"Now, Miss Silver —"

"The matter is urgent, Inspector. I shall not waste your time. Shall we say four o'clock?"

He said, "Very well." And then, "Where are you — where are you speaking from?"

"Tunbridge Wells," said Miss Silver, and rang off.

At a little after four she was sitting in his office, neat and dowdy in her old-fashioned black cloth coat with its faded fur collar and her felt hat with the bunch of pansies on the left-hand side. She was pale and looked tired, but there was an air of deferential obstinacy about her which caused Lamb to fear the worst. If he knew anything at all about women, she was going to try and get her own way, and it would probably end in his having to give her the rough side of his tongue.

She began by telling him about her interviews with Ivy Lord, with Mrs Underwood, and with Ella Jackson, after which she told him all about her visit to Tunbridge Wells.

By this time Lamb was no longer cross. He was considering what a feather in his cap it would be if Miss Silver's evidence should prove to be correct and enable him to pull in so notorious a criminal. It began to look as if she had hit on something. On the other hand, if she was wrong — well, no one liked making a fool of himself, and he wasn't going to be pushed into doing it. Miss Silver was now propounding a plan — one of those fancy stunts which women think up. He didn't care for them himself, but in this case, and with the possibility that the whole thing might be a mare's nest, well, it had some points — he wouldn't go farther than that.

Miss Silver was talking.

"— a meeting of everyone from all the flats at No. 8 — that would, I think, be the most suitable locality. I am convinced, and I shall hope to prove it, that the murderer had an appointment with Miss Roland and was admitted by the sitting-room window after ascending the fire-escape. If startled and cornered, I think an attempt will be made to escape by the same way. This is not a certainty, but in view of the character of the person concerned I think it very probable that such an attempt will be made. The window of course should be open — so large a gathering would make this seem quite natural. When we are assembled you could have a search made in the direction I have indicated. If the things I have described are found where I believe they will be found, a pre-arranged message could be brought up to you. Great care must be exercised not to arouse any suspicion. We are dealing with a most cunning criminal."

Lamb let his hand rise and fall again. It struck the blotting-pad before him and sent the pen which lay there rolling half across the desk.

"You seem to be sure that these things will be found."

Miss Silver inclined her head.

"I am sure," she said.

CHAPTER
FORTY-SIX

By ones and twos the inmates of Vandeleur House came out of their flats and took the lift or walked up the stair to the top of the house, where the door of No. 8 stood wide with Sergeant Abbott on the threshold to usher them in.

Mrs Underwood got into the lift, which already contained the Lemmings, but Meade and Giles walked up the stairs. Meade said low in his ear, her face upturned, her grey eyes dark, "I can't make Agnes out. Aren't people queer? Up to now she's just been anyone's slave who wanted one, and the way her mother trampled made me boil. She didn't seem to have a life of her own at all, she just did things for other people. But now it's all different. She's so taken up with what is happening to her, she hardly notices that there's been a murder and a suicide in the house."

Giles laughed.

"This is where I ask what's happening to her, isn't it?"

"Wait and see," said Meade. She slipped a hand through his arm and brought her voice down to a murmur. "Giles — what is all this about? I don't like it very much. Why have we all got to go up to Carola's flat? What was Miss Silver saying to you when she took you off and talked to you just now? Is anything horrid going to happen?"

"Miss Silver seems to think so," said Giles with rather an odd inflexion.

"Oh, I do hope not!"

"I don't know —" He bent and kissed the cheek that was nearest. "Hush — not a word!" he said, and hurried her on with an arm round her. Nobody could have heard what passed, it was all so quick and low between the two of them.

They came into Carola Roland's sitting-room, and found that the furniture had been shifted and rearranged. The writing-table had been pushed against the right-hand wall, and Chief Inspector Lamb sat with his back to it as if he had been writing up to the last moment and had then swung round to face the window. Between him and the door there were three chairs, which were occupied by Mr and Mrs Willard and Mr Drake, Mr Drake being nearest the door. Upon Lamb's other side was a vacant chair, and then Mrs Lemming, Agnes, and Mrs Underwood. The couch had been moved to the hearth, where it stood with its back to the fireplace. Someone had covered the mark which stained it with an incongruous tartan rug, and here in state sat Miss Silver and Miss Crane, the former still in her outdoor clothes, the latter in her customary drab attire of raincoat and old felt hat. Both ladies wore woollen stockings and very sensible shoes. Beyond the couch stood another empty chair. The silver dancer was back upon the mantelpiece, but the photograph of Giles Armitage had disappeared. It being a mild and muggy evening, both windows stood open, the lower sash of each being raised to the fullest extent. It was half past six and daylight outside — three quarters of an hour to sunset, but a dull sky and thickening air.

The ceiling light shone down upon the blue carpet, the blue and silver upholstery, the tartan rug, and the people in the room. It showed the Inspector looking solid and serious; Mrs Lemming, handsome and quite obviously in a very bad temper; Agnes in her new clothes, a flush on her cheeks and a dreaming light in her eyes: Mr Drake, who looked at her and looked away; Mrs Underwood, breathing quickly and looking as if everything she had on was too tight for her; the Willards, she flushed and untidy, her hair slipping, an inch of petticoat visible at the hem of her dark blue dress, he very much himself again, very stiff, very official; Meade between the Inspector and Agnes, small and young like a child who has got into a grown-up party by mistake — small, and young, and just a little bit afraid. Giles had been reft away from her and given the vacant chair on the farther side of the couch. Thus, starting at the door with Sergeant Abbott, the names run as follows. On the right-hand side of the room — Mr Drake, Mrs Willard, Mr Willard, Chief Inspector Lamb, Meade Underwood, Agnes Lemming. Across the hearth — Mrs Underwood, then the couch with Miss Silver and Miss Crane. And lastly, Giles Armitage on a gimcrack skeleton of a chair which must have been a great deal stronger than it looked, since it supported him without so much as a creak.

The first thing Meade noticed was that there were five absentees. Nobody of course would expect old Mrs Meredith to be here, or that she should be left alone in her flat. Since Miss Crane had come, Packer would of course be obliged to stay behind. But Ivy wasn't here either. Perhaps she was coming, or perhaps she had refused to come. She had been very queer and upset all day, bursting into tears and giving notice one minute, and relapsing into a sort of dumb misery the next. Bell wasn't here either, or Mrs Smollett. Bell would be glad enough to be out of any unpleasantness, but Mrs Smollett would never get over it. Meade felt thankful she wasn't there, but perhaps she too was coming. It looked as if somebody else was expected, because there were two chairs on the left of the door next to where Sergeant Abbott was standing. Perhaps one of them was for him. No, it wasn't, because here was someone else arriving. Of course — this must be Carola's sister, Mrs Jackson.

She came in, pale and slight, in the new black which spells mourning, followed by a delicate-looking young man with a limp who was Ernest Jackson. They sat down, marked out from the others by their mourning garb, their late arrival, their separate seats.

Sergeant Abbott shut the door and stood against it, not lounging now, but slim and upright and tall, his face expressionless and his blue eyes cool. Actually, he was conscious of some excitement. Was Maudie going to land them in a fiasco, or were they going to bring off something big? He had a tingling in his bones which he did not remember to have experienced over a case before. He looked at the quiet, ordinary people sitting round the room and wondered at himself. He looked at Miss Maud Silver and wondered at her, a quiet, ordinary spinster sitting side by side with another quiet, ordinary spinster, only a bit of Highland tartan between them and the stain made by the blood of a murdered chorus girl — murdered in this room, and perhaps by one of these very ordinary people. Fantastic, but — well, here they were. Ring up the curtain!

CHAPTER
FORTY-SEVEN

Chief Inspector Lamb cleared his throat and looked at Miss Silver. Miss Silver, sitting primly upright with her ungloved hands in her lap, began to speak. The gloves, a pair of worn black suede, lay on the tartan rug between her and Miss Crane. She used exactly the voice and manner with which she would have addressed a class of children. She showed no trace either of self-importance or nervousness. Her look was kind and grave. She said, "The Chief Inspector has called you all together to clarify a few doubtful points. He is very kindly allowing me to ask one or two questions. I shall begin by explaining my own position. I have been engaged upon a private investigation which seems to have some connection with the sad events of the last two days. The matter I had in hand, though trifling in itself, has acquired a certain importance from the fact of Miss Roland's sudden and tragic death. Murder," said Miss Silver in her placid schoolroom voice — "murder has a way of giving significance to the most insignificant trifles. Since yesterday morning we have, I think, all become aware of this. Our every movement, our simplest action, has had the searchlight of an official investigation turned upon it. This is a most

288

unpleasant experience, but in these tragic circumstances it cannot be avoided. I shall not detain you a moment longer than I can help. I am merely anxious at this time to make certain that the timetable which I have here is correct, and to fill in one or two gaps."

She paused, opened her shabby black bag, and took out a neatly folded paper from which she proceeded to read.

"Time-table of the events of Wednesday evening: — Between 6.30 and 8.30 Miss Roland had several visitors with whom I am not at the moment concerned. She was last seen alive, as far as the Chief Inspector has been able to ascertain, at 8.30, when she came out on to the landing and waved goodbye to a friend who was going down in the lift. It is from this time that speculation takes the place of direct evidence. There is reason to believe that Miss Garside paid a visit to this flat between 8.35 and 8.50. I think, Mrs Lemming, that you made several attempts to get into telephonic communication with her and failed to do so."

Mrs Lemming, leaning back in her chair with an air of complete indifference, was understood to assent. She was immediately and very directly addressed by the Chief Inspector.

"You tried to ring Miss Garside up — and more than once? How often?"

Mrs Lemming turned a bored glance upon him.

"Three times, I believe."

"You are not sure?"

"Oh, yes, I am sure."

He went on questioning her until he elicited that she had looked at her watch before ringing up and that it was then 8.35, and again at ten minutes to nine, when she decided that it was too late to get the game of three-handed bridge which had been the object of her original call.

This disposed of, Lamb looked at Miss Silver and nodded. She began to speak again immediately.

"After that we have a considerable hiatus. It is this gap which someone here may be able to fill. Mrs Willard, you were, I believe, in some anxiety about your husband that evening. He had gone out soon after seven, and he did not actually return until nearly ten o'clock next morning, having been detained at the home of his brother, Mr Ernest Willard. Being uncertain as to when your husband would return, you probably opened the door of your flat from time to time and looked out. You did in fact do this, as you informed the Chief Inspector. Now did you on any such occasion see anyone either going up in the lift, or upon the stair between your floor and the next one above it? Your flat being immediately beneath Miss Roland's, and the other top flat being empty, it would be fair to deduce that any person so seen was on his or her way to or from Miss Roland's flat. Did you see anyone, Mrs Willard?"

On being first addressed, Mrs Willard, who had been looking down at her own clasped hands, gave a start and looked up. As the enquiry proceeded, a distressing flush covered her face and neck. Her eyes took on a frightened expression, her hands clung damply together. At the direct question she swallowed convulsively but did not speak. Beside her Mr Willard stiffened, straightened his pince-nez, and took the word.

"If I may be allowed to reply for Mrs Willard, the answer is in the affirmative."

"She did see someone?"

"She did. When she informed me of the fact, which was not until this afternoon, my opinion — I may say my very strongly expressed opinion — was that the police should be informed immediately."

"I don't want to get anyone into trouble," said Mrs Willard in a stifled voice.

The Chief Inspector addressed her in an admonitory tone.

"Now, Mrs Willard, you must understand that this is a very serious matter. You won't get any innocent person into trouble, you know. You don't want to shield a guilty one — do you?"

"I don't want to get anyone into trouble."

"Mrs Willard — who did you see?"

It was at this point that Mr Drake got quietly to his feet and said pleasantly, "She saw me, Inspector."

A faint whisper of sound stirred in the room. It was as if everyone had moved a little — as if each had breathed more deeply.

Lamb said, "You came up here to No. 8?"

"I did."

"What time was this?"

"Half past nine."

"Why did you come?"

"To see Miss Roland."

His eyes went past the Inspector to Agnes Lemming. She was pale, but she looked back at him.

Lamb went on.

"Did you see her?"

"No — I didn't get in. I rang, and there was no answer, so I came away."

"Was the door shut or open?"

The eyebrows which gave Mr Drake his resemblance to Mephistopheles rose in an even sharper arch. After a momentary pause he replied, "The door was ajar."

"Did you go in?"

"Oh, no."

"It didn't occur to you that there might be something wrong?"

"Frankly, it didn't. I thought she was expecting a visitor. I was afraid that I might be de trop."

Lamb looked at him hard. Everyone in the room looked at him. Frank Abbott thought, "Here's a red herring with a vengeance! We put Maudie up to waste time whilst Curtis and the boys get busy downstairs, and she fishes this up. Well, well — on with the play!"

Lamb said in his weightiest voice, "May I ask what was the purpose of your visit, Mr Drake?"

To which Mr Drake replied, "Oh, just a little matter of business. She was blackmailing me."

"She was blackmailing you?"

Mr Drake smiled.

"Oh, not very seriously. You see, she had discovered my guilty secret. She didn't like me very much, and she thought it would embarrass me if she let it out. My visit was for the purpose of telling her that it was a matter of supreme indifference to me."

Abbott thought, "The Chief will spin this out. It's a good red herring. I like this chap. I wonder what he's playing at. He's got some game of his own. The Chief's playing up to him."

Lamb said directly, "Well, Mr Drake, if that's true, you'd better tell us what this guilty secret was."

Mr Drake looked past him down the room.

"Oh, certainly. I'm a pork butcher."

There was an electric silence. Mrs Willard stared. Mr Willard stared. Mrs Lemming looked disgusted. Miss Crane began to laugh in a silly giggling way, with little gasps for breath and little dabbings with a large white handkerchief. Agnes Lemming got up, walked down the room, and slipped her hand inside Mr Drake's arm. Mrs Lemming said sharply, "Agnes, have you gone mad?"

But Agnes stood there smiling. She looked radiant. She turned with that smiling gaze to the room and said in a simple, happy voice, "We were married this morning. Please, everyone, wish us joy."

CHAPTER
FORTY-EIGHT

Mrs Lemming's handsome features stiffened and set, her fine skin blanched. She turned the cold fury of her look upon the daughter whom she had bullied for so long. Never before had that look failed of its effect. It is to be doubted whether Agnes even noticed it now. She stood with her hands on her husband's arm, looking proudly and happily at her friends and awaiting their good wishes. But before anyone could move or speak there was a knock upon the door. Sergeant Abbott stood away and opened it, dislosing Sergeant Curtis, neat and brisk. He came in just over the threshold and addressed himself to the Chief Inspector.

"Anderson is below, sir."

Lamb turned a preoccupied face.

"All right — tell him to wait."

Curtis retreated. Frank Abbott shut the door. Pity Curtis couldn't be this side of it — he was going to miss the show. Or was he? So Maudie had done the trick. Astonishing woman. He took off his hat to her, metaphorically speaking. And to the Chief. Nothing small about him. He could take Maudie in his stride. To look at him sitting there, imperturbable and solid, no one could have guessed that Curtis' message was anything but the dullest routine stuff. Only three people in the room knew what it meant. The things had been found where Maudie had said they would be found. So now what?

Lamb was speaking in his steady, ponderous way.

"Well, we seem to have got a little off the rails. We'd better get back. Was there something more you wished to say, Miss Silver?"

Miss Silver coughed. She sat primly upright with no trace of triumph about her, a dowdy old governess with an old-fashioned decorum of manner.

"I should just like to complete my time-table," she said. "I think I can do so now. We will return to the moment when Miss Roland's friend went down in the lift, leaving her on the landing. This was at 8.30. At 8.35 or thereabouts Miss Garside let herself in with the spare key of No. 8, which she had obtained from the basement. She had reason to believe that Miss Roland had gone out for the evening. She had, in fact, seen her go down in the lift with her sister, Mrs Jackson, at twenty minutes past seven, and she did not know that Miss Roland had gone no farther than the corner of the road, and that she was back in her flat again by half past seven. Miss Garside remained in the flat for about a quarter of an hour, and during that quarter of an hour Miss Roland was murdered. I am going to tell you why she was murdered, and who murdered her. Carola Roland came to this house for a purpose. She was being blackmailed, and she was determined to discover her blackmailer, and to turn the tables. Mrs Jackson will tell you that her sister believed the person who was blackmailing her to be resident in one of these flats. She did not disclose this person's identity, but she was determined not only to free herself but to punish the blackmailer. With this end in view she secured a post in one of the flats for a girl with whom she had been friendly in the past, and who was peculiarly qualified to assist her. I refer to Mrs Underwood's maid, Ivy Lord. This girl had been an acrobat, she was devoted to Carola Roland, and she had a useful reputation for walking in her sleep. At Miss Roland's instigation Ivy got out of her window at night and pursued certain investigations."

Abbott looked round at all the faces and found them looking at Miss Silver — flushed, pale, eager, nervous, distressed. There was a general air of expectancy about them. Even Mr Willard's superiority and Mrs Lemming's hauteur were tinged with it.

Miss Crane said, "Dear, dear — how unpleasant!"

Miss Silver continued in her quiet, carrying voice.

"One day Ivy brought Miss Roland a letter which gave her the evidence she required. It was the answer from one of the blackmailer's victims to a demand for money. With Ivy's testimony as to where it had been found, it afforded conclusive proof of the blackmailer's identity. But Carola Roland had no idea of prosecuting. She thought she could make a good bargain for herself and get the upper hand. She communicated with the blackmailer, and a meeting was arranged for Wednesday evening at approximately 8.45. It will be remembered that Miss Garside was still somewhere in the flat at this time — probably in the bathroom, as a ring belonging to her was subsequently found there. She did not wish to be seen, and was waiting for a chance to get away unobserved. Miss Roland, awaiting her visitor in some excitement, probably had the sitting-room door ajar, if not wide open. She might have walked to and fro between the sitting-room and the hall. She might have been expecting that the bell would ring. Or she might have known that her visitor would come by another way."

"What way?" Giles Armitage asked the question which was in everyone's mind.

"By the fire-escape and the window," said Miss Silver. "And that, I believe, was in fact the way by which the murderer came. The sash was lifted, the blackmailer admitted, some talk perhaps followed. After which Miss Roland turned towards the table which stood on the window side of the room. She may have been going to produce the compromising letter. We do not know, but that is a reasonable conjecture. As soon as her back was turned the blackmailer caught up that little silver figure which you see on the mantelpiece and struck the fatal blow. It makes a very dangerous weapon. The head and bust are easy to grip, the pointed foot is sharp, and the blow would have the weight of the base behind it. Dropping the figure upon the couch, the murderer went to the door of the flat and set it ajar, thus widening the field of suspicion. Miss Garside, I think, had already gone. She may have heard the blow and the fall, or she may have slipped away as soon as the sitting-room door was shut. There is an uncertainty upon this point which can never be cleared up. This uncertainty was shared by the murderer — and murderers cannot afford this kind of uncertainty. Miss Garside was found dead last night after having received a visit from a smartly dressed woman with conspicuous fair hair. This woman was seen coming out of Miss Garside's flat, and her appearance noticed and described. There is reason to suppose that Miss Garside was having tea when her visitor arrived. I do not know how she explained herself, but I am convinced that she found an opportunity of introducing strong morphia tablets into Miss Garside's tea. The affair was very cleverly planned, and arranged to look like a suicide, but circumstantial evidence pointing to murder is now forthcoming."

As she spoke, Lamb sat with an elbow on the arm of his chair, a big hand propping his chin, his face heavy and expressionless.

Miss Crane said "Dear me!" in a very interested manner. Then she heaved a sigh and got to her feet. "You make it so very interesting — you do indeed," she said in the husky voice which always seemed a little short of breath. "You must come and have tea with me and tell me all about it. But I must go now. Packer will be busy with the evening meal, and we do not like to leave Mrs Meredith alone."

"Just a moment," said Miss Silver. "I was going to ask you a question about Tunbridge Wells. Mrs Meredith used to live there, did she not?"

Miss Crane had her foolish smile.

"Now who could have told you that?"

298

"She used to talk about the Pantiles and the Toad Rock when she first came here, did she not — and about her house on Mount Pleasant? To anyone who has ever been in Tunbridge Wells —"

Miss Crane laughed her giggling laugh.

"Oh dear — how clever you are! I should never have thought of that!"

"No," said Miss Silver. "You were not with Mrs Meredith then, I think? You have not in fact been with her for very long, have you?"

Miss Crane stopped laughing. She looked puzzled and concerned.

"I don't understand. No, really. There is no secret about it all. Oh, none at all. A very dear cousin of mine was with Mrs Meredith for many, many years. When she died I was only too pleased to take her place. I am sure I have tried to make up for her loss in every way. You will not ask me to neglect her now, will you? I really must be going."

She began to move towards the door. She still had the large white handkerchief in her hand. Giles Armitage, who had risen when she did, walked beside her. She lifted the handkerchief to her eyes for a moment, and then, still holding it, her hand went down into the pocket of the drab raincoat and there remained, gripped and held by Giles.

In a flash she twisted to free herself, and with such a sudden trick of the muscles that she was almost out of his grip.

It was Miss Silver who caught the other wrist and held on to it till Frank Abbott got there. There were some horrible moments. Meade sickened and shut her eyes. A woman struggling with men — three of them trying to hold her. Horrible!

Fierce panting breath. The men's feet scuffing on Carola's blue carpet. And then the sound of a shot.

Meade opened terrified eyes, got to her feet, and felt the floor tilt under them. Giles — the shot — *Giles!* And then what had been a swaying, struggling group resolved itself, and she saw him. He was still holding Miss Crane by the wrist, but she was falling back, limp and pale, between Sergeant Abbott and the Chief Inspector. A small automatic pistol lay where it had fallen at Giles' feet. As Meade looked, he hooked it dexterously and kicked it away. Mrs Underwood screamed on a high, shrill note, but whether this came first or next, Meade never was quite sure, because at the time everything seemed to happen together — Mr Willard saying in a horrified voice, "She has shot herself"; Miss Crane sagging against the two men, her head hanging, her eyes fixed, her pale mouth horribly open; Mabel Underwood's scream; and then Miss Crane suddenly, galvanically in action again. There was a yelp from Lamb as the hand which was holding her was bitten almost to the bone. With a violent twist she was free and with a single spring had reached the open window.

Giles and Sergeant Abbott reached it too, but not in time. Desperate haste had taken her over the sill to the ledge beneath, and from there on to the fire-escape. They could see her a yard or two below, going down at a speed which spoke of practice. As Giles threw a leg over the sill to follow her, Frank Abbott caught his arm.

"No need," he said. "They're waiting for her down there."

They watched her drop the last few feet and turn to find herself surrounded.

This time there was no break-away.

CHAPTER
FORTY-NINE

Miss Silver gave a tea-party a few days later. She was back in her own flat with *Bubbles*, *The Soul's Awakening*, *The Black Brunswicker*, and *The Monarch of the Glen* gazing from their maple frames upon the scene. *Bubbles* and the damsel in *The Soul's Awakening* could not truthfully be said to enjoy a view of anything but the ceiling, but that was the fault of the upturned gaze with which the artist had endowed them. *The Black Brunswicker's lady* and *The Monarch* had been more kindly treated. They looked down upon Nicholas and Agnes Drake, Meade Underwood and Giles Armitage, and upon Frank Abbott, off duty and very much at his ease.

Miss Silver's tea was of the excellent blend and making dreamed of but seldom achieved. There was enough milk, there was real sugar, there was even a little cream in a small antique silver jug. There were scones and buns of the valuable Emma's best. There was raspberry jam. It was like the pleasantest kind of schoolroom tea.

Miss Silver beamed kindly upon her guests. She was delighted at the happiness which radiated from the Drakes, and delighted to hear that Meade and Giles

302

were to be married without delay. She received with pleasure the admiring attentions of Sergeant Abbott. Altogether a very pleasant party.

But the dark background against which they had played their parts so short a time before could hardly be ignored. Behind the happiness and the agreeable talk it was still there, like a shadow which has been left behind but cannot be forgotten. At first they did not speak of it at all. The Drakes were leaving Vandeleur House. The lease of his flat was up, and they were looking for something in the country.

"It doesn't really matter where I live, you know," said Nicholas Drake.

Frank Abbott, with his lazy, impudent smile, now put the question which everyone wanted to ask.

"Are you really a pork butcher?"

"Selwood's Celebrated Sausages," said Mr Drake, looking more romantic than ever.

"Lucrative?" said Frank.

"Oh, very. I'll tell you about it if you like. I was going to the other day, but the roof fell in. I'd like to, because it's a story about some very nice people and some very good friends. I was reading for the Bar when the last war started. I hadn't any near relations, and I had quite a reasonable income. By the time I got out of the army in 1919 I hadn't any income at all. My gratuity went west, and by 1921 I hadn't the price of a meal. Then I bumped into Mrs Selwood. She'd been our cook, and she married Selwood from our house when he had a little shop in a little country town. By the time I met her he had three shops, and the sausages were beginning to take on. She made me go home with her, and they gave me a job. After three years they made me manager of one of the shops. Business boomed — the three shops increased and multiplied many times — the sausages became celebrated. When Selwood died two years ago I was stupefied to find he'd left the whole concern to me. He said I'd been like a son to them, and Mrs Selwood wouldn't want to be bothered with the business. He'd settled enough to make her comfortable, and he knew I'd look after her."

Miss Silver smiled her kindest smile.

"That is a very nice story, Mr Drake. It is indeed pleasant to realise how many kind and generous people there are in the world. It is particularly salutary when one has been brought into unwilling contact with crime."

Frank Abbott looked at her with a malicious gleam in his pale blue eyes.

"It was our duty and we did," he murmured. "Now you're going to reward us, aren't you — let us ask questions and tell us all the answers?"

He received an indulgent smile.

"I think, Mr Abbott, you know the answers already."

He murmured, "Call me Frank," and went on a thought hastily, "I'd love to hear them again. And I don't know them all — at least I don't suppose I do. Everyone else is perishing with curiosity, and what they all want to know is, how did you do it?"

Miss Silver coughed.

"It is really extremely simple —"

Frank Abbott broke in reproachfully.

"When you say that, you know, you put all the rest of us into a sort of C iii category below the infant class. It would save our pride a lot if you'd just set up as a superwoman and have done with it."

Miss Silver looked quite shocked.

"My dear Frank — *pray!* This talk of supermen and superwomen always seems to me to be rather impious. We are endowed with certain faculties by our Creator, and it is our duty to make good use of them. I have a retentive memory, I am naturally observant, and I was trained in habits of industry. When I came into contact with this case I was immediately struck with the fact that blackmail was at the bottom of it. The two people who were being blackmailed were both in a position to furnish the blackmailer with something more important than money. Ship construction, aeroplane construction — information about these two key industries was what had been aimed at. The money payments were in each case only intended to compromise the persons who were being blackmailed, and to render it impossible for them to break away. In the Mayfair blackmail case last spring there was a strong hint of the same procedure. But my memory took me back a great deal farther than that. The most dangerous organisation of this kind was that of which the Vulture was the head. This was smashed in 1928, but some years later it revived under a pupil of his, a woman known under the names of Deane, Simpson, and Mannister — the latter being her legal designation. I have taken some interest in her career, and have had the opportunity of talking it over with Colonel Garrett, the head of the Foreign Office

Intelligence Service. He told me that in his opinion Mrs Simpson was the most dangerous criminal he had ever come across. She was arrested three years ago for the murder of a woman who had been her cook, and who had had the misfortune to recognise her. I refer, of course, to the Spedding case. She shot this poor woman dead in cold blood, and attempted to murder two other people. After her arrest she managed to escape, and knowing her to be at large, the possibility that she might be involved in these cases of blackmail presented itself to my mind. There were other possibilities, but amongst them I considered this one.

"When it transpired that the occasion of one of the blackmailing demands was a trifling incident which occurred a good many years ago at Ledlington, the possibility which I had been vaguely considering became a sharply outlined probability. Mrs Simpson was, you see, the daughter of a Ledlington clergyman, the Reverend Geoffrey Arthur Deane. She was recently married to Mr Simpson but still resident in Ledlington at the time of the occurrence I have mentioned. Some of her father's parishioners were involved. The link was too significant to be accidental. I had now to consider the possibility that Mrs Simpson was one of the residents in Vandeleur House. I had studied her history, and found that when hard pressed she had always saved herself by assuming a new identity. She had in turn impersonated her own brother, an old professor, a chorus girl, an exotic medium, a middle-aged secretary, and an eccentric spinster. With this in mind I reviewed everyone in Vandeleur House, and at once discarded

Bell and Mrs Smollett who were well known local characters, Mr Drake on account of his height, and Mr Willard whose credentials were quite unimpeachable. Mrs Willard I rejected for the same reason. Mrs Underwood and her connections were known personally to friends of my own. Miss Garside and Mrs Lemming were of a physical type impossible for Mrs Simpson to imitate, both having the regular features which no amount of make-up can counterfeit. Miss Lemming I did not consider at all." Here Miss Silver paused for a moment and smiled at Agnes Drake. "Goodness, like classical features, is not to be imitated. I was therefore left with Mrs Meredith's household, and Ivy Lord. Mrs Simpson, at forty years of age, would certainly not be able to pass for a girl of eighteen. There remained Mrs Meredith, her companion, and her maid. When I discovered the connection with Tunbridge Wells the obvious course was to go down there and make enquiries."

"I hope," said Nicholas Drake, "that I shall never have a secret which you have set yourself to find out."

Miss Silver smiled benignly.

"Happiness is a secret which should be shared, not hidden," she observed.

"What did you find out at Tunbridge Wells?" said Giles Armitage. "The balloon went up before you had time to tell us what you did there."

"It was really very simple," said Miss Silver. "I telephoned to the leading house agent, and having discovered the name of Mrs Meredith's former residence, I paid one or two calls upon the neighbouring houses. A Miss

Jenkins who had lived next door for about fifteen years was particularly helpful, though I must confess that for the first twenty minutes or so it seemed as if I was to have my journey for nothing. Miss Jenkins, as well as a Mrs Black whom I had already interviewed, spoke in the warmest possible terms about Miss Crane — so kind, so conscientious, so devoted to Mrs Meredith. When I asked how long the association had lasted, she told me that it was already of long standing fifteen years ago when she made their acquaintance. It was only as I was rising to go that she sighed and said she really did not know what Mrs Meredith would do without her faithful Miss Crane, and a great pity she had not stayed among her old friends, whose society would have done something to make up for the loss. A few questions brought to light the astonishing fact that the devoted Miss Crane had passed away about six months previously. Mrs Meredith and she had gone up to London on a short visit. They stayed in a family hotel which Mrs Meredith had patronised for years, and whilst there Miss Crane was found dead in her bed, having taken an overdose of some sleeping mixture. I have not the slightest doubt that she was murdered by Mrs Simpson, who was in urgent need of a change of identity. It is now quite certain that she was the principal in the Mayfair blackmail case, and that it was necessary for her to disappear. It was by no means the first time that she had done this. The method was very simple. Some middle-aged woman of no importance and without relatives was selected, and removed. There is very little fuss made about the death of such a person, since none of the ordinary motives for foul play are discernible. Mrs Meredith was naturally in the greatest distress. When Mrs Simpson presented herself as a cousin of her beloved companion she was received with open arms and with no difficulty at all persuaded to take the dead woman's place. What followed is still a little obscure, but Mrs Meredith speaks of a visit from a doctor who advised a course of treatment which would necessitate her being within reach. He also told her that the air of Tunbridge Wells was very bad for her. There is no doubt, I think, that he was not a genuine medical man but an accomplice of Mrs Simpson's. Mrs Meredith was persuaded to sell her house. She never returned to Tunbridge Wells. The new companion acquired an unbounded influence over her. A very respectable maid who had been with her for some years was got rid of and Packer engaged to take her place. This woman's real name is Phoebe Dart. She figured in the Denny case, but disappeared and was never traced. She had been nurse in the Reverend Geoffrey Dean's household, and Mrs Simpson's influence over her has always been complete. The party moved to Vandeleur House, and from this safe retreat the blackmailing activities were continued. When the police searched the flat they found all the evidence they required."

"What did you really think we were going to find?" said Frank Abbott. "And did you know, or were you gambling?"

Miss Silver gave him a glance of mild reproach.

"That is not an expression which I should choose," she said. "On my return from Tunbridge Wells I saw the

Chief Inspector at Scotland Yard. At that time I was tolerably certain that a search of Mrs Meredith's flat would discover the fair wig and the smart black clothes worn by the woman who visited Miss Garside at tea-time on the day of her death. I thought it more than likely that there would be other disguises, and some compromising papers. On my return to Vandeleur House I confronted Ivy Lord with the evidence which I possessed. She then told me what I had already guessed, that, instigated by Miss Roland, she had entered several of the flats at night, using the fire-escape and the ledges which run round the house. She said she rather enjoyed doing it, and if she had been seen, there was a genuine history of sleep-walking to get her off. She had not, of course, the least idea that there was anything serious involved. She said Miss Roland told her that someone had been playing a practical joke and she wanted to get even. They quarrelled over the letter which Ivy found on her second visit to Mrs Meredith's flat. She took it from the drawer in which many similar letters were afterwards discovered, and she selected this one because she knew the writer. She showed it to Miss Roland, but she did not mean her to keep it. She said she did not think it would be right. In the quarrel that followed, a corner of the letter got torn off. This afterwards furnished me with an important clue."

"Why didn't Ivy come upstairs with all the rest of us?" said Meade.

"She was so much upset that suspicion would inevitably have been aroused. Also Mrs Simpson is an extremely vindictive person, and I was afraid of what she might do if she realised that Ivy Lord was going to be the chief witness against her. As regards the first point, it was highly necessary to keep everything going smoothly until Sergeant Curtis had had time to make a thorough search. Miss Crane having been separated from her accomplice, this search and Packer's subsequent arrest took place without any untoward incident. No resistance was offered, Mrs Meredith was not alarmed, and the compromising clothes and papers were duly discovered. When Sergeant Curtis appeared at the door to say that Anderson was below he was, in fact, notifying the Chief Inspector that the search had produced results which warranted the arrest of Miss Crane."

"The Chief has a good poker face," said Frank Abbott. "The bored official stare when Curtis showed up — good, wasn't it?"

Miss Silver coughed.

"If Miss Crane had been given the slightest warning, the situation might have developed very dangerously. I was quite sure that she would be armed, and Major Armitage had been warned to look out for any movement of her right hand in the direction of that capacious raincoat pocket. He is much to be congratulated on the promptness with which he acted. It would have been impossible to place one of the police officers next to her without putting her on her guard. Well, we have all cause to be grateful that so dangerous a criminal is now under lock and key."

"Do you really think she murdered Miss Garside?" said Agnes Drake in a shrinking voice.

"I think she did," said Miss Silver soberly. "It was, from her point of view, a perfectly logical thing to do. She knew from Mrs Smollett that the poor woman had exchanged a worthless ring of her own for a valuable one of Miss Roland's. She had also been informed of a conversation between Mrs Lemming and Miss Garside which made it quite plain that the latter was not in her flat at the time of the murder. And she had herself seen her coming up from the basement just before this time. It was perfectly clear that while Miss Garside's continued existence might be extremely dangerous, Miss Garside's death might be extremely useful. If it could be made to look like suicide it would be tantamount to a confession. We do not know how she effected this latest crime. She may have used the sale of the ring to introduce herself. She brought the morphia tablets with her, and found an opportunity of slipping them into Miss Garside's tea. It will not, fortunately, be necessary to prove all this. She will be tried for the murders of Louisa Spedding and Carola Roland, and with Ivy Lord's evidence there should, I think, be no doubt of a conviction."

They talked a little more, and then they said goodbye.

Meade and Giles walked slowly down the street. When they had turned the corner, he said, "They're sending me back to the States. Will you come too?"

She looked up at him, flushing.

"Will they let me?"

"I think so. Will you come if they do?"

Her look was enough. The hand on his arm shook before she could control it. She said, "When?"

312

"Next Clipper. But you mustn't tell."

Nicholas and Agnes Drake walked in a companionable silence. They had everything in the world to say, and all the time in the world in which to say it.

Frank Abbott remained alone with his hostess. Her room delighted him as much as she did. His gaze travelled reverentially from the flowered wallpaper to the curly walnut chairs, from Landseer and Millais to the silver-framed photographs which thronged the mantelpiece, from a monstrous pink china ornament in the form of a bee to Miss Silver herself in her best afternoon dress of a neatly patterned purplish material with collar and cuffs of Maltese lace, a brooch of carved bog-oak set with three small pearls and bracelets to match, the double eyeglass which she used for reading suspended about her neck by a fine black cord, her feet encased in beaded glacè slippers.

Having arrived, the gaze remained and was fixed. Miss Silver, aware of it, glanced at him with mild enquiry. She saw a tall young man who could be impudent, but whose demeanour at the moment was modest in the extreme. Whilst she looked up, he looked down. And then, without any warning at all, he was bowing over her hand and kissing it.

"You're a wonder, Maudie!" he said, and fled.

Miss Silver's eyebrows rose, but she did not appear displeased. She said, "Dear me —" and relaxed in an indulgent smile.

The Catherine-Wheel

Patricia Wentworth

There was certainly a heavy air of intrigue and mystery emanating from the old inn high up on the cliff top. The Catherine-Wheel had once been a home for pirates and smugglers, but now it looked like it was harbouring a murderer.

It had begun with a newspaper advertisement, inviting descendants of the late innkeeper, Jeremiah Taverner, to stay for a weekend at the inn. A mixed bunch arrived at the family reunion, eager to discover the secrets of their ancestry. But one of them is hideously murdered, bringing the inn's stormy past into frightening focus.

Scotland Yard, already suspicious of drug smuggling in the area, sends Maud Silver to investigate before the fireworks begin.

ISBN 978-0-7531-7826-3 (hb)
ISBN 978-0-7531-7827-0 (pb)

Eternity Ring

Patricia Wentworth

Wentworth is a first-rate storyteller   **Daily Telegraph**

*Patricia Wentworth has created a great detective in
Miss Silver*   **Paula Gosling**

Mary Stokes was walking through Dead Man's Copse
one evening when she saw, in the beam of a torch, the
corpse of a young woman dressed in a black coat, black
gloves, no hat and an eternity ring set with diamonds in
her ear. But when she and Detective Sergeant Frank
Abbott went back to the wood, the body had vanished.
This would have been mystery enough for Miss Silver
. . . but then a woman reported that her lodger had
gone out on Friday dressed in a black coat, black beret,
black shoes and large hoop earrings set all around with
little diamonds like those eternity rings. She never came
back . . .

ISBN 978-0-7531-7656-6 (hb)
ISBN 978-0-7531-7657-3 (pb)